DANCE OF SHADOWS

THE WINTER QUEEN SERIES—*BOOK 2*

ENDORSEMENTS

True epic fantasy at its best. Hogan presents an engaging world that bristles with danger, characters you love (and love to hate), and a thrill-ride story that keeps you guessing ... and turning pages!
—**T.E. Bradford**, author of *The Divide Series*

In the second installment of her breathtaking series, Hogan expands her intriguing fantasy world, deepens her unforgettable characters, and raises the stakes until the book becomes impossible to put down. I came into *Dance of Shadows* with high expectations and was far from disappointed! Each character is on a unique journey of hardship, self-discovery, joy, and heartache, and I look forward with great anticipation to seeing how the author uses her expert storytelling to bring each of the intertwining plots to a satisfying conclusion.
--**Laurie Lucking**, author of *Common*

People are talking about *Winter Queen*, Book One of the Winter Queen Series

Erica Marie Hogan has the unique gift of writing in living color. *Winter Queen* picked me up and dropped me into another place and time. Hogan's ability to take the reader from a comfy chair to great adventure is priceless. For those of us who enjoy escape reading--*Winter Queen* does not disappoint!
—**Shelley Pierce**, author, *The Wish I Wished Last Night* and *Battle Buddies*

Winter Queen drew me in immediately with its strong women characters, elaborate world building and ongoing tensions. It is everything a fantasy novel should be, and I can't wait to read more.
—**Sue A. Fairchild**, author, *What You Think You Know*

DANCE OF SHADOWS

SHADOWS

THE WINTER QUEEN SERIES—*BOOK 2*

ERICA MARIE HOGAN

PUBLISHING THE POSITIVE

ELK LAKE PUBLISHING INC.
Plymouth, Massachusetts

Cover and Interior Design: Derinda Babcock

Editor(s): Deb Haggerty

Author Represented by Hartline Literary Agency

PUBLISHED BY: Elk Lake Publishing, Inc., 35 Dogwood Dr., Plymouth, MA 02360, 2018

_____

Library Cataloging Data

Names: Hogan, Erica Marie (Erica Marie Hogan

Dance of Shadows—The Winter Queen Series Book 2 / Erica Marie Hogan

246 p. 23cm × 15cm (9in × 6 in.)

Description: The Winter Queen has brought the storm ... and the Abyss roams the halls of Blood Keep.

Identifiers: ISBN-13: 978-1-948888-60-8 (trade) | 978-1-948888-61-5 (POD) | 978-1-948888-62-2 (e-book.)

Key Words: Fantasy, Speculative Fiction, Justice, Female Protagonist, Tolkien, Robert Jordan, Relationships

LCCN: 2018957020 Fiction

DEDICATION

For my mom.
You are stronger than you realize.
I love you.

ACKNOWLEDGMENTS

First, let me say I am so happy *A Dance of Shadows* is complete! I am thankful to family, friends, and readers who have encouraged me for years to pursue my writing, even when others tried to diminish my dream. There were a few times I wasn't certain I'd make it through this book. But with the support I received, I survived to the end and am now full of energy for the next step in this journey!

Special Thanks to:

Deb Haggerty—for all the work you do for your authors! With every book we work on together, I learn something and grow more excited to continue this journey of writing.

Derinda Babcock—for my beautiful cover! You did such an amazing job putting together exactly what I wanted. Especially since I wasn't quite sure what I wanted and can be picky. Thank you!

Jim Hart—for being an agent who listens when I get nervous and reassures me to keep moving forward.

T.E. Bradford, Beckie Lindsay, Linda Wood Rondeau and **Laurie Lucking**—for joining my launch party! Thank you so much for your support, and thank you **T.E. Bradford** and **Laurie Lucking** for your beautiful endorsements of *Dance of Shadows*!

As always, I thank my Creator for His many blessings and love as I strive to live the life I believe He wants for me.

PROLOGUE

The City of Sunkai

A harsh winter wind howled against the walls of the Blood Keep. The streets were empty, market stalls overturned with food and clothes scattered across the marketplace up and down the Lower Village. Sunkai was silent, not a sound to be heard save for the scurrying of mice down the alleys and the angry roar of the Nfaros Sea crashing on the shore.

Lathan Jandry heard nothing amiss in the city that had suffered such a horrendous display of blood magic as he strode across the practice yard, taking the long way to the stables. He had discarded the king's colors of black and red, dressing instead in dull browns and grays. They would not distinguish him from any other traveler leaving the city. His gray cloak, fraying at the edges where caught by the wind, was tied securely around his shoulders—the hood protected his face from any who might recognize him.

Lathan moved as a shadow down the stone steps, turning sharply to the right at the bottom before he entered the stable yards. There was no boy to ready his horse—not at this hour of the night after the bells had been rung and all were to be in their beds. The law was clear and had been enforced with brutality this night after the rising up of the outraged rebels in the city. Lathan himself had taken up his sword, but had been unable to act. Not with his brother locked away in the Keep's dungeons. Not with everything else at stake. The guards had even been dismissed from the gates, all of them gathered close to the Blood Keep entries to watch for any who would seek revenge for the life of Brae Sundragon.

He winced just thinking her name. She'd been his sister by law—she'd been as close to him as any other member of his family, and he had failed her. He should've trusted her when she said Raphaela Kael intended to imprison her. He should've trusted she knew Raphaela's true intentions for her. Lathan shivered, buffing his arms to gain some warmth.

The first snow had fallen mere moments after Brae's death, leaving Sunkai covered in a thin layer of white frost quickly melting away. Winter had begun, and the wind grew colder with each passing moment. His sword swayed against his hip beneath the cloak, and he reached under, gripping the hilt securely. A foul scent was on the air tonight, one that filled the senses of every person in the city.

Blood. Brae's blood. Stale and cold on the streets. Lathan's lip curled in a snarl. He punched open the door to the stable, startling the horses within.

His trusted horse, Storm, stomped about in his stall, black eyes wild as he sensed his rider's tension. Lathan quickly saddled the animal and was buckling the leather bridle into place when he heard the creak of the stable doors. For a moment, he thought the sound was just the wind, but then the sound of a man's boots thudding against the weak wooden floors of the stable reached his ears. Lathan drew his sword with a sharp hiss, spinning to face the intruder.

"Blessed Sun, Lathan!" Maxx growled, holding up gloved hands. He glared at his brother. "Put that down!"

Lathan lowered the blade slowly, his eyes roaming over his younger brother cautiously. He was dressed just as Lathan, only in blacks, so he would blend into the night. The glimmer of his silver sword hilt peeked out from his left hip while the dagger given to him by Brecken upon his promotion to Lieutenant was strapped securely to his right.

"What are you doing here, Maxx?" Lathan snapped, thrusting his sword back into its scabbard before turning his back to finish preparing Storm.

"The same as you." He eyed his brother as Maxx went for the stall across from Lathan's, gently coaxing Wind Racer from his bed. "I'm going to find our niece."

"It's too dangerous. We can't both disappear on Brecken, and you have a stronger influence with the king then I do. He trusts you more than he trusts me, and we both know he'll order my arrest before long." Lathan gripped Storm's reins, guiding him out of the stall.

"With his sister running from him, the king trusts no one. He never thought for one moment Damari was working against him all this time." Maxx tossed his bag over Wind Racer's rump, tying it securely to the saddle. "Clea and Afra are in the wind, and there's no way to get to Brecken. Even if we tried, Raphaela would accuse us of treason for trying to see him and sentence us both. I've done all I can for Brecken. He's on his own now."

"I can't let you do this, Maxx."

"You can't stop me, Lathan." Maxx mounted, adjusting his cloak over Wind Racer's back before turning to his brother. "If you think I will sit back while Damari Kael runs blindly across all of Nfaros with our little niece, you are mistaken. Noelle is the one we must protect now. She is the only one we *can* protect now. She is all that is left of Brae."

Lathan closed his eyes, tremors rushing through him at the sound of her name.

"I think we both owe Brae this, don't you?" Maxx's voice lowered to an angry rumble.

Lathan nodded, swinging into the saddle before taking up his reins. He came alongside his brother as the horses moved slowly from the stable, carrying them leisurely out into the night air. The frozen wind stung Lathan's skin, but he ignored the cold as he turned to his brother.

"Let's find Noelle." He nodded. "Let's see her safe, far away from this cursed place."

"Then we will find Adlae." Maxx grinned.

"Yes. Then we will find Adlae Sundragon, Winter Queen, Sword Maiden of Sunkai and Queen of Nfaros by Blood and Birthright." Lathan dug his heels into Storm's sides.

Long live the Sundragon.

The Night Wood

Expelling a long breath, Dominant Gwylan turned her back on the swirl of white fire in the center of their circle. The Night Wood was eerily quiet, the first snow falling lightly on the Sisters' hair and shoulders, sprinkling them in white powder. A layer of silver coated the ground before melting ever so slowly to soak the dirt beneath their feet. The Intermediates looked at each other, whispering softly as their white cloaks rippled in the wind.

None of them felt the cold here, not with the white fire burning to warm the magic within them.

The Novices were huddled closest to the fire, their dark hoods pulled up to hold in as much warmth as they could. With their magic so new inside them, no wonder they sat so close in the circle, trying to draw from the flames—their only source of warmth. The Night Wood was one of the northernmost forests in Nfaros and when winter came, was deadly.

Gwylan sighed, clutching her black cloak around her, marching through the circle, ignoring the burn of the cold as she walked farther and farther away from that flame. There had been rumors of disturbances in their force all day. The power being drained from one of their crystals was undeniable, though most of the Dominants tried to brush the idea off as nonsense. Surely their magic hadn't been used improperly! Surely there must be some mistake they would rectify shortly. But Gwylan held the strongest power among them, and she knew the Abyss had touched the heart of one of their own. To know such things was a gift among the Eventide Sisters, and only a few of them were granted such power. Gwylan had never wanted to be one of them, but the gift had been given to her by the Creator, and she would not argue.

The horses were restless in their corral as she passed, dancing the perimeter of the crudely carved fence and swinging their heads as the steady snowfall draped them in white splendor. Gwylan summoned the Gentling, offering them a few moments of calm as she walked by, the golden embers sparking on the fence as she ran her fingers along the rough wood. The horses paused for a moment, their dark eyes watching her as she passed. But their calm lasted only for a moment before their feet began to stomp once more, the dark pools of their eyes brightening wildly. She knew then there was something truly amiss. Even their animals sensed the shift in magic—the shift in the world.

Only the Superiors will know for certain what has happened. Gwylan nodded sharply at the thought, quickening her steps between the trees to the next clearing. Their tents were scattered through their small part of the forest, canvas fluttering in the breeze. She mumbled under her breath, tugging on one of her multiple braids. Most of the Eventide Sisters were Draedin born, but the numbers of Quintarian and Kaldoner were growing among them, scattering their faction with a mix of colors and accents.

Having been a Novice when they came to this part of the world, Gwylan herself had reservations about bringing these women into their fold. She was pure Draedinian, as all those of the Blood of Eventide had been for years before her. But now, they had strengthened their numbers with these women who hailed from Northern Lands, which worried Gwylan. Never had she felt such a strong surge in their magic as she had this past day, and she knew the use was not from a woman of Draedin.

These women of the North do not truly understand the power they wield.

"Dominant Gwylan," one of the Novices whispered as she passed, bowing low until her nose nearly touched the ground.

Gwylan merely waved a hand at her before moving on, still unused to her title. Reaching back, she scratched at the incessant itch on her right shoulder. The ink had been etched into her skin, three circles intersecting each other with a long sword down the middle through them. The bottom circle was white, her Novice status, the middle red for Intermediate and the third black for Dominant. Each circle was given at the time of their advancement, as ordered by the Superiors. If Gwylan were ever to reach Superior, her left shoulder would be etched with a golden cord—the bindings of a Superior to the law of the Creator's magic.

Gwylan removed her hand from the most recent markings, knowing in the end scratching at them wouldn't help her. Taking a deep breath, she moved on, passing down the path, the ground worn out by so many feet marching from tent to tent. The Novices would be called in to their beds soon, so they might rest before the dawn when the Intermediates would rouse them from their sleep to begin their lessons. The Dominants would then gather their council, to discuss the turning of the world. Without them, the world would never make its turn—there would be no magic. Even the Winter Queen would be powerless against one of their top Dominants.

Before she'd taken the black garb, Gwylan hadn't fully understood how firmly Dominants controlled the magic of the world. Truly control was a gift, given to those deemed worthy. But placed in the wrong hands, such control could do great evil, and Gwylan feared such a thing had come to pass. Whichever Intermediate had done this, the Dominant who advanced them from Novice would be brought to trial for their misjudgment first.

Another breath tapered her lungs, misting before her face in the chill air. The snowflakes were falling heavily now, thicker than before, and

Gwylan wondered if perhaps the wind was preparing for a storm. Perhaps the snow meant to lay thickly on the ground tonight, testing the limits of the Eventide Sisters. It would be something the Creator would do, to test the strength of their hearts and the faith of their souls. A long time had passed since she'd felt the Frostling's touch. Not since the Sundragon had sat upon the throne and called Nfaros his.

Gwylan breathed a sigh of relief when she found the tent she sought, sitting at the farthest edge of the camp, nearest the border of the woods to Kaldon. Keeping Kaldoners away had been difficult. Some came to them for their healing powers, others came as though they were a traveling show—entertainment for the children. The pestering Gwylan would not tolerate. None of them understood they were the reason the world thrived, and none of them would ever understand. The Superiors said this was the way the world worked, and they had to be gracious and kind. Those were virtues Gwylan struggled with every day.

Stepping over the threshold of the council tent, she breathed easier, warmth flooding into her, forcing all memory of the cold outdoors from her mind. Gwylan looked back and forth at the other Dominants, gathered closely together around the crystal hanging midair in the center of the tent. Her friend, Ellia, spared her a glance and smile before returning her bright eyes to the glittering crystal.

Gwylan stepped up close beside her, squeezing her friend's hand for a moment. She and Ellia had crossed the sea from Draedin together as Novices, becoming good friends during their training. Now Dominants together, they'd learned what being sisters truly meant with this magic pulsing in them both—with this duty of sharing the magic with each other to help anchor the world in nourishment.

"Have you seen anything?" she whispered in Ellia's ear.

"Nothing." Ellia shook her head. "Intermediate Kaylah has been sent with a message to the Superiors. They have been so silent since the surge happened. Even the crystals do not speak to us. There seems to have been a shudder in the power, and we cannot reach the answers."

"Do we know the source at least? Do we know which city? We have Intermediates spread out from Kaldon to Sunkai, for their personal growth. If we know the city, surely the crystals will show us something."

"We have attempted everything, Gwylan," Haileah's strong voice made Gwylan wince, and she turned to the Dominant who had once been her teacher. "If we knew the city, do you not think we would tell you?"

"I meant no disrespect, Haileah. I am only suggesting options. Even the smallest answer is still an answer." Gwylan tugged on the edges of her cloak, pulling it taut around her. "I meant only if we can discover the city—"

"We could send horses?" Haileah sniffed, tossing her dark curls over her shoulder. "We are not sending any more of our Sisters, Dominant or Intermediate, out into this turning world. The Abyss seeks to corrupt our purity and he's seemingly succeeded with at least one."

"Sending horses is not a horrible idea, Haileah," Young Calli whispered, looking up from beneath her long, thick lashes at the circle of women. "We could send our strongest Dominants, once we know who we seek."

"And any one of us could go on trial any day. If one of our Intermediates has done this, then the Dominant responsible for offering her this greater magic will pay the price first."

"We know the laws, Haileah," Ellia snapped, her brow furrowing in a glare. "You needn't impress them upon us. Who knows? One of *your* Intermediates might very well be who has done this, so do not speak as if you were judge over us all!"

"Enough!" Symber, a tall Kaldoner, lashed her hand at them as though slicing the thick tension between the group. "Remember we are all sisters here, and we stand together. No matter what is to come."

"Complainers, us," Jhaedra giggled, her Quintarian accent thicker than usual. "Used to getting our own way, we are. But answers soon will come. Tea?"

The woman spun, practically skipping away to snatch up her teapot. Gwylan caught the tremor in her hands as she attempted to pour a cup.

"I am going to be ill if I have to endure one more cup of Quintaria mint tea," Haileah growled.

"Herbal, this." Jhaedra waved one of the teacups at her before turning her back again.

"The fighting must stop between us." Gwylan sighed heavily. "Perhaps we should try the crystals again."

"Yes. Standing here doing nothing is futile," Symber agreed, knocking the cloak from her shoulders to hang heavily against her back. She tugged off her long gloves. "The crystals will not—"

She was interrupted by a gust of wind as Intermediate Kaylah came bursting through, falling to one knee before the circle and holding up a parchment. No one moved, not even Haileah as they all stared at the golden sealed letter. The young Intermediate was shivering where she knelt, the tent flap still rippling wildly, allowing the cold wind to flow through. Gwylan grumbled under her breath as she stepped forward, snatching the letter from the girl's hand.

"You are dismissed, Intermediate."

"Thank you, Dominant Gwylan." Kaylah shot to her feet, running back out the way she'd come. Gwylan secured the tent door behind her.

Turning back, she held up the letter. "Let us see what the Superiors had to say, shall we?"

Ellia nodded vigorously, her eyes aflame with curiosity as Gwylan broke the seal, carefully peeling back the folds of the paper. Her eyes skimmed over the words, pausing at the very end. The silence in the tent was deafening as they all waited for her to speak. Gwylan looked up at each of them in turn, pausing for a moment on one in particular before she finally spoke.

"The Superiors have spent the day in meditation, seeking answers from the Creator and they have been given one." Gwylan's chest swelled. "The fault lies with an Intermediate in Sunkai. Brae Jandry, once known as Princess Brae Sundragon of Sunkai, has been executed by order of one of our Intermediates. Her blood has been used as a sacrifice to the Abyss. The Intermediate at fault ..."

Gwylan again scanned the group, her stomach twisting. "The Intermediate at fault is Raphaela Kael, raised to the advancement of Intermediate upon the judgment of Dominant Jhaedra."

Gasps rang through the tent, and Jhaedra's teacup thudded to the ground. Gwylan plunged on before anyone could speak, knowing the fear would be tenfold when announcing the second piece of news.

"There are to be four Dominants to cross out of the Night Wood to seek out Adlae Sundragon, the One Thought Dead, to offer her our numbers and strength in the fight to reclaim the throne of Nfaros from the usurper, Roderick Kael, and the evil follower of the Abyss, Raphaela Kael. These are the Dominants chosen; Dominant Ellia, Dominant Symber, Dominant Haileah ... and Dominant Gwylan."

The tent exploded in chaos.

The City of Sunkai

"You did not seek my counsel!" Roderick roared, ramming his chair into the table. "I am to approve executions, Raphaela! You had no right!"

"Hush, brother," Raphaela cooed, braiding her hair over her shoulder as she stared out the window.

The cloud had passed thick and dark into her heart. She felt him with her. Whispering in her ear, telling her where she needed to go. His presence filled her, and the power was hers alone to have. Now magic flowed freely, without the supervision of the Dominant who had *permitted* her to rise to Intermediate. Raphaela's lip curled at the thought, as she tied off the end of her braid. Lifting her hands, she pressed her fingers together, her veins turning to black vines beneath her skin as the magic streamed through her.

"I told you, everything will be fine now. I will have my army soon and we will crush Adlae Sundragon."

"What army? Half of my men are in Quintaria, and they have not answered my call. You have imprisoned my best captain, and now, my two lieutenants have run from the city!" Roderick stalked across the room, slamming his fist against his palm.

"He tried to kill me." Raphaela froze at the mention of Brecken. Her fingers curled around her braid, and she tugged, shaking herself free of those feelings. She had no time for them, not now, not with everything *he* had given her. She didn't need Brecken Jandry, and the blood sacrifice had worked—had strengthened her.

"What do you intend to do now, sister?"

"I intend to lead your new army." Raphaela turned to him, straightening her shoulders when she faced him. "We will have the greatest army in all of Nfaros, Roderick. A great power has come to me, and we will take back what is rightfully ours. Soon, the whole world will kneel before us and there will be no one to stand in our way. *He* has come to me, Roderick. Not even our little sister Damari will challenge us once she sees the power we have been given. She too will kneel before us and beg our forgiveness for her treachery. The world is turning, and it is *our* time. *He* has blessed us, my brother, and with me at the head of your army, we cannot fail."

Her surety resounded in her voice, sending ripples of darkness through the palace as the Abyss roamed the halls of the Blood Keep.

CHAPTER ONE

The Road to Molderëin

A frozen wind whistled through the trees bordering the wide dirt road. The crisp air filled her lungs, sharpening her senses as her red gelding moved leisurely down the path. Winter had been long in coming, but with its sudden arrival came a fierceness that spoke of the Winter Queen's rage. All who felt this wind knew her devastation; all who saw the storm clouds rolling over the world from the Ice Mountains knew her wrath. There was vengeance laced in the wind, and none could stop her now.

Clea Jandry breathed deeply, pulling in more of the cool air as she urged Copper to the front of the line. Her household had gathered around her when she'd announced her intention to leave Quintaria before her brother's army arrived. They refused to leave her side, insisting on accompanying her to her family's home in Molderëin. Together they looked like quite a caravan, the Head Mistress of her household having insisted on packing much more than Clea needed for the journey. Perhaps some of them thought they wouldn't be returning to Quintaria at all. But Clea had every intention of coming back here—once she discovered the purpose her brother had in sending her to the home of their birth.

The thought that she held the fate of the world in her hands troubled her. Brecken had never spoken in riddles before. He was always straightforward; a simple man with simple answers. But the world was turning and everything was changing.

Brae is gone. Nothing will ever be the same for my brother. Clea trembled, her gloved hands gripping the reins tighter at the thought of her sister by law.

The news had reached her on the road when one of the King's Guard had ridden as fast as he could on the road through the Aulend to spread the news of Brae Jandry's scheduled execution. Clea had known there would be nothing she could do, and the messenger would reach Maxx in time. But knowing neither of her brothers arrived in time to save Brae was like a knife to Clea's heart. The woman had been family, and Jandrys always protected their own at all costs. To lose her to a woman they once trusted—a woman whose power was supposed to nourish the world, not pollute it—was unbearable and awakened a rage in Clea that had not reared itself in years.

Her silk cloak did little to keep out the wind, and Clea wished, not for the first time, she had one of those thick, woolen cloaks common to Woodlanders. They might not be at the height of Quintarian fashion, but they were known for keeping out the cold. For the journey ahead of her, Clea could find a lot of use for one. She shivered, clasping a hand to the fur-trimmed collar of the cloak, holding the fur tightly at her chin.

The wagon lumbered beside her, carrying all the trunks and supplies her Head Mistress had insisted on bringing. She frowned again when she saw Izeana and Rheatha shuffling along beside the horses. Raised as slaves in Molderëin, they still believed sitting a horse was disrespectful to their master, no matter how Clea insisted they could have their own mounts so they wouldn't have to walk on the cold ground. She didn't know how they managed without the warmth from a horse's body. But they walked proudly, their heads held high and their arms tucked beneath their cloaks out of sight.

Rheatha caught her eye, and a wobbly smile touched her pale lips before she returned soft brown eyes back to the road ahead. Rheatha was the first slave she'd ever freed, but who'd chosen to stay and serve her. Clea wanted Rheatha to begin her own life, to put aside the customs of a Molderëinian slave. But the woman had said with the brand on her arm, she could never put aside her memories or the customs that came with them. Serving a noble was her whole life and to change now would be impossible. Clea only hoped the woman would put aside the custom of solitude, because she only had to look at her Captain of the Guard, Morgren, to know how he felt about the beautiful Molderëinian woman. But Clea also knew Rheatha would never leave her, not unless she had to. Having her was comforting.

Ever since Clea's mother died, Rheatha had become more a part of her growing up than any other woman. With Afra fulfilling whatever duties she had as a noblewoman of House Malaki, and her brothers having made their permanent home in the Mother City, Clea had little influence from family. Rheatha taught her everything she'd needed to know about Molderëin. The studies had prepared her for a day like today, when circumstance and trouble drove her from her home to her birthplace.

Clea cleared her throat, tugging on Copper's reins as they approached the border of the Aulend. Once across the borderline, she would go west, skirting a large circle around Sunkai. Avoiding the Mother City at all costs was vital, even though going that direction would cut the time to reach Molderëin in half. If she were to enter the Mother City, they could take a ship that would sail them directly into the port of Molderëin. But saving time wasn't worth the risk of being caught at the docks in Sunkai. If she was, she would be thrown directly into the cell beside her brother. Just the thought of Brecken rotting in one of those damp dungeons chilled her skin more than the winter wind ever could.

Shaking off those feelings, she squeezed her heels into Copper's sides, the young gelding leaping forward to come beside Morgren. Her Captain of the Guard smiled, reaching out with a slight frown to readjust her cloak on her shoulder. The man wasn't just her protector—he was like a father to her. He had taught her everything he knew about the sword, and she in return, had trained him in the ways of Northerners, helping him put away the savage ways of the Molderëinians.

"You will have no need for that cloak the closer we come to Molderëin," he commented, patting her shoulder lightly. "The south is never touched by the cold. Not even the Winter Queen could reach that far."

"I wouldn't be so sure, captain," Clea murmured, wrapping her reins around the pommel of her saddle so she could clutch her arms to her ribs beneath the cloak. "The world is turning and everything is changing. The Winter Queen has attacked Nfaros with a vengeance now the first snow has fallen."

"Your brother is wrong sending you on this mission," Morgren snorted. "Brecken knows better than this. I taught him well to protect his sisters, not force them into danger. Molderëin has worsened in savagery these many years. Slavery is twentyfold, the masters corrupted by darkness."

"Be that as it may, there is good magic there also. Brecken would not send me if he didn't think I could help. You know this, Morgren," Clea said, picking up her reins once more to keep Copper steady on the path.

3

"These masters you speak of may be corrupt, but I am made immune to the darkness. You know that also."

Morgren mumbled something under his breath before rolling his eyes to her. "That does not mean the darkness cannot touch you, my lady. You have not crossed the borders into Molderëin in a long time."

"I will be fine, Morgren. I'm sure." Clea scratched Copper's neck, combing her fingers through the gelding's freshly washed mane. Izeana always insisted on washing and combing Copper's hair until his mane was shiny and soft. Clea tried many times to tell her the extra grooming wasn't necessary, but Izeana would only smile, muttering it was no trouble before she continued with her work. She loved the young Molderëinian woman, but she couldn't seem to help her get passed the strict rulings of her previous owners in Molderëin. Clea had tried everything she could think of, but Izeana clung to the old customs as though clinging to life, and Clea wouldn't try to change her if this was what made her the sweet, gentle woman she was.

"Lady Clea!" Ryker, her stable boy and new soldier, came galloping from the front of the line, looking over his shoulder frantically. His eyes wild and his hair disheveled, he brought his brown packhorse to a skidding halt beside Clea. "There are shadows ahead! At the borders of the woods!"

"Talk sense, boy," Morgren growled.

"I am talking sense, sir," Ryker gasped, breathless. "They are shadows. Large shadows that move as a man would move."

"Morgren, gather the men!" Clea spun Copper around, pushing him to a brisk canter back down to the wagons. Rheatha and Izeana were already arming themselves with their Molderëinian longbows and quivers brimming with iron-tipped arrows. "Pick up your swords! Tighten the lines! There are Black Ones ahead!"

Behind her, she heard Morgren shouting orders, the clatter of the men's spears and swords easing from their resting places as they jogged forward, forming protective lines in front of the women who were taking charge of the wagons. Clea grinned. One of the many good qualities she could credit Molderëinian women with was they knew how to take over and keep calm in a dangerous situation. Spinning Copper back around, she dug in her heels, leaning far over the gelding's neck to spur him quickly to the front line.

Her men had come together in perfect formation, spears and swords in their hands as they waited for the order to march. Clea brought Copper up beside Morgren, a small smile tilting the corner of her mouth. The man very nearly rolled his eyes at her but caught himself. He knew how she felt about eye rolling, and he would never purposely dishonor her. Clea sighed, wondering if there was anything Morgren wouldn't do for her. She knew to him she was the daughter he never had, but the facts remained the same. She was not his daughter, she was his Lady, and he had sworn a vow to obey and protect her, which sometimes posed a problem for them both. Not helping matters was Clea's inexplicable excitement at the mere thought of danger that irritated him to no end.

You go looking for danger and then when it finds you, and I'm not around to help you, what will you do? His voice resounded in her ears even now, and Clea's smile quickly turned to a scowl.

Taking a long draw of air, Clea reached down, tugging her sword from its sheath. Mountain-wrought steel molded into a crescent shape, glittering sharp and silver in the sunlight rays gleaming through the treetops. The blade was engraved with foreign markings along one side and had been passed down to Clea from her uncle, a loyal Kaldoner noble. Spinning the sword between her fingers, Clea watched as the blade glinted and flashed at her side, the soft *swoosh* cutting the thick, cold air and sending tremors up her back.

"If Black Ones are this far south, then the rumors must be true," Morgren said at her side, hefting his iron-tipped spear in his right hand. "The Abyss has entered the heart of Raphaela Kael."

Clea trembled. "And if that is true, then my sister by law really is dead."

"You don't know for certain."

"Yes, I do. Only with pure Sundragon blood could Raphaela have made a sacrifice deemed worthy of the darkness—you know that as well as I, Morgren. Brae is dead." Clea's fingers tightened around the hilt of her sword.

"The shadow is approaching, my lady!" Ryker appeared at her side once more. "May I have permission to join the ranks?"

"You have it." Clea dipped her head. "Be safe, Ryker."

The young boy grinned before he slid down from the saddle, handing the horse off to Izeana before he jogged up the line to join the front ranks. Clea ignored the sinking in her stomach. Ryker was so young, nearly as young as she, and to have him fighting at her front line was something she'd never expected. But Molderëinians believed the moment a boy was old enough to pick up a sword, he was old enough to fight. Denying Ryker this right would be a great insult to him, and she refused to do that.

When she had taken all of them in and offered them their freedom, she promised she would not change the way they were raised, only attempt to soften their hearts and encourage them to different paths. They had all stood up and refused to leave her, despite her desire for them to begin their own lives, lived in freedom far from the cruelty of Molderëin.

"They're here, my lady," Morgren hissed, pulling one of his two short swords from his back. With spear in one hand and sword in the other, Morgren looked as fierce as he ever had. He attempted to edge his mount in front of Clea to protect her, but she skirted his effort, tiptoeing Copper around him.

Part of her wished she'd let him shield her when she saw the darkness descending on her men. The creatures were rolling like thunderclouds in the shadow, long claws curved and reaching as sharp as any blade, large yellow eyes gleaming in the blackness and crooked fangs protruding from between bleeding lips. They were as black as the shadow, their big ears pointed and quivering as they roared their warning.

Wraith Spawn. Black Ones. They were one and the same. Until she'd grown up and learned better, they'd only been a frightening children's story. Clea closed her eyes, raising her sword high into the air.

"Prepare to loose!" she shouted above the snarls of the Black Ones.

The creak of bowstrings and hiss of arrows filled her ears. "Loose!"

Bolts hissed through the air, and she opened her eyes, watching as the arrows formed a perfect arc over her head before falling upon the enemy. The creatures howled, some of them dissolving into thin air when an arrow hit the heart. But they still came, pushing forward around the trees to try to overwhelm them. Clea raised her sword again.

"Another round! Loose!" Again the arrows flew, invoking more screams of agony from the dark creatures.

"They're still coming, my lady. I fear we will have no choice but to come face to face with them."

"They are clever creatures, and they know the woods better than we do." Clea's head swayed back and forth as sudden panic began to set in. "We won't survive this ... unless ..."

"No!" Morgren grabbed her arm. "Not when you need to conserve strength for Molderëin!"

"We will never see Molderëin if I do not do this! The power is mine to use when I am in need. I will not let my people die here! Not at their hands. Not like this."

Clea leaped down from Copper and took off, pushing through the lines of men as she ignored Morgren's call for her to return. In a moment like this, there was no time to waste, and Clea wasn't about to let an innocent boy like Ryker die if there was no need. No matter the risk Morgren thought she was taking, Clea knew this was the only way and her strength would be sufficient.

"Into the hands of the Creator, I commend my spirit," Clea intoned as she broke through the frontlines, brushing off one of the men who tried to stop her. "For this reason, I have given my mortal soul to the One who gave me life and know with this sacrifice, I am made pure and strong by the power that emanates from my soul."

Clea raised her hands, a golden glow glittering around her sword as she faced the darkness. Her power pulsed in her now, magic so strong, so a part of her, she could hardly bear it. Her eyes burned, her heart racing as she stretched out her palms to the oncoming throng.

"Let no man here fall, but instead let these animals of darkness come into the light and see the true Master of the World." Clea thrust the blade point down into the ground. The sword cut through the frozen dirt, sliding nearly to the hilt before she released.

A bolt of lightning shot from the ground, expanding until the power rose up as a wall between her and the enemy. The Wraith Spawn continued on, unperturbed by the light. Clea took a deep breath, the magic still throbbing within her soul. The light grew brighter, and she heard her men groaning behind her, shielding their eyes from the blinding white. But Clea looked on, keeping her eyes on the creatures.

The first one hit the wall, his screech deafening her to any other sound as he was trapped in its rays. The light grew like vines, wrapping around his throat until his screams were silenced and he dissolved in a burst of black blood and ash. One by one they came into the light, some pulled there against their will. Sweat beaded on Clea's brow, but she held firm to the weavings, pulling air into her lungs for life. She could feel herself being drained, her magic growing weaker, but she pushed on. Her mortal life was in the Creator's hands, and she would not question His purpose for her.

Clea closed her eyes, her neck arching back as she surrendered herself to the magic, letting power fill her to brimming over, until she thought she would be torn apart. Suddenly, the woods were silent, the magic leaving her so quickly she gasped, her ribs throbbing as she fell to her knees. Her sword lay flat at her side as Clea pressed her hands into the dirt, her entire body trembling against the sudden cold washing through her—the loss of the magic cutting deep into her soul. Letting go of so much power always weakened her this way, and Clea had never used so much at one time before.

"My lady!" Rheatha was at her side now, cupping a hand under her arm to pull her back to her feet. "You've used too much, you have."

"I ... I'm fine," Clea answered, closing her eyes and breathing deeply. "I'll be fine."

"I told you not to," Morgren growled, lifting her right off her feet. Her head lolled against his shoulder weakly. "The entire Mother City will have seen that."

"Had to be done," Clea replied, her eyelids growing heavy.

"And if your soul is spent from so much magic?" Morgren glared down at her.

"If my soul is spent, then it is the will of the Creator," Clea answered as he hoisted her onto Copper's back. "Let death come to me as it wishes. Death is not stronger than the One we serve, Morgren."

Rheatha passed her sword up to her, and Clea sighed with relief as her fingers curled around the hilt. This weapon was not something she was willing to lose, and without the blade, her strength was half. Clea slid the blade carefully into its home and picked up her reins.

"Gather the men into lines," she ordered, ignoring Morgren's constant glare now. "Let's move on."

"We cannot continue on this trail," Morgren objected.

Clea smiled. "This is the path chosen for us, and we will walk on it without fear. I will not go through the Gracian and risk wasting more time. My family has already lost too much. We go where we were always meant to, and if we risk the wrath of the Mother City, then so be it. I am not afraid of the Kael King, and he cannot hurt me. Not anymore."

Without another word she marched Copper out in front of the men, making them scatter to catch up as she launched herself down the path to Molderëin.

The City of Sunkai

Brecken breathed deeply, the gashes across his chest burning. The dried blood from his wounds cracked and dribbled afresh down his ribs. He snarled, lip curling as he yanked on the chains holding his arms to the wall. The iron scraped deeply into his wrists, peeling already raw flesh away from the bone. Brecken bowed his head, his shoulders trembling as he fought the moisture gathering in his eyes. He had been like this for ten days. Moments of harsh struggle, anger rising to the surface before the memories of his wife's dead body in his arms came flooding back, trying to weaken his resolve. But worse were the dreams of Mirae.

They'd risen up somewhere deep within him, the same feeling he'd resisted when he saw her on the battlefield rearing itself at his weakest moments. She looked like Brae, she walked like Brae, and at least in his dreams, she even sounded like Brae. But, as had Brae's life, his dreams always ended with blood. Brecken pulled on the chain again, shouting until his lungs hurt.

Ten days had passed since Brae was slaughtered on the streets of Sunkai. Ten days since his brothers disappeared into the Aulend Forest. Ten days since the Blood Keep received any news of the progress of Adlae Sundragon, the Winter Queen. His family was scattered across Nfaros. Rumors of a band of Quintarians, led by raven-haired Clea Jandry, whispered through the halls of the palace. Brecken was happy—prouder of his sister than he'd ever been. She would go to Molderëin and seek her destiny, just as Brecken knew she would. He knew she would be all right. The magic within her pulsed strong, fueled by the Creator Himself. Brecken knew she would find what she needed in their birth country. No matter what came, he knew Clea could handle any situation. The only one he needed to worry about was Afra.

No one knew where she was, not even her family by law, the Malaki's. Widowed so young and left alone with a small fortune from her husband, Afra had been living in Kaldon. But she disappeared mere days before

Brae's execution. Some said she was in Sunkai, others said she was the veiled woman who walked the streets of Kaldon at night. Brecken didn't know which story was the truth, he only knew Raphaela would be looking for her, and Afra was not equipped to protect herself the way Clea was.

Brecken closed his eyes and saw Brae, her bright eyes glistening, red hair fluttering in the wind. The hole in his heart grew larger and Brecken filled it with his fury. Another face flashed behind his closed lids and his lip curled, a low rumble emanating from the base of his throat. The door to his cell creaked open, and Brecken raised his head, shifting his bare feet against the rough stone floor so he stood steady, eyes narrowing in a heated glare. A flash of red and white passed swiftly in front of him, but he didn't let his eyes follow her. He wouldn't look at her unless he had to.

"My brother wants me to release you," Raphaela's voice echoed softly in the dank chamber. "He believes you are still loyal to him. That you will run to his side and rally his armies back to him. Is that true, Brecken? Do you remain loyal to my brother?"

Brecken straightened his spine, jutting his square jaw. "I am loyal to the true heir to the throne."

Raphaela stepped in front of him, and he now had no choice but to look her in the eye.

"Roderick Kael," Raphaela whispered, searching his gaze.

"The Sundragon," Brecken hissed.

Raphaela stepped back, crossing her arms. "This is what I feared. How could you, Brecken? After so many years of loyalty and friendship to my brother?"

"You killed the woman I love!" Brecken lashed forward, straining against the harsh chains. "She was first in my heart! Her loyalties are mine also!"

"Not always." Raphaela shook her head, her long braid whooshing back and forth against her back. "You were loyal to Roderick all these years. You love my brother. You didn't love Brae, Brecken. You and I—"

"I hate you!" Brecken roared, pulling the chains taut, wrapping his fists around them as his anger grew to tremble his body. "My hatred for you runs deep within my soul and will never go away. I never loved you, Raphaela. I never could. You are a cold, evil witch, and you killed the only woman I ever loved! The *only* woman I ever will love."

Raphaela's eyes glistened and she turned her back. Brecken felt nothing—her tears meant nothing for she had no right to shed them.

"You will not reform me, Raphaela. You will never have me." Laughter bubbled up his throat and burst forth, drawing her back around, her eyes wide in shock. "You will have to kill me. Then I will go to the arms of my wife, and you will be left alone—as you always have been and always will be."

Raphaela spun away. "If that is what you want, Brecken, then so be it. I offered you a chance ... I will not offer one again."

Her delicate hand rose above her head, slicing through the air sharply. Brecken looked up, the familiar black cloud gathering, swirling, and descending upon him. Closing his eyes, he surrendered to Raphaela's wrath.

CHAPTER TWO

The Aulend Forest

Damari had lost all sense of time. A soft snow fell in the woods—the light, frozen flakes whispering through the tree branches to add a dusting of powder to the already foot-high layer covering the ground. Holding Noelle tighter against her chest, Damari curled herself closer to her horse, drawing his warmth into herself. Noelle sighed contentedly against her, and Damari knew the child didn't feel the cold, just as she didn't. She knew as long as she kept Noelle close to her, the child would never feel the harsh bite of winter.

Damari tugged on the reins, halting the horse. A heavy sigh slipped between her lips as she looked back and forth, brushing a loose strand of her golden hair from her face. There was no sign of the Woodland Paths, nothing to draw her to them—no glitter of magic. She'd been riding through these woods for days. If she'd found the Paths, she would have already been in the Shadow Lands by now. But instead, she feared she was riding in circles, with no true destination. This had to be the work of the Abyss, and if not, then Damari was simply lost.

Breathing deeply, Damari tugged on the reins, pulling the old animal farther north. Or at least, she thought they were going north. After leaving the caravan, direction had been simple—finding the Aulend wasn't difficult. But she hadn't expected the first snow to fall so thickly, marring her path ahead through the forest. Damari wished she'd thought of the many more provisions she would need in order to keep Noelle warm and safe. She'd been relying on finding the Paths, now everything was falling apart all around her.

Time had no meaning in these woods, and soon Damari would have to forage for food. Their last loaf of bread was already half gone, and already they'd resorted to eating snow in place of the water they had finished. Noelle shifted, murmuring in her sleep as she buried her face against Damari's chest. Damari rested her hand on the back of the child's head, tears springing to her eyes. This child didn't belong to her, but to Brae Sundragon, her dear friend. Damari couldn't even imagine what Raphaela was putting Brae through, but in her heart she had to believe her friend was still alive. Perhaps Brecken had arrived in time, perhaps he'd stopped Raphaela's torture before too late.

Damari stroked the gelding's neck, and he snorted, mist puffing from his nostrils. She smirked, pulling back on the reins to bring the animal to a full stop. The snow had stopped for the moment, leaving a glittering layer of powder on the icy ground. Damari scooped Noelle up on her right arm as she slipped carefully down out of the saddle.

"Are we there yet, Mama Damari?" Noelle whispered, snaking her little arms around Damari's neck.

"No, sweet one." Damari sighed. "Not yet, but soon."

A heaviness fell upon her heart when she heard the name Noelle had taken to calling her. The child understood only that to anyone who crossed their paths, she had to pretend Damari was her mother. Damari was troubled to hear the name, knowing the little girl couldn't possibly understand what was happening to her parents, or how her life had already been altered beyond repair. Damari wished she could ease the fear she sometimes saw in the little one's eyes. But there would be plenty of time to comfort her later.

Creator willing, Brecken will see all those we love out of the city safely. Damari's chest swelled with a breath before she bent, carefully setting Noelle down on the cold ground. The child shivered the moment she left Damari's arms, her small cloak bundled tightly around her for warmth as Damari led her to the biggest tree she could find. The loyal old horse followed her without urging, staying close to her shoulder as though to lend his own warmth. Damari settled Noelle against the tree before she hurried deeper into the woods, collecting armfuls of frozen sticks until she couldn't carry anymore before she returned. Noelle's eyes widened when she saw her, a sparkle glittering in her eye.

"Are you going to do the magic again?" she asked, clapping her little hands together. "Do the magic again, Mama Damari! Please?"

Damari avoided looking at the child as she dug the snow away until moist dirt appeared beneath, creating a perfect circle for their campfire. Her heart raced over little Noelle's request, knowing magic was the only way they would have a fire tonight, but reluctant to do what had come so naturally in a moment of dire need many nights ago. She hadn't known where the power came from, unless it had originated from her fear Noelle would freeze to death in these woods without a fire.

The magic was strange, something foreign that had risen up inside of her and boiled her blood, but did not scorch her. Something Damari never wanted to do again, yet the fulfillment of her soul the moment the magic touched her had been keeping her awake at night and feeding her desire to feel that way again. She breathed deeply, looking up at Noelle again. The little girl was trembling in the cold, but her eyes were wide with excitement and hope. How could she disappoint her? How could she deny her anything?

Closing her eyes, Damari rested her hands on the mountain of sticks she'd made, relaxing herself. The wind whistled through the tree branches, pulling her hood from atop her head to catch her hair in a whirlwind. Tilting her head back, she arched her slim neck, exposing it to the cold. Her mother's necklace, the intricately shaped golden eagle of the Winter Queen, began to burn, infusing warmth throughout her body to keep out winter's chill, as it had done since Damari was a little girl. Heat pooled in her belly, swirling and reaching to flow like a river through her veins. Her breaths quickened, rasping through her parted lips as her fingers erupted in flames.

Gasping, she opened her eyes, watching as stark white flames flickered out of her fingertips. Noelle squealed in delight, falling forward on her knees to hold her little hands close to the heat. Damari fell back, wincing when her tailbone slammed onto the hard ground. Grumbling under her breath, she rubbed the now tender spot before distancing herself a little more from the flames. They were magic in its purest form. She had never seen white fire before, but she had the strangest feeling such a flame could only come from her, and her alone.

Damari scooted forward cautiously, situating herself behind Noelle. The child curled against her chest, a sweet sigh slipping from her little lips.

Damari wrapped her arms around her, resting her chin on top of the girl's head as she drew her cloak around them both, scanning the woods for any unusual movement. She could only hope they were deeply enough in the woods not to be detected by any of the men she was sure her brother sent out after her. How many of them were brave enough to enter the forest, she did not know. But she knew Roderick and Raphaela wouldn't stop until they had her and Noelle locked in the Blood Keep dungeons.

The wind picked up, tree branches creaking as they swayed and bent at sharp angles. Damari shivered, even though the cold didn't touch her. Noelle's little arms curled around Damari's waist as she settled in, seeking sleep. A smile tilted her lips, holding the child coming more easily to her now than before. She didn't have much experience with children, having stayed close to her family her entire life. None of her cousins had any children, and with little progress toward an unwanted marriage with Roderick, there were no signs of any children coming any time soon. Damari knew as long as Brecken was married to another, Raphaela would never subject herself to another man's will. A shudder wracked her body and she turned her thoughts from her sister.

"Mama Damari?" Noelle groaned, rearranging herself in Damari's arms.

"Yes?" Damari tilted her head back against the tree trunk, closing her eyes.

"Is my Mama going to be at the mountains? Will she and my Papa meet us there?" Noelle's voice was sluggish as she fought sleep.

Damari opened her eyes, staring through the roof of tree branches to the glittering golden sky as the sun descended in the distance. Her grip on the child tightened, holding her against her warmth as she whispered,

"I hope so, my love. Creator's Blessing, I hope so."

Quintaria

"How much?" The silver chain glittered in the light of the sun, the tiny diamonds embedded in the set sending streams of rainbow lights across her face.

"Five gold," the merchant replied, glancing up at her briefly before he continued with his work.

"Hmm." Shaking her head, she set the chain down, tapping her finger against the edge of the wooden stall. The market was quiet today, unusual for the city of Quintaria. At least, that was what she'd been told. In all her years, she'd never been this far north before, and the customs of these people were still strange to her.

"I would pay three for such a piece," she murmured, running her hands along a few of the smaller chains. "Or five silvers. There are not enough gems in this for such a high price of gold."

"You would know much about gems," the merchant mumbled, his eyes narrowing on the veil hiding her face. "Being of the mountains."

"Indeed." Navaria was grateful her amusement was hidden by the veil, glancing from the corner of her eye at her *Chalqüin*, Krow.

He rolled his eyes, crossing his big arms over his chest. "Nothing here is worth our coin, Navaria."

"I would not say so." She lifted one of the golden chains, a simple piece with a single white diamond at the center. "This one is pretty."

"This one is barely worth two silvers," Krow grumbled, taking the necklace in his big palm to hold it up to the light.

"I like it." Navaria lifted her money pouch, turning back to the merchant. "How much is this one?"

The merchant grinned, revealing a missing front tooth. "Two silvers."

Krow snorted, but Navaria ignored him as she dug in her pouch for the coins. She dropped them one at a time into the merchant's hand before gently slipping the necklace into the small casing at her belt. She had changed out her simple gray robes for a bright blue dress. Adlae said Navaria needed to look like a Quintarian, and she hadn't argued, taking on the stiff black belts and brightly colored boots that seemed most common in this merchant town. But she had kept the veil.

No one this far north had ever seen one of the Mountain People before, and if she removed the veil, then the stories would fly across the country, and the false king would find them. He knew Adlae Sundragon, the Winter Queen, left Sunkai with two visiting Mountain People. Navaria was certain he suspected they were in Quintaria. But he would never move against the Winter Queen, one of the purest creatures of magic in Nfaros, without knowing for certain she was as helpless in this city as she appeared.

Navaria sighed, moving on down the street, Krow's shadow falling over her with every step. He'd kept close to her since the first snow fell, sharing his warmth. Navaria knew his proximity was the reason her heart was still beating. Feeling the cold was a burden the women of the Mountains had to bear, this weakness to the cold which seemed not to faze their men at all. The first snow hadn't even drawn a shudder from Krow. He did not flinch in the wind or waver under the frosty breath of the Winter Queen.

The cold was one of the many the reasons a woman of the Mountains like Navaria needed a *Chalqüin*. If it was possible for her to never leave the Mountains, then she wouldn't. But with her Gift, coming to these northern lands was imperative, and she would only survive with Krow. Yet even with him, her survival here was fragile. They both knew at any moment these strange elements could overwhelm her, and there would be nothing Krow could do to save her.

Shivering, Navaria pulled her new red cloak closer around her body, sealing in her own warmth. Krow stepped closer, and she smiled up at him. She didn't feel the cold as much since they'd left the woods—because the magic of her blue fire was still pulsing through her blood, like a piece of home had returned to her, renewing her strength.

After the Frostling's magic nearly killed her, embracing her own magic had most certainly saved her life, feeding her desire to return home, to finish her real purpose here. But she couldn't leave the Winter Queen. Not yet, not until she knew she was in the safe hands of people she could trust. They were close to such a goal, but Navaria knew finding the army Brecken Jandry left behind, finding the men who refused to return to the false king because of his actions against their captain, would be more difficult than anticipated. Convincing those men to fight a war with Navaria and Krow would be harder still.

"What are we doing here, Navaria?" Krow grumbled at her ear, glaring at any passing Quintarian who looked at Navaria strangely because of her veil. "Why are you spending our coin on worthless trinkets?"

"Perhaps they're not worthless." Navaria's brow twitched beneath the veil as she glanced up at the big man beside her. "The diamonds are of the Mountains, Krow."

Krow glanced at her doubtfully. "Mountain diamonds would never come this far."

"Yet some did." Navaria placed her hand over the pouch at her belt. "Every diamond has a purpose, Krow. You know this as well as I."

"Do you intend to give them to the Winter Queen?" Krow growled. Navaria winced at the sound as she turned slightly to him, wrapping her hand around his arm. "They belong with our people, Navaria."

"In the days to come, the Winter Queen will need all the strength and power the Creator has given to this world. Our diamonds can anchor her power, to preserve her strength for the fight." Navaria shuddered.

Krow paused in the middle of the street, which made Navaria turn to face him. "Has your Gift come to you again?"

Navaria swallowed. Being able to See was considered a blessing, but many times Navaria felt the power was a curse. Knowing what the future held for her friends was the hardest, but the few divinations she'd had recently troubled her. She'd always known the Winter Queen would have to go on alone soon, but she hadn't expected events to happen like this. Now that the world knew the Winter Queen was Adlae Sundragon, the lost heir to the throne of Nfaros, all of the people across the land were rising up against Roderick Kael. Yet as many as spoke for the Sundragon, the same number also ran to swear loyalty to the false king and his sorceress sister, Raphaela.

Taking Krow's arm again, she gently tugged him forward, weaving her way through the thinning crowd toward the inn. Finding an inn where they could hide hadn't been difficult. No one knew the Winter Queen rested in the smallest room on the second floor of the Golden Dragon. Navaria and Krow had acquired the room before Adlae used her power to slip in unnoticed.

Their small band of soldiers—the captain of Navaria's army, Glaydin, and the men he'd selected—had taken refuge at a much smaller inn at the gates of the city, knowing too large a party of such unusual people would draw too many questions. Navaria couldn't risk the false king catching up with them, not with Adlae Sundragon's life at stake—not with Damari Kael's whereabouts still unknown. All of Quintaria had come alive with the rumor Damari Kael had defied and betrayed her brother the king, taking Brae Jandry's daughter out of Sunkai and to safety in the Aulend Forest.

The thought of Brae Jandry, once Brae Sundragon, provoked a strange pain in Navaria's heart. She hadn't known the young woman very well, but Brae had offered Navaria and Krow shelter when they needed it most. She'd shown them kindness, and Navaria had never been able to thank her. There was no doubt in anyone's mind Brae was really dead, that the news from Sunkai was true, and the Sundragon Princess had been executed. Navaria could only hope her Sight hadn't betrayed her, and Brecken Jandry was still alive. He still had a part to play in Adlae Sundragon's life, but Navaria knew how ambiguous Seeing was; how the actions of evil could change what she had Seen in an instant.

If anything happened to Brecken Jandry, then the world might be altered beyond repair, and the thought alone set Navaria's knees to knocking. Even if the greatest powers in this world came together as one against the Kael princess and her brother, Navaria knew they might not be enough. *Everything* depended on the Jandry bloodline surviving.

Navaria gasped suddenly, gripping Krow's arm tighter. She felt his concerned frown as his arm snaked around her waist, keeping her upright. Her eyes rolled, the images flashing so swiftly across her eyes she could barely make them out. But the message was clear, the thousands upon thousands of faces blinking in and out of darkness and light. The whispers filling her ears until she heard nothing else.

The Shadows are coming.

The Shadows are coming.

Follow the golden path. Follow the moonlight trail. Follow the Frostlings' touch.

The Shadows are coming.

The Shadows are coming.

Follow the Queen's road. Follow the King's sword. Follow the Almaër Dominje.

The Shadows are coming.

The Shadows are coming.

Navaria wheezed, her breath haggard as she drew deeply into her lungs. The images left her as quickly as they'd come. She slumped against Krow's side, his thick arm the only thing keeping her on her feet. A tear slipped down her cheek, as hot as her skin, but it didn't burn. Wrapping her thin arms around Krow's waist, she tried to bury herself in him as he half carried her back to the inn, ignoring the curious stares from the people they passed. The pearl smooth scales on her face chafed, strangely hot—a sensation she didn't recognize. They were something she'd been born with—something she couldn't help—but every year they'd seemed to spread a little more until finally they stopped, curling around her eye to curve across her forehead. Then they had ceased, and her people knew she'd attained her full growth.

"Another vision," Krow growled, the center of his chest vibrating. "It's this place. You cannot survive so many visions, Navaria. It is dangerous for you to be here."

"We knew the dangers when we made the voyage, Krow. Nothing has changed," Navaria managed to say, readjusting her veil as they stepped over the threshold to the inn.

Krow looked down at her as she peered back up at him from beneath the veil. "Everything has changed, Navaria."

Her veil fluttered when she sighed, pressing her palm against his side to steady herself on her feet without his support. Her strength was slowly returning as they made their slow ascent to the second floor of the inn. The establishment was quiet today—the common room practically empty and the innkeeper nowhere to be seen.

A gust of wind rattled the shutters as Navaria and Krow stepped into the little room. Glaydin merely glanced up at them from his seat in the corner, his wide sword sitting across his lap and fingers curled around the hilt. The rest of the men were probably hiding in the shadows of the alleys surrounding the inn, keeping watch for any King's Guards who might threaten Adlae. Navaria nodded to him before her gaze fell on the Winter Queen.

Long white hair glittered like snowflakes down her back, nearly to her knees now, the white satin gown she wore clinging to her slim waist and hugging womanly curves. Her staff leaned against the wall beside her, the glass globe at the top swirling with dark clouds as the Winter Queen whispered to herself. Navaria had started to grow accustomed to the woman's strange way of speaking to herself. She'd never learned much about the legends of these northerners, but she had begun to believe in the stories they told about the Winter Queen and her predecessor.

Only Adlae would be able to tell her if the stories were true, or if her powers had turned her mind soft, but Navaria didn't care. The woman was always lucid when she spoke to her, which was all that mattered. Keeping Adlae safe was vital, especially now the whole world knew she was the Winter Queen.

"There has been no sign of Brecken Jandry's army?" Navaria whispered, settling herself on the edge of the bed near Glaydin's chair.

"They say his Second, Klade, hides on the border of the Aulend Forest, near the gates of Quintaria, with what is left of Brecken Jandry's army. But if they do, then they hide their fires and use some sort of magic to keep themselves invisible from even my eyes," Glaydin grumbled. "I am certain the Queen could find them, if she would leave this room."

"She has suffered a great loss, Glaydin." Navaria bowed her head.

The captain mumbled something she didn't hear. Navaria sighed. He had pledged himself to Adlae, he would give his life for her if he had to, but there was still uncertainty in his eyes. He had made such a pledge for Navaria's sake. But trusting a northerner was not in his nature, especially not one who had the power to kill nearly their entire race. Navaria reached into her pouch, fingering the necklace she'd bought in the market. Just feeling the diamond that had come from home was comforting, even though she knew she would need to part with the gem soon.

"Navaria had another vision," Krow announced suddenly.

Navaria glared at him behind her veil as Adlae turned slowly from the window. Her blue eyes pierced Navaria's *Chalqüin*, studying him closely before they turned on Navaria herself. She shivered under the woman's stare, feeling the bite of Winter's chill just when Adlae looked at her. The woman embodied winter and all the power that came with the season. Navaria had not known how strong winter truly was until she'd met Adlae.

"What did you see?" Adlae whispered, her voice a low rasp yet echoing in the empty room.

"It is not for me to say," Navaria answered, rising slowly to her feet. "Not yet. When the time has come, I will tell you, but you will already know the answer."

"You speak in riddles." Her pale brow arced.

"Many of us with the Gift often do." Navaria smiled, even though she knew Adlae couldn't see her expressions. "What you have not seen, you know, and what you know, you have not seen. A quandary and a solution. A shadow and a light. This is mine to hold in my heart until the Creator tells me you are ready."

Adlae tilted her head, her crystal lashes batting twice before she turned her back once again to look upon the city. Navaria didn't like her standing so boldly at the window, but she would not question her reasons. After the grief she'd been battling these past ten days, Navaria would demand nothing of her.

Krow sidled close to Navaria, frowning at Adlae's back worriedly. Navaria knew Krow hadn't been capable of holding much trust in his heart for the young Winter Queen, but things had changed when Adlae saved Navaria's life on the Woodland Path. She could only imagine how difficult letting Adlae weave her winter magic over Navaria had been for her *Chalqüin*. The magic could kill Navaria, and Krow had been shielding her from the moment they stepped onto the docks in Sunkai. But now Krow's heart had changed, and his loyalty to the Winter Queen, the true heir to the throne of Sunkai, was growing.

"Brecken Jandry's Second will ride before dawn tomorrow," Adlae announced, her eyes never leaving the window. "We must intercept Klade before he steps upon the path to the Shadow Lands. If he takes the men north, they will come to the Night Wood and be lost to us forever. This I know."

"You cannot know this." Glaydin shook his head. "My scouts have not reported such activity in the woods."

"Klade is a leader, and he knows the woods. He knows how to move in the shadows," Adlae replied. "The darkness will do whatever necessary to keep me from him. We must move tonight if we have any hope of catching him before he takes the army north."

"And if he doesn't wish to join you?" Navaria whispered, taking a step closer to the Winter Queen. "If he instead chooses to fight on his own to free Brecken Jandry?"

Adlae turned around, looking Navaria in the eye. "Then we will cross the Kliat Plains, join my sister, Mirae Sundragon, and face whatever fate she offers us."

Navaria closed her eyes, shuddering.

The Shadows are coming.

The Shadows are coming.

The chant whispered in her ear and Navaria bowed her head. Now wasn't the right time—she couldn't tell her now. Not yet. Not until they faced Klade and his choice. Then she would tell Adlae Sundragon her true fate. Then she would tell her what she thought she already knew.

The Shadows were coming, and Adlae Sundragon could not escape them.

CHAPTER THREE

Kaldon

Another cloud passed across the sun, shrouding Kaldon in darkness. The city was strangely quiet today, the people scurrying down the streets with heads bowed and hoods lifted to hide their faces. Never had the large city seemed so small to Afra Malaki. Kaldon had been engulfed in silence since the news had arrived. Adlae Sundragon lived. She was the Winter Queen, and she had come to reclaim her father's throne. But with this joyous news came devastation.

Brae Jandry had been executed—brutally murdered at the hands of Raphaela Kael. The false king was gathering his armies to march upon Quintaria in search of Adlae. Afra had listened to the messenger in the Malaki Manor with little emotion, holding in the grief she felt at the loss of her sister by law. None knew she was here; none were supposed to. Her presence in Kaldon would only endanger the city, this she and her brother by law, Jabon, knew. She must remain a shadow; imperative she dance in the darkness, gathering what little information she could from the whispers of the people and fulfilling her destiny through the power the Creator had given her.

Yet she was troubled Clea had disappeared. Rumors abounded her little sister was on the road to Molderëin. The darkness had descended upon that road, and Clea hadn't been seen since. With three of her siblings' whereabouts unknown and her oldest brother locked away in the Blood Keep dungeons, Afra knew only a matter of time would elapse before some of Roderick's guards would come looking for her. Becoming invisible had been Jabon's notion, and Afra admitted invisibility was the only way. But keeping her presence a secret even from Jabon's younger brother Tyrese was difficult for her. She loved her brothers by law and didn't want harm to come to them, especially not by her hand. She didn't know what her husband would have said if he were still here, but Afra did know he would support her in this new life she found herself living. Everything had changed since Brax died. The Creator had given her new purpose and a reason to live, no matter how difficult her task sometimes was. She knew her husband would have been proud of her for accepting such a life from the Creator. But knowledge of his approval didn't make what she had to do any easier.

Afra sighed, tugging the hood of her black cloak further down over her forehead. Her cheeks puffed as she took the long, curving stone steps to High Town. Low Town was much like the Lower Village of Sunkai, only had been preserved and cared for by the Ruler of Kaldon. Unlike the Lower Village of Sunkai, which Roderick Kael was willing to let waste away and eventually disappear. Afra's lip curled at the thought, her anger rising hot in her heart as she pressed her hands to the stone buildings on either side of her. The path grew narrow the closer she came to High Town. This path would open right beside the gates surrounding the Malaki Manor.

From there, Afra could go in two directions, south and deeper into the city or north to the private back gates that would take her out of the city and directly onto the Kliat Plains. Many times since Brax died, she'd been tempted to step through those gates and let the Plains decide her fate. Moving on without the man she loved had broken her, robbing her of her joy. Until the Creator had come for her and told her she held a higher place in this world than she believed.

Afra shivered in the darkness as she stepped out onto the street once again. Kaldon had been her home for the past three years—two of which she'd spent with her husband until the Creator had seen fit to take him from her. Her brothers had disapproved of Afra marrying so young. They'd said sixteen was too young for a girl to know her own heart. But Afra was just as stubborn as they, and she knew her heart had not deceived her about Brax Malaki. But to be left alone now, childless and with a brother by law protecting her from the evil magic of Raphaela Kael, was beginning to weigh heavily on her soul, and Afra didn't know how much longer she could stay in Kaldon.

She breathed deeply and marched toward the gate of the Malaki's Manor. This place had become her home when Quintaria couldn't be anymore. Brax had made it so, and she'd been so grateful to leave that place. With her sister's power growing, and her brothers making Sunkai their home after Roderick took the throne, Afra had been anxious to make her own change.

The gates to the Manor were iron, intricately woven in metal braids by the Malaki's personal blacksmith. The hinges creaked when she stepped through, metal clanging when she let the gate swing shut. She had to get into the Manor before the first ray of sunshine, so she wouldn't be seen entering. Night was the only time she could walk the streets, letting the rumors of the black-veiled woman live, and speculation rush through the dark alleys that the figure was indeed Afra Malaki, formerly Afra Jandry, the sister of the traitor Brecken Jandry.

Shivering, Afra stepped briskly over the pebbled path, the small stones crunching beneath her boots as she hurried around the Manor to the back door. The servants knew to ignore her when she used their door, none even looking up as she passed like a ghost through their kitchens and up the servants' stairs. Jabon had decided this was how she must live until he discovered where the last of Brecken's army had taken refuge.

The people whispered the moment Raphaela Kael killed Brae, the moment she had thrown Brecken behind bars, Klade Overlage had rushed what was left of the army into the woods and hadn't been seen since. Klade was known for his ability to move unseen, even in the brightest of places, and Afra knew Jabon would never be able to find him, no matter how hard he tried. Only one person would be able to find Klade Overlage.

Adlae Sundragon. The Winter Queen. Afra sighed heavily. Even if she was the only one who would be able to find Klade Overlage, she too had disappeared into the forest and no one had seen her since.

Afra stepped quickly through the kitchen, sprinting up the back stairs and around the corner toward the long hall that would lead to her bedchamber. The Manor was not the largest home in Kaldon, but close. Most people considered Jabon to be the true Ruler of Kaldon, but Thornlay Neverly currently held the title.

Afra's lip curled at the mere thought of the man. He was a true supporter of Roderick Kael, raised to the appointment of Ruler over Kaldon on the same day Roderick had killed Vihaan Sundragon and stolen his throne. He was trying to turn Kaldon into another Sunkai, their stone city undergoing years of reconstruction. Afra would never forgive him for turning a once beautiful city into something so ugly.

Once, there had never been a Low Town and High Town. Once they were a city of equals, no wealth of family changing the station of those who had once been friends. This was one of the reasons Afra had loved Kaldon. Now, since Brae's execution, the city had felt the harsher side of Thornlay Neverly, and people were afraid if they left, they would be accused of treason and killed.

Turning another corner, Afra came to another set of stairs. Ascending, she made a sharp turn to the left at the top. Jabon would be in his council chamber now, studying the same parchments he'd been reading since the messenger delivered them. Roderick was calling all the Nobles in Nfaros to gather in Sunkai and prepare for the battle against Adlae Sundragon. But Jabon had yet to answer the call. Afra urged him to be true to his own heart. Jabon had never completely supported Roderick Kael for many reasons, but there was one reason that surpassed the rest.

His love for Adlae. Afra buffed her arms, warming herself against the winter chill sweeping through the Manor.

She knew better than most the one you loved could decide your fate—could make decisions for you that you may never had made before. When they thought Adlae was dead, Jabon had done what the rest had. He became a follower instead of a leader, which had pained Afra to see. But there was little choice, especially with his sister, Gelsey, choosing rebellion and disappearing into the Night Wood and his brother Tyrese joining the king's army. Brax himself had bent the knee to Roderick, all the while hiding his true loyalty to the Sundragon. He told her, in the privacy of their chambers, that one day the Sundragon would rise again, and he would be there to support her. He'd not lived to see that day.

Afra rapped her knuckles lightly on the large oak doors, waited until she heard Jabon's quiet murmur and then, stepped inside. The walls were built as shelves, books and parchments lining them from ceiling to floor. As she had expected, Jabon was sitting behind his large oak wood desk, hands clasped together with elbows on the surface as he glared down at the king's messages.

Shaking her head, she closed the door behind her, throwing the bolts before she removed her veil. Her dark brown hair splayed across her shoulders as she removed the drape completely. The one feature that separated her from her siblings were her brown locks. The Jandrys were known for their raven heads, but Afra had inherited the slightly lighter color from her mother, who had been only half Molderëinian. Stepping forward Afra carefully tucked her veil over her arm before smoothing a hand over her hair.

"You have read them so many times, brother," Afra murmured, stopping a few feet away from the desk. "The command will not change, Jabon. You know this."

"If I do not respond before the next dawn, I will be proclaimed a traitor. If I do respond … then I will have betrayed myself," Jabon answered, his deep voice echoing against the domed ceiling. Lifting dim brown eyes to look at her, the head of the Malaki family sighed. "There is no choice, Afra."

"Of course there is." Afra smiled. "Do you remember what Brax once said? It is better to betray a king then to betray your true heart. We all know who your true heart is, Jabon. The world knew how you felt long before she disappeared."

"Nothing could come of my feelings then and nothing will come of them now," Jabon growled, rolling the parchments and tucking them away out of sight. "The laws are clear."

"Laws can be changed. Already Mirae Sundragon has spoken freely of new laws. Laws that will allow any and all to marry whomever they wish." Afra smoothed her finger along the slick surface of the desk. "Royals will not be prevented from marrying nobles or even soldiers if they wish. We once longed for a world with such freedom—the world Vihaan Sundragon tried to build before he was killed."

"No matter." Jabon stood, combing his fingers through his dark, unwashed hair. He marched to the window, clasping his hands behind his back as he looked out. "She has disappeared again, and the future once more is bleak."

"How can you say such a thing?" Afra hurried to stand directly behind him, peeking over his shoulder at the Kliat Plains beyond. "She is out there, perhaps even with Mirae by now. If you stand for her, then the rest of Kaldon will follow. The people have no love for Thornlay Neverly. They will follow you to the death before they will stand behind that man. If you choose Adlae, then the people will rally and so will your brother."

"Tyrese is still in the king's hold." Jabon shook his head.

"Tyrese is clever. He will find his way home, and when he does, he will be ready to take up the sword. You and I both know this, Jabon Malaki."

Afra leaned her head to his shoulder. "It's time, brother. It's time for both of us to—"

A banging on the door silenced her and Afra spun, rushing to snatch up her veil to hide her face.

"My lord! The Lady Afra is needed!" Cal, Jabon's serving boy, called from the other side. "There is a soldier come with a message, and he is wounded!"

Afra's heart leaped into her throat. *No, not today. I cannot bear it today!*

Jabon was up the moment he heard her name pass the servant's lips. He yanked the door open, reaching out to pull the servant in quickly before slamming the door after him.

"Do not speak her name so loudly!" Jabon shook the boy by the scruff of the neck. "Do you wish for her death?"

"No, my lord!" The poor boy's eye's widened. "Forgive me, my lord."

"Let the boy be, Jabon." Afra stepped forward, squeezing between the man and boy. "There is someone in need."

"Greta says his wounds cannot be healed. Someone did not wish him to survive the journey." Cal licked his lips, his eyes darting nervously back and forth between Jabon and Afra. "The Passing is coming, Lady Afra. Greta says he needs you."

"You have done the right thing, Cal." Afra smiled gently, squeezing his arm even as her stomach turned.

"Afra, you cannot!" Jabon grabbed her wrist, pulling her back around when she tried to leave. "The act requires too much power. Do you not think the Plains will feel the shift? Or perhaps the Eventide Sisters themselves? You have not completed a Passing in nearly a year and the act will weaken you to any threat that comes."

"The days of Passing are coming swiftly, Jabon. I will need to strengthen this gift, and the time has come." Afra cupped a hand to his unshaven cheek. "I love you, brother, but you know I cannot let this soul suffer. Not when he is under our roof. Not when he has sacrificed so much to bring us this message."

The moment Jabon released her, Afra flew, her feet moving faster than humanly possible, floating down the stairs to the kitchens. Pots and pans had been tossed to the floor, flour and gravy spilled around the table where they'd made room to lay the poor soldier down on the hard wooden surface. Afra glided into the room, taking her veil from her face once again. The servants whispered and scurried, none of them looking directly at her.

Still they obeyed their master, pretending they didn't see her even when she was right before their eyes. Jabon and Cal appeared behind her moments later, Jabon standing protectively at her shoulder as she bent over the soldier. His breath came short, rasping through dried and cracked lips as he clung desperately to life. Afra shuddered when her eyes found the gash in his side. The wound was too wide, too deep to sew and already he had lost so much blood.

"You have given much to deliver a message to the House of Malaki," Afra whispered against his ear as he wheezed, blood dripping from his side into a puddle. "Deliver this message to me now. In return, I shall see you swiftly and peacefully into the hands of the Creator."

"Y-You are A-A-Afra M-Malaki," he stuttered, his face twisting in pain. "It is f-for you I d-deliver this message."

"Then tell me what you know." Afra stroked his hair soothingly.

"The Shadows are coming," the soldier spoke clearly now, and Afra drew back, her eyes widening as she watched the soldier's eyes cloud, fogging until his natural eyes were shadowed in glittering silver domes. "The Shadows are coming, and no one is safe. The Shadows are coming for the Winter Queen. They have a message. Gather the swords. Gather the men. Gather the willing hearts. The Shadows are coming."

He gasped, his eyes clearing once more before he grabbed her, yanking her down until his lips touched her ear. "Raphaela Kael rides with Black Ones. They know this message and will seek the Winter Queen at her weakest. The time has come, Afra Malaki. The time has come for the Passer to roam the earth once more."

Afra closed her eyes, tears streaking down her cheeks. She straightened her back, looking back at Jabon briefly. He looked so confused—his brow knit in worry. She could not ease him now. The time for comfort had passed.

"The message is clear. I understand." Leaning in once more she raised her hands palms up, resting her forehead on the man's temple. "Let me pass you now into the hands of the Creator."

He closed his eyes. Afra breathed deeply, seeking the depths of her power, seeking the fulfillment of souls given to her by the Creator's blessing. This magic was as natural to her as breathing, coming to her without effort,

31

without force. Afra smiled as the sweetness filled her—overwhelmed her. Looking down, she saw the man's face ease of tension, peace smoothing the creases in his face as his soul lifted from the earthly body gifted him at birth. Afra gasped as the prophet's soul floated, glittering and golden before settling on her palms.

The moment his soul touched her, the world blackened. Afra heard Jabon call her name before she vanished.

The Aulend Forest

A breeze rustled the leaves as Gwylan crouched. She frowned, running her hand over the uneven ground, her finger tracing the horse's hoofprint left behind. The imprint was fresh, that much she knew. But how fresh, she was unsure. Sighing, she stood, the wind plucking her cloak from her shoulder. Her Sisters shifted on their horses behind her, waiting for her to make a decision.

Ever since she'd read the letter from the Superiors, Gwylan had been uneasy. To be so far away from the crystals as the world made its turn was frustrating—almost painful. Gwylan had never been this far away during the turning. But to be on a mission such as this, to be searching for the true heir of Nfaros to swear loyalty ... this enterprise would cause a rip in the turn. Already the search had caused a rift between the Sisters.

Their camp was split between loyalty to Jhaedra, the one who had given Raphaela the power to do what she'd done, and loyalty to their Superiors' wishes. Gwylan had been glad to leave before Jhaedra's trial began. Such things were never pleasant. Watching one of their sisters go on trial was painful for all of them, even those passing judgment. As innocent as Jhaedra seemed, Gwylan couldn't believe she'd actually missed Raphaela's true nature—her true intentions.

Yet it's done and cannot be undone. May the Creator have mercy on her. Gwylan closed her eyes, pressing a hand to her heart before she turned. Smiling, she stroked her mare's nose, cooing softly to the animal as she swung lightly back into the saddle.

"There are two riders in the forest," she announced. "They have not detected us yet."

"Then they are not on the Path," Ellia breathed, relief flooding her dark eyes. "They merely crossed over."

"Their purpose must not hold need of the Path," Haileah murmured curiously, tilting her head. "Or perhaps their purpose is not right and true."

"Do not make judgment without knowing who we have found," Symber clucked, wagging a finger back and forth at Haileah. "They may simply be travelers."

"There are no travelers in the Aulend," Haileah snorted. "Only the false king's men or the creatures of the Abyss."

"How quick you are to search for discord," Gwylan muttered, looking back and forth.

The Path obscured the rest of the forest, making each small step they took seem like a leap. Her eyes widened when she saw the figures, approaching from the side. They could not see them yet—not with all the trees between them. Not with how quickly she and her companions were moving on the Path. Raising a hand, she pointed.

"There."

"Two men." Ellia nodded, a frown creasing her youthful brow. "There is something familiar about them. I have seen them before."

"We should move now." Haileah pulled her daggers loose. "Be done with them before they come upon us."

"If they become aware of us, we will confront them." Gwylan reached over, pressing her hand against Haileah's wrist. "Be still, my sister. Only in need will we raise our weapons against them. Let us wait and see what they do. We will know soon if they are worthy of life … or death."

CHAPTER FOUR

The Aulend Forest

Lathan Jandry bent to the ground, running his fingers beneath the ice that covered the moist earth. His hand slipped easily into the dirt, caked in his fingernails and sent shivers rushing up his arm from the cold. Looking up, he glared at the roof of tree branches, inwardly cursing them for shadowing the path. These trees had a mind of their own, the power pulsing in them keeping him from his purpose—from the one he sought. He felt his brother watching, and he turned, looking up into Maxx's eyes.

His younger brother shook his head before turning away, black hair swaying in the winter breeze chilling them both. They'd been searching the forest for days and still no sign of Damari Kael or the Woodland Paths they knew she had been seeking. The thought they would find both her and their little niece Noelle dead beneath a snow drift somewhere chilled him to the bone. Gooseflesh rose on his arms and he growled, slapping the dirt from his hands as he straightened to his full height, pressing a hand to the pommel of his saddle. Storm snorted and stomped, his breath steaming in a small puff around his face.

Climbing back up into the saddle, he turned to his brother. "She was heading for the Shadow Lands, that we know for certain. It's the only place she would take Noelle—the place of her grandmother's birth."

"You think we should keep north." Maxx rolled his eyes as they both urged their horses to a leisurely stroll through the woods. "Even though the Kael girl has no sense of direction and could be anywhere in all of Nfaros by now. Especially if she took a Woodland Path."

"Damari is smarter than you believe," Lathan snapped, glaring.

"It's Damari now is it?" Maxx chuckled, a gleam lighting in his dark eyes. "When did you start calling her by her name and not her title?"

"When we were children," Lathan grumbled. "What I call her doesn't matter. She deserves your respect, Maxx. She saved Noelle."

"Only to bring her out into this deathly winter," Maxx argued, spreading an arm wide. "The Aulend is lethal in winter, Lathan, you know this."

"Yes, I know. It doesn't mean they're not still alive. Damari is … special. Like Clea."

"She has no power, Lathan."

"I would not be too sure, Maxx."

Lathan squeezed his heels into Storm's sides, urging him faster through the forest. The trees were at their thickest here, hiding any sign of a path. The snow lay thickly on the ground, another foot having been added the previous night. When the storm had come, it did so swiftly, attacking Nfaros' forests and cities with a vengeance. Lathan didn't want to think of the damage done to the Shadow Lands, as they rested nearly in the heart of the Ice Mountains. But the Frostlings showed mercy to those who were deserving, and Lathan could only hope their grace had fallen upon Damari and Noelle.

Closing his eyes, he could see her. Her long blonde hair rippling in the wind and sharp, blue eyes piercing him until he ached. There had always been something about Damari, something so warm and compelling he'd been drawn to her. When he discovered she'd gone missing with his niece Noelle, an old protectiveness he'd held for her when they were children had risen like a flame in his heart.

The feeling came so naturally to him when they were children, offering her his strength against the bullies. She'd been so secure, so safe with her brother for so many years Lathan had forgotten those feelings. Now she needed him again, and he would protect her even if it meant his death. He would never let her from his sight ever again. Despite what Maxx said, there was something magical about Damari Kael, and no one knew.

Which could be to our advantage against Roderick, if it comes down to it. Lathan snarled at the mere thought of the man. He would be coming after Damari now, Lathan was certain. She would need protection more now than ever before.

Maxx pulled up abruptly, and Lathan frowned, looking over his shoulder at his brother. Maxx was a good tracker. Their sister Clea had even said he possessed special gifts of his own. The Second Sense she called the power, and Lathan had slowly come to trust Maxx's instincts. Tugging on the reins, he backed Storm until he stood directly beside Wind Racer. Maxx's horse danced and stomped, swinging his brown head as tension filled the air.

"What is it?" Lathan whispered, his eyes narrowing as he searched the woods.

"Something's coming." Maxx bared his teeth. "Or *someone*. They're coming fast."

"I don't hear anything, brother." Lathan bent forward slightly, his fingers curling around the hilt of his sword.

"Trust me, Lathan. Someone's coming."

Lathan pulled his sword loose with a low hiss. The sunlight glittered on the blade as the tip reached above Lathan's head toward the sky. His weapon had been specially crafted by the best blacksmith in Sunkai when he'd been made lieutenant by Roderick. He remembered so well those days he'd followed the path of the false king. Roderick had made the people rise up, claiming Vihaan Sundragon was going to destroy Nfaros with his new, secret laws. King Vihaan had never been given the chance to even offer these laws to the people before Roderick threw him from the Tower of Truce. Now Vihaan's vision for Nfaros would never be realized.

The brothers moved forward together, their eyes trained to the shadows in the woods. Lathan's heart leaped at the thought the intruders might be Damari. But the pensive look on Maxx's face told him that whatever or whoever was coming, wasn't a friend. A whoosh of air chilled his face and Lathan spun Storm around. He heard the sharp hiss of Maxx's sword releasing from its scabbard. Another whoosh brought Lathan back around, his eyes widening as he watched.

Flashes of black flew here and there all around them, faster than any normal animal could move. They seemed to be everywhere and nowhere—a mere blur of black cloaks. Lathan turned Storm in a circle, Maxx guiding Wind Racer the other way so they were always watching each other's backs.

They must be on a Woodland Path. Lathan licked his lips.

"Should we step on the path?" Maxx whispered as the figures continued to circle.

"If they wanted to hurt us they would've done so by now," Lathan answered, carefully sliding his sword back into its sheath.

"I don't—"

Lathan reared back, eyes widening when the woman stepped off the path. She was Draedinian—he knew the moment he saw her naturally sun-kissed skin and oil black hair, separated in multiple braids. She glared daggers at him and Maxx as her brown mare clomped forward until she was nearly nose to nose with Storm. In her hands, she held a long bow, glazed dark brown and slick to allow arrows to fit and slide with ease.

But it wasn't seeing a Draedin born woman this far north that startled him as much as the black uniform she wore. The leather bodice, crisscrossed laces down the front and a silky skirt, split for riding. Her arms were covered above the elbow with matching black gloves and her black cloak billowed behind her, fluttering in the breeze. She was a Dominant of the Eventide Sisters.

Raphaela. Growling, Lathan yanked his sword out again and Maxx hissed, baring his teeth.

The woman's lips tightened and her eyes sparkled with amusement. "You have nothing to fear from us."

Her voice was like music, deep and sweet. Lathan shuddered at the sound, gripping his sword tighter.

"Raphaela Kael did not send us," she continued, smoothing her hand down the mare's neck.

"How many of you are there?" Maxx asked, glancing at Lathan.

"There are three others with me," she replied, tilting her head curiously at him. "I am called Gwylan. We have come in search of the Winter Queen."

"Then you're going the wrong way." Maxx snorted, putting his sword away. "The Winter Queen was last seen entering the Gracian Wood. She's heading north as fast as she can and no one has seen her in ten days."

"Hmm, how smart you are, young warrior." Gwylan's lip curled. "Do you consider yourself a creature of magic that you would understand the working of the world as well as a powerful creature like the Winter Queen, better than I?"

"Do not bother with them, Gwylan," another voice rasped, stepping off the path.

The woman didn't sit as tall in her saddle as Gwylan. She was dressed in the same uniform, a little plumper and with silver sprinkled at her temples, but her eyes were as sharp as a young woman's—her hands strong where they gripped her daggers. "They are of Sunkai, and if they are of Sunkai, they are our enemies."

"Let's not be hasty." Lathan held up his hand, easing his sword halfway back into its sheath with the other.

"Not all who have stepped from the gates of Sunkai are our enemy. We have a score to settle with one in the city. The one who still wears Intermediate red." Gwylan sighed heavily. "Forgive my sister, Haileah. The world is making its turn and to be so far from our home is troubling to us."

"You are Lathan Jandry." Another woman stepped from the path, this one as young as Gwylan and also Draedin born. "And you are Maxx Jandry. You are the brothers of Brecken Jandry who is imprisoned for his loyalty to the Sundragon."

"Who they are does not matter, Ellia." Gwylan waved a dismissive hand at the woman. "What matters is what they are doing in the Aulend. Why do they wander aimlessly while the Winter Queen is in need?"

"I do not believe that concerns you." Maxx moved Winder Racer closer. "These are not your woods."

"No, but my sisters and I must now make a decision." Gwylan tilted her head.

"And what is that?" Lathan asked.

Gwylan turned to him, a gleam in her eye. "We must decide now if letting you live would benefit the world."

Maxx's brow rose. Moving slowly, he pulled his dagger from his belt, meeting Gwylan's glare with his own. He felt Lathan grow tense beside him, his shoulders hunched as he inwardly prepared to fight. They both knew they didn't stand a chance against four Eventide Sisters, but to do nothing while they chose to slaughter them was not an option. Maxx had never actually faced one of these women before, but he had trained for a day like this.

The Eventide Sisters were a mystery. No one truly knew if they were friend or foe, though they seemed kind enough to the Kaldoners. But this woman seemed to be just like his father always described them. Stern and cold. There was no warmth in her eyes. Maxx flexed his fingers around the hilt of his dagger, his chest swelling with a deep breath when the third woman stepped from the path. Her golden hair, shorn to her chin, and her sharp blue eyes declared her a Kaldoner.

"Have you asked them their purpose, Gwylan?" the woman intoned, her thick voice echoing around the trees. "We are not to bring judgment without reason."

"We are searching for our niece," Maxx answered before Gwylan could, drawing the woman's gaze back to him. "She disappeared before her mother was killed, taken for her safety by Damari Kael."

"If they fled into these woods, then they are both dead," the one called Haileah said, shoving her daggers back into their sheaths at her belt. "Winter has come harshly to the Aulend. No lone woman and child could survive."

"You don't know the woman," Lathan growled.

Maxx eyed his brother and Lathan was silenced. "Forgive my brother, he holds a fondness for Damari Kael."

"Friendship," Lathan corrected. "She is dear to me as my own sister."

"Hmph," Maxx snorted.

"What reason do we have to believe you?" Gwylan waved a hand at them, her pretty brown eyes narrowing on Maxx. "Your name might be Jandry, but you have served the false king for years, and this is not a time of peace, but of war. There is no one we can trust."

"Perhaps not." Maxx shrugged a shoulder. "But my brother and I have no desire to start a war. If war comes to us, so be it. We only want to honor our brother's wife by finding her child and keeping her safe."

Carefully, he urged Wind Racer forward, a little bit closer to the Draedinian woman. She was beautiful, he had to admit, with those multiple braids swaying against her back and her silky olive skin. Maxx swallowed, ignoring the race of his pulse when her sweet honey scent came to him on the wind. Gwylan was watching him, her eyes roaming from the top of his black hair to the tip of his scuffed boots. He knew he had to look like a pauper, dressed as he was, but he didn't care.

There was something oddly appealing about the stiff Eventide Sister who, at the moment, held his life in her hands. If the way her eyes raked over him was any indication, she felt the same, and Maxx knew he could use that. This wouldn't be the first time he got something he wanted because a woman thought he was handsome.

It would be the first time my Molderëinian looks saved my life though. Maxx grinned and Gwylan's brow arced.

"You don't want to kill us." Maxx reached out and pressed his hand over hers where she clutched her bow.

Her spine straightened, eyes sharpening to toss daggers at him. For a moment, he thought he'd made the fatal mistake. But she didn't move and her companions merely gasped before falling silent, their horses shifting nervously as they backed away. Maxx curled his fingers around hers. The glove she wore was thin black leather, made more for her uniform than for comfort. The outside was cold, but when he pressed his palm deeply against her knuckles he could feel her warm skin through the material. Her pretty eyes widened to another size before she looked down, fixating them on his hand holding hers.

"Maxx," Lathan snapped, but he didn't turn.

"I can see in your eyes you're a good person, Dominant Gwylan," Maxx hurried on, drawing her eyes back up to his face. "There's a little girl in these woods, and she just lost her mother. She needs her family. My brother and I are her family, and we intend to find her. I don't want to hurt you or your companions, so please, let us pass."

Gwylan blinked, her frown smoothing from her brow as she lowered her bow, strapping it carefully to her back. Maxx smiled.

"Thank you."

"Do not thank me." She sounded breathless as she pulled on the reins, tugging her mare away from him. "I cannot kill you now."

"Maxx," Lathan whispered again.

"I don't understand, but I'm still grateful." Maxx pressed his hand to his heart. "In return, we will help you find the Winter Queen."

"We don't need help," the one called Ellia said, inching herself closer to Gwylan. "The Creator guides us."

"Quintaria is still miles from here. We could help each other." Maxx watched Gwylan, her eyes once again moving over him carefully in observation. She was weighing his words—weighing the possible consequences of riding with him and his brother. "Everyone here knows the Winter Queen is in Quintaria, it's just a matter of finding out where in the city. You're Eventide, so leaving the forest is difficult for you but can be done."

"You seem to know a lot about my people," Gwylan whispered. "About my Sisters."

"He knows nothing." Lathan grunted, suddenly beside Maxx.

"Lathan what—?"

"Shut your mouth, you've done enough!" Lathan snagged Maxx's sleeve and yanked. Wind Racer shrieked in protest as he stumbled, bumping into Storm when he staggered. "Forgive my brother, Dominant Gwylan, he didn't know what he was doing."

"Lathan—"

"We could be great allies if we traveled to Quintaria together, but you have been given a mission by your Superiors, and we would not want to interfere in Eventide business." Lathan bowed slightly, to Maxx's shock. "Let us each go in peace from one another and pray the Creator doesn't call on us to meet again in war."

Gwylan straightened, readjusting her cloak on her shoulders. She seemed to calm at Lathan's words, collecting herself once more as she stabbed Maxx with an icy glare. He shuddered.

"Indeed. You have spoken sense, Lathan Jandry. We will depart from each other in peace and fulfill our missions, such as they are. I do not believe you or your brother are a threat to my Sisters."

"You cannot make such a judgment alone, Gwylan!" Haileah squawked.

"But I can, Haileah." Gwylan's brow twitched irritably at the woman. "Who was appointed leader of our mission?"

"She's correct, Haileah." The Kaldoner smirked. "Gwylan has declared these men will go unharmed. They are not our enemy."

"No." Gwylan looked at him again, and Maxx straightened—tried for a smile but quickly changed his mind. She was angry with him now, and Maxx couldn't understand why, not since she'd decided to let them live. "They are most certainly not our enemy."

Gwylan turned her mare about, body swaying easily with the movement of the animal. "Come sisters, let us leave them to their task."

"Creator's Blessing," Lathan called before they stepped on the Woodland Path once more, disappearing in a flash of black. Then he turned on Maxx. "You're a greater fool than I thought, Maxx Jandry."

"I don't know why you're angry with me," Maxx grumbled, stretching his neck from side to side to relieve the tension. "Because of what I said, we're still alive."

"No, it's because of what you did," Lathan snarled, raking his fingers through his hair. "Did you never listen when our mother taught us the ways of Draedin?"

Maxx grinned. "Her looks were Draedinian, but she didn't dress like one."

"Your mind is soft, Maxx. It must be. Is that all you know of Draedin-born women? The barely decent drapes they wear?"

"What else is there to know? Any Draedinian woman who isn't Eventide is a promiscuous husband seeker."

"You really do know nothing." Lathan pulled Storm up short and Maxx frowned, turning Wind Racer around to face him. "Draedin women might dress to attract, but they have strict rules they live by."

"What is your point, Lathan?"

"You touched her, you fool! That's my point! That's why she said she *couldn't* kill us now!" Lathan leaned forward, his eyes sparking. "When a man intends to take a woman as his wife, he will touch her."

Maxx's eyes expanded, his heart racing. "I ... I just touched her hand!"

"One touch is all that's necessary. By the laws of her country, you have to marry her now. She is a touched woman and no one else would have her."

"But Eventide Sisters don't—"

"This one will," Lathan growled. "If she has stayed true to her Draedinian ways, she will, and if you refuse, she has the right to kill you for dishonoring her."

His brother brushed passed him without another word, urging Storm into a quick trot through the woods. Maxx sat there for a moment, his fingers tightening around the reins as he stared into the forest at nothing. Closing his eyes, he saw her face. Cold and calculating as she watched him, ready to plunge a dagger through his heart. Then he'd touched her and her entire manner had changed.

Now I know why. Creator's Night! I'm betrothed! Maxx snarled, yanked the reins and galloped after his brother deeper into the Aulend.

"You should not have let them go!" Haileah shouted in her ear.

"I had no choice," Gwylan murmured, her breath coming short and raspy. Ellia reached over, placing a gentle hand on Gwylan's shoulder. She smiled, grateful for her friend's compassion. She was a marked woman—a woman who had been touched by a man, and now her fate was sealed.

"You should have accepted the younger one's offer and let them come with us! Then we could have kept a watch on them!"

"Leave her alone, Haileah," Symber grumbled, puffing a stubborn strand of her hair from her cheek. "You understand the laws of Draedin as well as I. You know what this means for her."

"So she has a husband, what is the difference?"

"He's not her husband. Not yet." Ellia chewed her lip. "But if he is honorable, he will be."

Gwylan shuddered. "Let us not speak of this. It has nothing to do with our task. *They* have nothing to do with our task. We are on the Woodland Path, as the Creator wished."

"If those Jandry brothers were—"

"They're not!" Gwylan snapped at Haileah and her brow rose. "We will not speak of them again! We are here for the Winter Queen. We are of Eventide, and we do not need the protection of mere men!"

"Gwylan—"

"Enough talk. Ride!"

Gwylan launched down the path without a backward glance, her mare's feet flying down the path, floating on the Frostling's magic with ease. She would not think of the Jandry boy and what he'd done. She had been given a mission, and she would not let anything distract her. Especially not Maxx Jandry's beautiful eyes.

CHAPTER FIVE

Quintaria

You continue to torture yourself when there is nothing you could have done. You could not have changed the prophecy. You could not have changed the future, no matter how you wanted to.

"I thought the prophecy was about Mirae. If I had only seen the truth in the foretelling, I might have been there. I might have stopped her."

You couldn't. Once a prophecy is told, it is impossible to stop. If it had not happened now, it would have happened another way, perhaps worse.

"What is worse than being slaughtered in front of your people? What is worse than being stabbed through the heart in front of your husband? What is worse than your blood being used for a sacrifice to the Abyss?"

Do not do this, Adlae Sundragon. You are the true heir to the throne. You are the Sundragon, and Brae sacrificed herself so you might live. So you might go on and become who you are meant to ...

Adlae shuddered as Winter's voice grew faint, leaving her as it so often did in these days. Winter was elusive, leaving her to her own will and mind. Adlae never wanted her comfort more than she had in these days. But Winter seemed reluctant to speak, as though she were watching her from a distance, letting her make her own way.

Adlae scratched at the rough material on her arms. She'd known dressing as a Quintarian would be necessary today as she made her way through the city and into the woods to find Klade. But she had grown used to her silky white gowns—to the light material that fit her body perfectly. This blue woolen dress and plain brown cloak was foreign to her, offering a strange sensation. Not exactly warmth but close, which made her discomfort worse. She could not feel earthly warmth as others did. Ice was in her blood now, flowing strong and steady—keeping her alive.

Turning, she ignored the sting of Navaria's gaze beneath the veil she wore. Adlae had kept her distance since she'd saved the mountain woman's life on the Woodland Path. Doing so had been a risk she had to take—one she was thankful she had. Coming so close to Navaria was enough to kill the woman.

For while the cold kept Adlae alive, heat and fire was vital to Navaria's survival. She could not live without warmth, and winter was lethal to a woman of the Mountains. That much Adlae knew. But she had no knowledge of what Navaria hid beneath her veil. Her face was a mystery Adlae was not meant to solve—an answer only Navaria could give when she was ready. Just as the answer to her riddles were hers alone to keep until the time was right.

Adlae breathed deeply, her ribs expanding against the corset restricting them. She was unused to such undergarments, having been free of them during her years on the Ice Mountains. But Navaria said the Quintarian clothing would not fit her properly without them.

"Brecken Jandry's Second will be upon the path north soon." Glaydin paced across the room, slipping daggers into hiding in different parts of his clothing.

Adlae's lips twitched slightly at the desire of a grin at the thought. Since none of the Mountain men wore shirts, how he could find so many places to hide weapons was surprising. Glaydin caught her looking, his brow curving slightly in question. As he turned again, his copper hair swaying against his back to his hips, Adlae's amusement quickly faded. The man's back was marred with scars, from battle or whippings she could not tell. But he had shed blood throughout his life for one purpose or other, and Adlae could only hope she would not take even more from him than he'd already given.

The warrior buckled his sword to his belt and turned around again to face her. "We should be on the move now, Your Highness."

"Adlae," she whispered. "I am not the Queen yet."

"To me, you are." He stepped forward, towering over her until his breath touched her face. His eyes—one blue, one green—stared into her own. "You are the Winter Queen. I have pledged my life to you, and that makes you my queen."

"Thank you, Glaydin," Adlae sighed, the weight on her heart growing heavier. "Have the men done as I asked?"

"Yes." Glaydin dipped his head. "Navaria and Krow will leave first. I shall be the only one to escort you from the city walls."

"Good, that's good." Adlae closed her eyes, pulling in another long breath. "I must be the only one to speak to Klade. He was once loyal to my father, perhaps he will be loyal to me now."

"He refused to return to the king. He's sentenced himself to the life of a traitor." Glaydin marched passed her, peeking out the door. "He has no reason not to join you."

"And every reason, if he chooses to save himself and his men. Raphaela could strike him at any time."

"You will strike back then," Navaria's muffled voice whispered from beneath her veil.

"I could not save my sister," Adlae snapped. "I will not be able to save them."

She spun away, raking her fingers through her snowy hair. Winter's presence filled her, a comforting pressure building inside her heart.

Enough, Adlae. The time for torturing yourself is finished. Brae would want us to fight now.

"I will fight only to avenge her."

And that, my friend, would ruin her. Brae may be gone, but her place beside the Creator grows strong with each passing day, and she sees you. Do not trouble her heart now, for she has been given a new one that beats strongly.

Adlae shook her head. "Forgive me, Navaria."

"There is nothing to forgive." Navaria's smile filled her voice and Adlae returned it.

Reaching out, she clasped her hand around her staff. The ice cracked and swirled, vines forming to curl around her knuckles, formed to her as a part of her own hand. Adlae ran her other hand over the slick globe at the top, her finger tracing the slope. The dark clouds didn't part but grew larger, blacker as they rumbled like a thunderstorm. Adlae sighed, wishing the object offered her some sense of what was to come.

Winter said when the staff first came to her, what she now held was a cruel thing. A dangerous thing that could cause her grief. Adlae had not believed her, but now she understood. She did not rule over this magic. It was too powerful. This weapon had come to her and already tortured her.

47

Do not be fooled. The staff is an asset and an enemy. We will need it before the end, but it will abandon us.

"When?"

I cannot tell you.

Adlae's heart trembled with Winter's frustration.

You will have many allies before the end, Adlae Sundragon, but the truth is coming to you swiftly. We cannot escape it. I grow weak. You know what this means.

"You cannot leave me."

I never will. My spirit will remain, but my mind grows weary.

"I will not speak of this!" Adlae clapped the staff against ground. The floor shuddered beneath their feet, and all eyes turned to her. Adlae ignored them, used to the strange glances—the unblinking stares. "You are in me, and I am in you, remember?"

I remember.

"Then let us not speak of losing one another in the madness." She bowed her head as her voice lowered to barely a whisper.

The madness may not touch you. It never did me. But I was taken from this world younger than most Winter Queens. We are like the Prophets. Like Navaria. Our magic cannot extend to endlessness without a price. There is no one to keep us sane. No one who loves us enough to keep our minds balanced.

"Your Grace?" Glaydin touched her elbow and she turned, raising her head. "We need to move."

"Yes." Adlae nodded.

"Creator bless you, Your Grace." Navaria approached, keeping at least a foot between them.

"I will see you soon. Stay with the men in the cover of the trees and wait for my sign."

"You will win his heart, Adlae," Navaria whispered.

Adlae watched her go, Krow hovering close. He looked over his shoulder once at her, a concerned frown creasing his brow before he closed the door behind him. Adlae's shoulders slumped once they were gone, the breath whooshing out of her. Glaydin was watching her—she could feel his eyes on her as she moved back to the window, staring down into the streets. Navaria and Krow stepped out of the inn, hurrying through the crowds toward the Lower City. Klade wouldn't be very deep inside the forest, but not close enough to the border of the trees to be detected by the guards patrolling the walls surrounding Quintaria. Adlae pressed her fingers to the glass, closing her eyes.

"Do you grow weak?" Adlae jumped at the rumble of his voice at her ear. "Can you … See? As Navaria does?"

"No, Glaydin." Adlae smiled. "I do not See."

"Winter is a strange magic. Still I do not understand this cold." Glaydin's hand scorched her where he placed it on her shoulder and she winced, drawing back. "Forgive me."

"It's not you." Adlae turned, tilting her head back to look at him. He was taller than any man she'd met; taller even than Krow. "It is the world you were born in. People of the Mountain burn me, a heat from the outside I can feel."

"It pains me that my hand harms you." Glaydin swallowed, eyes searching her face.

"You are a good soldier, Glaydin," Adlae whispered. "A good friend. I see trust in your eyes for the first time, and I am gladdened."

"We must go." Glaydin stepped back. "They are out of sight now."

Adlae looked over her shoulder and nodded, seeing the crowds move in a sea of bright colors. There was no sign of Navaria or Krow in the crowd, and they could not be missed. As much as they tried to blend, Krow's height and strange hair color made him stand out. Adlae moved to the door, pulling the hood of her cloak over her head to hide her white hair.

Glaydin hovered close, a strong hand on his sword as he followed her out of the room. Adlae stepped silently down the stairs, her heart racing when she heard music coming from the dining hall. Glaydin's shadow fell on her as they walked silently through the hall to the front door. Adlae wished she could disappear under his shadow. Wished she could blend with it so no one would see her.

They stepped out onto the street, and Adlae pulled fresh air into her lungs. A relieved sigh slipped between her lips as the breeze washed through her, infusing her with the Frostlings' strength. A long time had passed since she'd spoken to the Frostlings, which weighed on her. Adlae wished she could go to them in her dreams, but they had brought the storm as she'd asked and their task was done. They had no stake in the war to come. They had no reason to risk their delicate lives in this fight. Adlae would not begrudge them their silence.

Glaydin's presence close beside her offered some comfort as they walked in the shadows of the buildings. He provided a block between the prying eyes of the Quintarians and her all too recognizable staff. Quintaria had always been a kind, gentle city. But since Brecken came with an army, they'd grown frightened—suspicious of any travelers coming to set up their stalls in the marketplace. Getting passed the city gates without notice had been nearly impossible.

Adlae slipped in and out of the shadows, keeping her head down as they passed into the Lower City. Glaydin had discovered another way through the gate, an old door that hadn't been used in years—built there as a way out for the people if the city ever fell under attack, but not used since Roderick marched across the Plains on his journey to conquer Sunkai. A sharp breath expanded her lungs, making them ache as she quickened her steps, Glaydin grumbling under his breath as he rushed to keep her hidden. She'd been hiding for five years and finally revealed herself to the world only to go back into hiding.

Her fingers tightened painfully around her staff, eyes growing moist as the ugly truth slammed into her once more. Because she had come out of hiding, because she had told the world her true name, her sister was dead. Her beloved, one of only two people in the world she loved most, was killed for knowledge of her real name.

This is the reason no one asks us—the reason we keep our true names a secret, Winter whispered in her ear. **To protect the ones we love. We are creatures of magic, and creatures of magic can be used for evil if those they love are in danger.**

"If I hadn't told the world, then I would never retrieve what was lost," Adlae murmured.

The Creator's will is for you to take back what was once yours. Brae has offered us a way. The people rise up against Roderick and Raphaela for what they did to her.

Adlae reached for her necklace, once a link between her and her sister Brae. "Mirae is happy today. The first time since Brae."

Take comfort in her then, Adlae Sundragon. Your sister will also rise up in support of your name and you will find each other. This you already know.

"And if the price is too great for both of us? If we cannot survive this, even together?"

You will.

"Your Grace." Glaydin's hand to her arm brought her around. "We're here."

Adlae turned, her breath catching when she saw the small door. She moved forward without hesitation, Glaydin watched the walls to be certain they weren't detected as she rested her hand on the bolt. A scattering of ice spread over the lock, and she heard it snap before the door came loose on its own, creaking as the hinges turned. Adlae slipped through and Glaydin followed right after, breaking into a sprint as they hurried from the walls.

The wind blew in her ears, muffling any sound the guards might have made at the sight of them running toward the border of the woods. Her feet sunk into the snow, crunching ice as she stepped across into the woods. The leaves cast dancing shadows across their faces, and Glaydin grinned at her. Adlae turned away, her eyes narrowing as she searched the woods.

He will be nearest the northernmost Woodland Path. Navaria and Krow will have found him already. To reach the Night Wood, he would need to begin the trek north already. He would not stay too close to the city walls.

"I know." Adlae nodded and moved forward, Glaydin following silently behind her.

The man moved as though he were stalking prey, silently and swiftly. She knew if he wanted to be, Glaydin could become invisible too, disappearing into the atmosphere before her very eyes. Adlae paused for a moment, closing her eyes as she reached out to the Frostling's magic. Glaydin's men would be nearby with the horses, waiting for her sign.

There, Winter gasped, her joy flooding Adlae's heart when she felt the Frostling magic. **Right there, my friend. We're close.**

"Your Highness," Glaydin murmured.

"We're almost there, Glaydin." She smiled up at him, her neck tilted so far the hood of her cloak nearly slipped from her head.

"No, Your Grace." Glaydin stepped in front of her, easing his blade from its sheath with a low hiss. "We're surrounded."

Adlae's eyes expanded and she turned slowly, the vines on her staff twirling tighter around her knuckles until she could barely feel her fingers. "I don't see anything, Glaydin."

"They're here." Glaydin's chest deflated as he released a calming breath, the air turning to steam as it slipped from his lips. "You should stand behind me, my Queen."

"I can better protect you if I stand at your side." Adlae narrowed her eyes, searching deep within herself for the magic to sense the beating hearts of the men in the woods.

The corner of Glaydin's mouth twitched in the desire of a smile. "I thought to protect *you*."

Adlae shook her head and took another step forward. At that moment, the woods seemed to spring alive, the men leaping from their hiding places with arrows to bows and swords raised. Glaydin rushed in front of her with a growl, baring his teeth as his brow furrowed in a deep glare. Adlae's breath quickened, her chest rising and falling as she worked to control the sudden rush of adrenaline calling to the ice in her veins. A horse snorted and shrieked, bringing both Adlae and Glaydin around.

Her heart leaped when she saw the man, still dressed in the king's colors of black and red, come riding through the circle of soldiers. Klade's chestnut hair was loose around his neck, clinging to the curve of his throat, and his face was shadowed in a week's growth of beard. Hazel eyes narrowed on Glaydin as a strong hand reached for the sword at his belt. He was just as Adlae remembered him. Stocky and stern, his fair skin reddened by the sun and thick arms straining within his shirtsleeves. Klade had always intimidated her when she was young, and when he'd stood up with Roderick Kael against her father, he'd terrified her. Now, he was exactly the man she needed to stand up beside her.

"You have been searching for my trail." Klade broke the silence, sliding his sword an inch from its sheath. "Why?"

"Do you not know Winter when you see her?" Glaydin tilted his head, his brow smoothing slightly. "Even I know her by sight."

"The Winter Queen disappeared. She has not been seen since the murder of Brae Jandry," Klade replied.

"Klade Overlage." Adlae stepped around Glaydin, lifting her staff slightly before snapping it to the ground again. The snow parted, clearing a smooth, iced path to Klade's horse. The gelding danced nervously, eyes wide as he grunted and trembled. "Were I you, I would not challenge a man of the Mountain."

Klade's eyes widened as Adlae pushed back her hood, allowing her white hair to be swept up in the wind. Bowstrings creaked as the men lowered their arrows, swords glinting against the sun as their weight tilted in the men's hands. She walked slowly along the little path she'd created, stopping in front of the horse to rest a hand on his nose. The animal calmed at her touch, bowing his head. Adlae looked up at Klade, eyes shimmering with tears.

"I have sought you out, now I've found you. I am come to summon you to my side, to ask you to bend the knee and swear to me—to the Sundragon. I ask you to fight for me, Klade Overlage. To raise your sword in the name of the Sundragon as you once did. Will you do this, Klade Overlage? Will you give me your sword?"

Silence echoed in the woods.

Navaria slowly lowered herself beside the creek, sinking into the snow. Krow mumbled something as he joined her, always hovering so his warmth filled the space between them. He cupped his big hands into the creek to splash his face. Navaria giggled when he grunted, the icy water raising gooseflesh on his arms and neck. Shaking her head, she bent to the water, merely touching her lips to the surface.

She sighed, the water rippling beneath her breath before she carefully slipped her hand beneath the surface. Navaria hissed through her teeth, the water burning her, but she ignored the sensation, raising the water to her lips. Most dripped between her fingers, but she swallowed enough to quench her thirst. Sitting back, she dried her hand on her dress, shivering in the breeze. Krow inched closer, and his warmth skittered across her skin, filling her with strength. Navaria smiled, hesitating only a moment before she lifted her veil. Krow turned to her fully now, his eyes roaming over her face.

Heat rushed up her neck at his intimate stare, but her heart leaped at the same time. His big finger stroked up her neck, trailing the pearly smooth scales on her face and throat. Navaria closed her eyes, placing her hand on his wrist. She raised his hand, leaning her cheek into his large palm. His hand filled her blue skin with heat, even more than the rest of her body. It was a different kind of fire filling her, lighting the subtle ridges of her sapphire scales.

Navaria slipped away from his touch, arching her back in a stretch as she rose to her feet. Shaking her head, she combed her fingers through her hair, readjusting her skirts around her legs to allow better movement.

"Navaria, *che hædorên yïlth?*" The language of their people floated off his tongue in a deep lilt. The familiarity of it warmed her inside, reminding her of the mountains, of home. She would see them again soon.

"No." Navaria smiled. "There is no need for concern, my *Chalqüin.*"

"You should cover your face." Krow stood, his great height forcing her to tilt her head back. "*Brögern sâlfe.*"

"I am safe here, Krow. You are with me." Navaria placed her hand against his ribs lightly before she turned, lifting her feet high as she stepped across the way through the snow. A few of the men bowed as she passed, acknowledging her nobility, though it meant nothing in this land. Not to these northern people.

"There has been no sign of them, my lady," one of the men murmured when she came to his side, looking out into the depths of the forest. "My heart worries."

"As does mine," Navaria whispered. "The sun will set soon. If Klade Overlage has rejected her …"

"She lives," Krow spoke strongly at her shoulder. "Your Gift does not lie."

"No. But Glaydin is with her, and his future is hazy in my Sight."

Navaria buffed her arms, leaning back against her *Chalqüin's* chest. They both knew what it would mean if Adlae returned and told them Klade Overlage would fight with them. They both knew she would have to tell the Winter Queen about her vision, then they would have to go. Then would be the time for them to seek out the *Almaër Dominÿe* once more.

"Glaydin is a great warrior, Navaria. He will—"

"Navaria!"

She turned, her heart jumping into her throat when she saw Adlae approach. Turning back just as quickly, she covered her face, Krow helping her with her veil before she faced Adlae again. The Winter Queen didn't even hesitate, and Navaria didn't know if she'd seen her true face or not. If she had, she gave no indication as she marched through the forest, Glaydin close on her heels. She stopped a few feet away, her fingers flexing around her staff. She looked into the woman's eyes and her stomach turned.

"Klade Overlage?" she rasped.

Adlae's blue eyes twinkled, and Navaria's blood raced.

"He's with us. We ride for Kaldon tomorrow."

CHAPTER SIX

The Pilvaa Forest

A swirl of flurries rose from the ground, whistling through the camp as the wind picked up. The Pilvaa had been quiet, eerily so as the Woodland People made slow progress through them toward Kaldon. They were finally on the move again, after storms had nearly devastated them since the first snow fell. Being this far north and coming closer to the Ice Mountains meant the storms would be fierce—harder than they ever were in Sunkai. But this was different. This storm was full of rage, sweeping the country with its ferocity. Mirae Sundragon knew why now—she understood now. Shivering in the cold, she reached for her dragon necklace and closed her eyes.

Adlae. My sister. The only one I have left. Mirae sniffled, fighting back the tears coming against her will. When Brae was murdered, she was certain the emptiness would fill her—the magic gone from the necklace keeping her linked to the only sister she thought she had left. But not so. Another presence had risen up stronger than ever. Then the rumors began, spreading far and wide. Out of the mouths of travelers on the road to safety, from passing soldiers who abandoned the false king in the name of the Sundragon.

Adlae Sundragon, the true heir to the throne of Sunkai, was alive. The news spread like wildfire, reaching the ears of the Woodland People and igniting them with hope … and confusion. Mirae herself was confused, knowing now she had no right to the throne she'd been fighting for. Her sister, the one who sent her off on her own in the Gracian Wood five years ago, was alive. Mirae's anger rushed through her but quickly dissipated into relief.

Adlae was alive, she was the Winter Queen, and Mirae would find a way to join her. There was nothing else to do. She would continue on her path as Queen of the Woodlanders and gather as many people to her side as possible in the name of Adlae.

Mirae continued through the camp, stopping every few steps to comfort a cold child, before she came to Astra's tent. Already, she could hear Jaeger inside, speaking in low tones with Braven and Griyer about their next move. She dreaded facing him, knowing he was angry about Adlae coming back from the dead. He wanted to see her on the throne, he wanted to see Astra's prophecy fulfilled. But Mirae knew Astra's foretelling's changed with the passing of time. They changed with the actions of the people, and there was nothing anyone could do to stop it. Mirae's future did not rest in a prophecy, but rather, her future rested in what she chose to do with her life. She could accept that.

If only my Second would as well. Shaking her head, she yanked back the tent flap, marching inside.

Warmth flooded her immediately, and she turned slightly in the direction of the fire, the flames crackling and spitting near the corner where Astra's cot had been set up. The tent's arrangement had been Braven's doing, she was certain. Everything the man did was for Astra's comfort. Mirae smiled, wondering if such a love would ever come to her.

The vision of a tall, dark-eyed man flashed across her eyes and she shook off the memory, her troubled heart pounding faster in her chest. Gooseflesh rose on her arms when she remembered how he'd towered over her, his sword gleaming in the sun, trembling in his hands, threatening her. Mirae hadn't been able to conceal her surprise when he'd spared her life. Brecken Jandry had been sent to take her life, of that she was certain. Instead, he'd let her go. Now he was rotting in the Blood Keep dungeons, and there was nothing Mirae could do to help him.

I will repay the debt. *I must.* Her jaw tightened as she stepped forward, pushing the hood of her cloak back from her head.

"Do you have news, Griyer?" she asked, resting her hands on the small table covered in maps.

"Only that she was seen entering the Aulend, just bordering Quintaria," Griyer answered, rubbing his hands together as he stepped back. "If she encountered Klade Overlage, she could be dead by now, Your Grace."

"No, she's not." Mirae touched her necklace, shuddering. "I would know."

"The link does not lie," Astra hissed between clenched teeth, her silver eyes glistening. "The link offers no rest."

"The link is a curse!" Jaeger growled, glaring at her necklace. "You should be rid of that bauble."

"As you would have me be rid of my sister? Of my flesh and blood?"

"She abandoned you to the Gracian Wood!"

"She saved my life!" Mirae slammed her fist on the table.

The silence in the tent was deafening as Mirae and Jaeger glared at each other across the space. Shaking her head, Mirae ignored the hot tear rolling down her cheek.

"Do not challenge me, Jaeger. I am Queen of the Woodlands—you made me so, and I do not believe you regret your action now. Let that be enough. Stand with the Sundragon. The *rightful* Sundragon."

"You are the Sundragon."

"I am *a* Sundragon. Adlae is *the* Sundragon. You do not know her as I do. She saved my life, Jaeger, and paid a dear price for doing so. I am your queen, and I say we stand with her." Mirae looked around the room, breaking away from her Second's hot stare. "Does anyone else wish to challenge this choice?"

Astra stepped forward. "We, the Woodland People, have sworn to stand for the rightful heir to the throne of Sunkai. The rightful heir, the true Sundragon, Adlae is. Treason, worthy of death it is, to not stand by her."

Jaeger bowed his head.

"There is none other to follow. You are our queen, Mirae. If you follow her, then we do also." Griyer put his arm around his wife, Lara.

"Good." Mirae stepped back, clasping her hands behind her. "Now that's settled, shall we talk about the wedding?"

Braven grinned, stepping forward to take Astra's hand. Jaeger snorted, turning his back as he paced to the other side of the tent.

"Preparations are being made." Lara brightened, the tension beginning to ease. "The women are glad for a celebration, and the children have not danced for a long time."

"The wedding shouldn't interfere with our plans to continue north toward Kaldon," Griyer added. "Staying on the Kliat was made impossible by Brecken's army. But if we continue along the Crescent Path, we should circle the border of the Pilvaa and come around to the other side of the plains, just outside the Kliat."

"Better news, that is." Astra shifted uncomfortably, her glittering eyes darting about the tent. Mirae grinned at the way the woman's strange accent thickened in embarrassment. "Silly, this is. Love this man, I do. But such fuss! Simple loyalty vows and cherish promise is enough before the Holy Man. No dance. No sweets. Silly that, silly."

"This is a celebration of us, my love." Braven kissed the woman's temple and her lips pursed resisting a smile. "Let them alone."

"I must speak to the queen privately." Jaeger turned suddenly from his isolation in the corner.

Mirae's brow quirked, and he bowed slightly. "With your permission, of course."

She dipped her head, gesturing for the others to go. Astra paused at her side, her black braid tilting when she leaned her head to the side. "Careful, you. The Shadows are coming."

Mirae frowned, but Braven pulled Astra from the tent before she could say anything more. Turning back, she crossed her arms, looking Jaeger over. Her mentor had been frustrated ever since the battle on the Kliat, ever since their great loss. When news had come from one of their spies that Adlae was alive and the Winter Queen, Jaeger's mood only soured all the more.

Mirae tried to talk to him about his feelings, but he wouldn't listen, which was beginning to worry her. The people loved Jaeger, as they loved her, but he'd raised half the young men in her army. He had taught them the sword, and they all looked to him as their father. She had chosen him as her Second, knowing when the people doubted her, they would rally to him. But if he began to doubt her now, only a matter of time would pass before some of the people chose to follow him instead of her. Then everything would fall apart.

"What is it, Jaeger?" Mirae whispered, her brow twitching nervously.

"We have suffered a great loss in battle. We have the Winter Queen gathering support, and the storm raging between us and Kaldon worsens. With all of this, you wish to stop and have a wedding?" Jaeger growled.

"I think our people need some joy, don't you?" Mirae's hand clenched on her arm, tightening across her chest. "That Astra agreed to this in the first place is a miracle. She loves Braven, but she knows the kind of life he will lead married to a prophetess—she knows the risk. The only reason she's doing this instead of ignoring her feelings is because of the world's turning. She is one of us, and we must support her."

"Then let her marry as she wishes!" Jaeger stalked forward, banging his hands on the table. He leaned across close to her. "Let them speak the vows quickly and quietly before the Holy Man, instead of delaying our journey."

"There is going to be a wedding, Jaeger." Mirae pressed her hands to the table as well, meeting his glare with her own. "Did you see the despair in our people's eyes? Did you see how they wept, how they still weep, for the loss on the Kliat Plains? Do you see how the hope has left them? Astra and Braven's union will be a beacon of hope to them. That life, as we know it, continues and will always continue. Life will not stop."

"A wedding cannot accomplish that, Mirae. Taking the Tower of Righteousness would," Jaeger hissed.

"No. Seeing love will remind them what we fight for." Mirae stepped back. "We fight for the common people. We fight for love and justice and truth. We fight for people like Braven and Astra. If you have lost sight of that Jaeger, then I pity you."

"The world is changing, Mirae. Nothing is going to be the same, and no matter what you think, having this wedding now will not change anything. Tomorrow, the people will still be cold and hungry, devastated by the loss."

"You knew there would be losses, Jaeger. We all did. If we let our losses alter our souls, then we have already let the enemy win. They cannot take our joy, Jaeger. If they do, then when the fight is over, we will have nothing left to live for." Mirae stepped back, pulling in a long, calming breath. "I know about loss just as much as you do, Jaeger. I lost my father and sisters within days of each other, and just when I thought I would get one of them back, Raphaela killed her. She killed Brae, and I could not stop her. But I can support Adlae. I can join the only family I have left and fight. I can remind myself the world is good—there is still joy. We *will* do this for Astra and Braven—while we still have the chance."

Mirae turned away, stepping outside. The cold wind bit her, slicing through her until she was chilled straight through to the bone. Trembling, she pulled her hood up over her head, hunching over as she strode through the foot of snow layering the ground. She had never thought she would lose him, but she could feel Jaeger slipping away from her, and that frightened her more than anything else. He had always been there for her—she'd always followed him. But now their paths had separated, their purposes changed, and Mirae knew if she lost him, she'd lose half her army.

Then what will I do? Then what will I have to give to Adlae? Mirae pulled her cloak taut around her to block out the cold as she stalked to her own tent, seeking solitude. She felt the eyes of every person she passed on her and the weight of who she was grew ever heavier on her shoulders.

"How is she this morning?" Mirae asked over her shoulder as Lara laced up the back of her dress.

"Lucid, thank eternity!" Lara laughed softly, shaking her head. "If she had been overcome with one of her visions, we would not be able to celebrate."

"Indeed," Mirae murmured, smoothing her hands down the silky green material. She hadn't worn a dress in nearly five years. Having this constricting material fitted to her body so perfectly, hugging every curve and cinching her waist ever smaller was a strange feeling. She took a breath. "Braven seems to keep her grounded, though."

"Do you know where she comes from, Your Majesty?" Lara tilted her head, peeking over Mirae's shoulder. "We have never been able to place her accent."

"I know only that her country is full of trees. That's why she never likes to leave the forest." Mirae's chest rose and fell as she breathed deeply, turning to let Lara twine the plain, golden tiara into her hair. "She says she thrives on trees."

"Considering her magic, that makes sense." Lara chuckled. "You look beautiful, Your Majesty."

"Thank you, Lara." Mirae sighed, wiggling her bare toes on the rough surface beneath.

"They've started the music. Won't be long now." Lara turned on her heel, practically skipping to the tent opening to step outside.

Mirae closed her eyes, listening to the gentle tunes of the lute and harp, filling their circle with happiness. She could feel joy, radiating in the air as the women laughed and whispered, the men clapping each other on the back as they brought barrels of ale down from the wagons. The entire camp was ready to celebrate, as they so often used to. This would be one night they didn't have to worry—one night they could pretend the world was at peace and be who they always had been. The simple Woodland People, whose circle of life was never ending, who thrived on nature and never had to raise a weapon to anyone.

Mirae shook her head, bending to pull on her boots. They looked out of place with such a fine dress, but they would guard her against winter's chill. Twirling her cloak about her shoulders, she stepped outside. The night air turned her breath to steam and she smiled, remembering how curious she'd been about that her first winter as a child. She had been nearly five when winter returned to Nfaros, the first one since her birth. Her father always said winter had stayed away in grief for her mother, who had not survived the night Mirae entered the world.

Still she wondered if her father blamed her for her mother's death, but he never said and she'd never had the courage to ask. Adlae became her mother then, raising her and teaching her as only a loving sister could. Brae had been her rock, the one she leaned on during times of trouble when Adlae had to stand beside their father in defense of their country. Together, they had been a force to be reckoned with; a force that had not been allowed to blossom and grow stronger. Roderick Kael had stolen that from them.

But I will get it back. When I stand beside Adlae once more, I will have what was lost. Mirae marched between the line of tents, the people pausing to bow as she passed.

Still she wasn't used to that. She'd tried to keep them from doing so in the beginning, telling them she would rule under the belief all men were equal. But the bowing started after the battle on the Kliat. Her survival renewed their faith in her, and the number of people she'd saved awakened their respect.

Mirae pulled her cloak around her as she approached the growing crowd near the edge of the circle. The trees were thickest here—just the sort of place Astra would pick to say her vows to Braven.

Squeezing through the crowd, Mirae found her way to the edge of the circle, standing near the stones Astra herself had placed to form the invisible wall protecting them. Hugging herself, she smiled, swaying back and forth on her heels in tune with the music. Cohdel, Astra's other bodyguard, was standing as still as a statue across from her, his head dipping only slightly in acknowledgment.

Cohdel had always been quiet, not a man of many words, but like Braven he would give his life for Astra. He'd been with her since she had her first Sight when she was a young woman. Braven had joined them, creating their trio, years later. Mirae didn't know what the Woodland People would have done if Astra had not left her home behind to live in these forests. She didn't know what they would've done if Astra had not followed them from Quintaria into the Pilvaa. She knew this was the only forest that disturbed her—the only one with such strong magic even Astra worried.

The music stopped, and Mirae looked up, breathing deeply when she saw the crowd parting for the Holy Man, Braven and Astra close behind. Mirae remembered how unusual she'd found the custom of marriage in the Woodlands. These Holy Men had been appointed by the Creator to advise and comfort the people, to join them in marriage and teach them the will of the Creator. Mirae smiled. In Sunkai, her father had been the one to rule over a marriage. One of the king's duties was to hear the vows and declare them wed under the laws of Nfaros.

Here, any man who was called by the Creator could become a Holy Man and claim the right to rule over such things under the law of the land. After having spent most of her life following the laws of Sunkai, Mirae had not so easily fallen into the traditions of the Woodlanders. But Jaeger helped her see things their way, and she'd opened her heart to these traditions.

Thinking of Jaeger made her heart tighten. She put those thoughts from her mind as the Holy Man passed her. She reached out, brushing her hand against Astra's as the woman went by. Astra glanced at her, silver eyes twinkling in the moonlight. The young prophetess looked beautiful, her dark skin aglow with happiness and her trim body fitted into an ivory gown—sleek satin with fur lining around the collar in the style of Kaldon. Her black hair was roped in three braids, twined together down her back to her knees. A light snow had begun to fall, flurries dancing all around them. The crowd thickened, the people coming from their tents dressed in their finest clothes to witness the union.

The Holy Man stood before them, Astra and Braven clasping their hands together between them. Mirae watched as the Holy Man twined the green silk scarf around their hands, braiding the ends together beneath their palms. Astra tilted her head, watching every move the man made. Mirae knew this was strange for her as well, though she didn't know what a traditional marriage looked like in her country. She didn't really know exactly where Astra came from.

"Tonight we gather to see this man and woman vow love and devotion before you, their witnesses," the Holy Man's voice echoed through the camp. "We celebrate their love for one another as they enter this new and exciting life. We gather here in happiness, to secure the Creator's blessing on Astra and Braven ..."

A strong hand touched Mirae's and she turned, looking up into Jaeger's eyes.

"I'm sorry for what I said," his whisper in her ear drowned out the Holy Man's voice. "You were right. The hearts of the people have never been lighter in these dark times then at this moment."

"We will still succeed, Jaeger." Mirae turned away, watching Astra. "Everything we want, we will receive. My sister will see it so."

"I hope you're right." Jaeger squeezed her hand before letting her go. "The vows are beginning."

Mirae turned back, focusing her attention on Astra and Braven. The braided scarf swayed beneath their bound hands as they began to speak together.

"Before the Creator, with the blessing of the people, I vow to be yours. Tonight, I pledge my heart is yours, my soul is yours, my life is yours. Tonight, I pledge that my love will never end, my heart will never grow weary. You are the one I will spend eternity with, in this life and the next. Until the moment death parts us, I will remain at your side. Even in death, I am yours, until you join me in the Creator's blessed hands. This I swear, before the Creator and these, the people."

Jaeger put his arm around her and she smiled, patting his knuckles lightly. The Holy Man unfolded the scarf and Braven took the cloth from him. She watched as he wrapped the soft silk gently around Astra's neck, a symbol of their union, before he gathered her close and kissed her. The people cheered, filling the woods with their joy and Mirae closed her eyes.

Creator's Blessing this wonderful feeling will last. Let this happiness strengthen them, push them on to the ultimate goal. Mirae leaned into Jaeger's side, her knees trembling. He frowned down at her, and she forced a smile as she whispered, "We ride for the Tower of Righteousness at dawn."

CHAPTER SEVEN

The Aulend Forest

Maxx clasped his hands over his chest, staring up through the roof of tree branches above him. Lathan was grumbling as he tried to start a fire, the damp sticks making the task nearly impossible. Maxx shifted on his blanket. He never thought he'd be coveting one of the stiff cots in the guardhouse back in Sunkai. The ground was frozen solid, even with the snow brushed away. If he looked beneath him, he was sure he'd find he was trying to sleep on solid rock.

The Aulend was full of night sounds, winter birds hopping from branch to branch as they sang their songs and deer leaping lightly around the trees as they sought their homes. A long time had passed since Maxx lingered in the woods, enjoying the quiet peace the trees offered. He frowned, wishing his heart was as unperturbed as the forest seemed to be. He wasn't here to take pleasure from the woods, he was here to take his niece back from Damari Kael.

His lip curled in a growl. He didn't care what Lathan said, he still didn't know what to think of Damari. The girl had always been strange, keeping to herself and acting the part of a privileged princess in her brother's presence. There was where Maxx's confusion began. Her whole life was an act, he was certain. Lathan always claimed to see the sweetness in Damari, the kindness setting her apart from her brother and sister. Maxx had only seen such attributes recently—the moment he discovered Damari's treason.

Everything became so clear then. The way she'd manipulated words, her nightly walks for *her health*. He knew now she'd been planning, scheming to take down her brother all along. Damari had been working with Brae, and while that awakened the desire to trust her in Maxx's heart, he was still unsure. She'd practically kidnapped Noelle, taking her from the city instead of delivering her safely to Lathan. If she didn't trust them, then how could he trust her?

Maxx grunted, turning over onto his side to prop himself on his elbow. Lathan was still mumbling under his breath as sparks flew out from the rocks he was cracking together. One branch lit, and Lathan leaned in, blowing lightly on the ember until it burst into a flame. He quickly added twigs and leaves, feeding the fire until the flames filled the circle of stones he'd made. Maxx moved closer, watching as the snow melted away gradually beneath the heat. His brother stood, striding back to the horses.

Lathan had the look of Brecken, with his tall and lean physique, hair as black as a night void of stars. Only his blue eyes set him apart from their older brother, a feature none of the other Jandry children had inherited. While blue eyes were unusual for a Molderëinian, Maxx never thought anything about his eye color. Their mother always said Lathan was special— he was meant to be set apart. None of them knew what she meant, but with the way the world was turning, Maxx sometimes wondered if they were going to find out and wished she was still here to see.

Some claimed his mother, Tsia Jandry, formerly Tsia Midlander, had been of the Mountains. Others claimed she was of the Shadow Lands, like Queen Zelaria. Maxx hadn't cared, as long as she'd been alive. But Tsia perished, fighting alongside his father during one of the wars against Molderëin. Vihaan Sundragon had called upon his father many times when the Lord Ruler of Molderëin rose up, attempting to take the whole of Nfaros. His father was valuable, knowing the savage ways of the people and wanting to change for the sake of his own family.

But during the last battle, his mother had insisted on fighting with her husband. Maxx shuddered, remembering the last time he'd seen them both, dressed in their armor with swords raised and heads held high with pride. Tsia looked beautiful ... then she was gone. Maxx had never seen her or his father again. His sisters grew up under the guidance of Brecken, with only their nursemaids to teach them the way of women.

The way of women. Maxx grunted again, turning onto his back.

Closing his eyes, he saw the dark-haired girl of Draedin, and his body quivered. What had he been thinking? Where had his mind been? His mother would have thrashed him within an inch of his life, he was certain, if she'd seen how careless he'd been. He hadn't even thought about Draedin traditions when he acted, seeing only a girl attempting to hide kindness in her eyes. Maxx was so certain with a little kindness in return, she would not kill them. Now he was tied to her forever.

"What are you stewing about?" Lathan grumbled, returning to the campfire.

"It's not your concern," Maxx answered, crossing his arms.

"If it's about women, you can ask me brother." Lathan's grin grated on Maxx's nerves. "I have some experience in that area."

"And I don't?"

"True. We both have more experience than our departed mother would like to hear about, I'm sure." Lathan tilted his head, curious. "You know I always know when you're thinking about her."

"And I always know when you speak nonsense." Maxx sat up, brushing away the snow clinging to his shoulders. "You don't actually believe she can hear us from the Creator's Realm, do you?"

"I believe there is a Creator, and there is a Creator's Realm. I believe the Abyss is out there—that he and his creatures exist. Why should I not believe those we love, who have gone from this world, still watch us?" Lathan tossed another stick onto the fire. "Tsia Jandry was never one to let us rest. Why do you think she'd let herself be at peace while we're here, fighting another man's battle?"

Maxx raked a hand through his hair.

"But we were not talking of mother." Lathan sat back on his heels, pulling his dagger loose with a sharp hiss before he began swiping it lightning quick, side to side against a stone. His gaze never broke from Maxx as he continued his work. "What are you going to do about the Draedin girl?"

"Nothing." Maxx maneuvered himself on the ground, facing the fire. "There is nothing to be done. She's an Eventide Sister. They don't marry. If her law states we are bound, then we are bound, and I will never commit to another. But clearly, we cannot be committed to each other."

"I don't believe that has to be the way." Lathan frowned. "True, not many of them marry, but it is not unheard of."

"Perhaps, but rare enough. Even frowned upon. Unless she were to forsake her vows to the Eventide, we will never be wed. I really don't think she will leave her life, her very existence, for me."

"You'd be surprised what a woman will do, if she's properly wooed."

"That will never happen, brother." Maxx stood up, going for his bow. "She is far away from me, now. We will never see her again."

"Where are you going?" Lathan's dagger stopped against the stone, eyes narrowing as he watched Maxx stride through the snow, away from their fire.

"To find supper." He raised his bow. "I'll stay close."

"Take care, Maxx. You don't know what lurks in the shadows."

Maxx waved a hand over his shoulder and jogged into the thick of the trees.

Lathan watched his brother go, shaking his head. Maxx had certainly gotten himself into trouble, and they hadn't even found Damari yet. He'd always known Maxx was trouble. From the moment he was born, Lathan had known, and he'd only been two at the time. But Maxx was different from the start. Chubby and curly-haired as a child, he'd grown into the stocky, domineering man he was today. Their mother had foreseen trouble in Maxx as well because of the differences. She said he resembled Lathan's great-grandfather.

Maxx wasn't short, but he did stand inches shorter than Lathan and Brecken, his stocky shoulders and broad chest stood out in stark contrast to Lathan and Brecken's identical builds. There was nothing about Maxx that resembled either of his brothers, or really their father, save for his skin and hair. Those features were what marked him a Jandry.

Leaning close to the fire, Lathan warmed his hands, ears attuned to every noise floating through the woods. Ever since they'd come across the Eventide Sisters, he'd felt uneasy. There was no sign of Damari, not even an old, dead campfire on the path. If she was still heading north, then they should've come across one of their campsites by now. But there wasn't a shred of evidence they were on the right path—no sign they were closing in on the woman protecting their niece.

Lathan knew Brecken would tell him not to lose hope, but to push on and complete the mission. His brother was counting on him, but Lathan wasn't sure they'd be able to succeed anymore. Damari was proving to be clever, more so than he thought she was. But her secrecy—her ability to hide as she had—only proved to him she was willing to do anything to keep Noelle safe.

Lathan's thoughts turned to Clea, and he wished not for the first time his youngest sister was with them now. Her insight would be useful, her heightened senses valuable in these powerful woodlands. Lathan still didn't understand how the Woodland people thrived with so much magic overwhelming them. This power crept up as a dense fog, attempting to choke them. Covering their eyes in terrifying images of the past, present, and future. Lathan had fallen under forest spells before. He knew their power, and he'd learned to counter that magic with his own strengths.

Rocking back from the fire, he rested his hand on the hilt of his sword. Closing his eyes, Lathan listened to the wind, the depths of the forest whispering with the sounds of the animals. A frown creased his brow when a twig snapped, a bird flapped its wings in fury and the branches rustled, disturbed by the sudden gust of wind.

He stood, drawing his sword silently from its home at his hip. Lathan tugged his scarf up over the bottom half of his face before moving around the trees, following Maxx's path through the woods. His brother would never be so careless as to make so much noise. Not while hunting, not unless he wanted to be heard. Lathan's frown deepened, and he rubbed his thumb across his forehead where his family cord used to be.

The Jandry colors were too bright and distinct, so he'd had to forsake the tradition of wearing the cord, marking him the second son in his family. Maxx too had put away his mark, the scarf their mother had gifted him to wear round his neck. Removing them had felt like they were leaving behind their family forever. Deep down, they knew nothing would ever be the same. Especially if Brecken didn't survive his captivity.

Lathan moved with stealth through the forest, his blade glinting off the glittering icicles hanging from the tree branches. Winter continued to rage through the land, covering the countryside in pure white. Still, he could hardly believe the woman they had kept as a guest in the Blood Keep a mere fortnight ago was really Adlae Sundragon. She'd been unrecognizable, the mark of the Winter Queen changing her so entirely none would have ever guessed she was the true heir to the throne. One only discovered the true name of the Winter Queen if she wished them to, otherwise it was considered an insult to even ask. Lathan grumbled under his breath, wondering if he'd even be able to find her. Being in hiding was beginning to chafe, since there was no news coming to them from any part of the world.

Murmurs reached his ears, and Lathan hunched, bending close to the ground as he sprinted forward, taking cover behind one of the trees. Breathing deeply, he peeked around the trunk, frowning when he saw the trio sitting around the fire. The woman was veiled, wearing a simple brown woolen robe with a braided rope around her waist. The man at her side was silver-haired, half-shaved from his head. His dark eyes darted around the forest in a way consistent with a soldier's training.

The other was bending close to the fire, as though protecting the strange blue flame, a dagger in each hand. Lathan thought he recognized the one man with silver hair, but he couldn't be certain. Mountain people in the north was extremely rare, and to see three this far from their home was practically unheard of. But the world was turning, and Adlae Sundragon once again walked the land, so he supposed anything was possible.

Instinct driving him to take the chance, Lathan stepped out of hiding, in full view of the trio. The two men bounded to their feet, weapons ready while the woman rose ever so slowly from her seat, her small hands clasped in front of her and her veil fluttering in the slight breeze. Lathan held up his hands, cautiously sliding his sword back into its sheath.

"I mean you no harm." He stopped halfway to their campfire, eyes darting as they searched the woods for his brother. A light songbird's call to his left alerted him to his brother's proximity, and for now, invisibility to the travelers.

"Why do you approach, good soldier?" The woman's voice was sweet, a low purr that rippled her veil. "We have nothing of value."

"I do not wish anything from you, and I'm not a soldier. Not anymore." Lathan winced, lowering his arms back to his sides. He pulled his scarf away, revealing his face. "I am searching for my liege lady, and wondered if perhaps you passed her in your travels."

"We have seen no one." The woman spoke again and Lathan found it curious that the men remained so silent. "You say this woman is your liege lady. Are you her *Chalqüin*?"

Lathan frowned. "Pardon, my lady?"

"Navaria." The silver-haired man spoke to her, his eyes never leaving Lathan. "*Mëa glodain hœr Chalqüin.*"

The woman, Navaria, nodded. "Forgive me. Are you her Loyal One? Her trusted guard?"

"Yes." Lathan bobbed his head. "She travels with a child, a precious child who must be protected. She is relying on me to find her."

"As my lady said," the silver-haired one growled, his eyes narrowing to slits. "We have seen no one."

"Who is this woman you seek? What is her name?" Navaria asked.

Lathan hesitated only a moment before he replied, "She is the escaped princess, Damari Kael."

The woman's gasp echoed in the space between them and she turned to the silver-haired man, grabbing his arm. "Krow, *lae mörgrin hâlafat glodain hœr Almaër Dominjë!*"

The two men lowered their weapons, the blades disappearing so swiftly Lathan didn't even see where they put them. He heard Maxx whistle again, but didn't respond, knowing it best they weren't alerted to his brother's presence.

"We have traveled from Quintaria in search of Damari Kael." Navaria stepped forward, the man called Krow a constant shadow over her. "We have left Adlae Sundragon to find the Kael princess. She is destined to follow us to the Mountains."

Lathan's eyes grew wide, his heart beginning to ram unevenly against his chest. Breathing in and out, he tried to think of how to respond. Who did these people think Damari was? What exactly did they want from her? His blood grew hot, and he gripped the hilt of his sword until his knuckles turned white. He had not come all this way, searched for Damari for so many days without sleep, for these people to take her from him now. Noelle had to be protected. Damari was the only one keeping her alive, and if these people reached her first and took her away for their own strange purposes, what would become of the child? Would they steal her too? That wasn't a risk Lathan was willing to take.

He opened his mouth, beginning to slide his sword loose once again, when Maxx came bursting through the trees.

"Lathan!"

"You are not alone!" The man who had not spoken until now rushed forward, tugging his daggers loose again.

"Be still, my soldier!" Navaria held up her hand.

"Lathan, they're coming!" Maxx rasped, pointing behind him with his bow.

"What, brother?" Lathan yanked his blade free.

"Wraith Spawn!"

A low hiss emanated from Krow. "Black Ones."

"Call them what you will." Maxx pulled an arrow from his quiver. "They're upon us."

"Have you ever fought Wraith Spawn before?" Lathan asked.

"Do not fear." Navaria stepped forward, raising her hand palm up. "We have faced many enemies in the darkness."

Lathan's eyes expanded when a blue flame erupted in her palm, crackling and whispering as it fluttered in the cold wind.

"I will give you what strength I have. The rest is up to your swords." Navaria stood between him and Maxx, her veiled face swaying back and forth. "You are Jandrys, yes?"

"Yes." Lathan nodded.

"Your swords are blessed. You have great purpose in your futures." Navaria stepped ahead of them, Krow shouldering them aside to join her.

"Who said she was in charge?" Maxx grumbled before aiming into the woods.

"Does it matter as long as she uses her fire on them and not us?" Lathan shook off his unease, glancing at the other soldier who stood with his back to them, watching the perimeter of the campsite.

Then the drumming began. Echoing around the trees, the sound of their paws trampling through the snow, slamming into trees as they pushed through, leaving darkness in their wake. Lathan resisted the tremors racking him. Navaria stood still and calm with her hand up, the flame growing larger.

"Shield your eyes," she said. "They are coming."

"Not a chance." Maxx shook his head.

"My fire will blind you. This power requires great strength. Shield your eyes!" Navaria shouted over the screams crashing through the air—the horrible sound resonating through the entire forest, striking terror in the hearts of all creatures.

"Do we trust her?" Maxx began to lower his bow.

Lathan crouched close to the ground and raised his arm, covering his eyes as he whispered.

"We have no choice."

The screams grew louder and the crackle of Navaria's flame rose to a roar as the Wraith Spawn closed upon the clearing.

"*Krow!*" Navaria shrieked, scrambling on hands and knees through the snow.

The Black Ones were retreating into the woods, screeching and hissing as Lathan and Maxx pursued them. Navaria felt her *Chalqüin's* pain the closer she came, the bond between them overwhelming her senses as his blood stained the white ground. Her long veil caught beneath her knee and she gasped, tearing it from her face. She didn't care if the Jandry brothers saw her true face, it no longer mattered. Not while her Krow lay dying.

"Navaria," Krow whispered as she sobbed, raising him up onto her knees. The Black One had torn through his shoulder, nearly dislodging his entire arm from his body. His breath grew weak, his heartbeat faint when she pressed her palm to his chest.

"No, you will not do this, my *Chalqüin!*" Navaria shook her head, her hair falling from its loosely roped braid. "This is not your fate. This is not my vision!"

"Hush," he rasped. "Let the Creator take me."

"No." She pressed her palm to his face. "I will get you home to the Mountains. You will live, Krow."

Lathan and Maxx came jogging back into the clearing, both of them with black blood smeared on their swords. Navaria looked over her shoulder at the soldier Glaydin had sent with them, but he averted his eyes, lowering himself carefully to his knees in preparation to bid farewell to his brother soldier.

Krow coughed, blood spilling on his lips. "It is time, Navaria."

"No!" She leaned in, her lips brushing his ear. "There is another way."

She felt his surprise. "No! We agreed years ago …"

"I will not lose you. My heart will not survive without you." Navaria kissed his lips lightly. "This is my wish. For you. For us."

"No, Navaria."

She smiled, a hot tear slipping down her cheek. A small puff of steam rose where it fell on the icy ground. Bending, she placed her forehead to his, her hand pressing deeply on his hard chest.

"Krow, my *Chalqüin*, Brother of the Mountain, Son of the Haven Star, I give you my heart and soul. I offer up my life for you in a pledge of eternity. I give away this mortal soul for a life of the Creator's Power—for a life with you. You will rise now, in this immortal life with me, to always be at my side. To be mine, for all eternity. Be healed. Be whole. Be mine."

Navaria opened her eyes, the blue light burning from her hand engulfing Krow entirely. Then, it was done. Her breath came, short and strained, but Krow's wounds were gone. An elated laugh slipped between her lips as she smoothed her hand over his shoulder, down his arm. Not even a scar remained where the Black One had mutilated him. Her soul weighed heavy now, the change growing and burning in her belly as the Creator's power worked through her. Nothing would be the same now.

She leaned over, pressing her lips to Krow's. "Oh, my love. My darling love."

Krow groaned, and she sat back, stroking his hair. His eyes grew heavy, closing as he passed into sleep. Tears streaked her cheeks when she looked at Lathan.

"I must take him to my home." With a snap of her fingers, Glaydin's soldier came to her side, lifting Krow as though he weighed no more than a feather to place him upon the back of his large horse. "He will only grow stronger as we travel closer to the mountains."

She picked up her veil, feeling their eyes on her sapphire dragon skin. Avoiding touching her scales, she turned to the brothers.

"You must find Damari Kael. You must find our *Almaër Dominjë*. With each hour that passes, her power grows stronger, and she begins to change. She will tell you this herself when you find her. Send her this message. Tell her Navaria and Krow journey back to the Mountains. Tell her we will wait for her, as long as we are able, in Draedin. If she does not find us there, then she must make the voyage to the Mountains herself. We will see her there, to grant her the Rebirth."

Turning, she went to Krow's side, stroking her fingers through his hair where he lay hunched over the horse's neck.

"Who are you?" Lathan's voice drew her back and she twisted her neck to look over her shoulder at him. "How do you know this?"

Navaria smiled. "I am Navaria Lightmaker, Daughter of Hadroul's Mountain and Mistress of the Crystals. I am the *Almaër Dominjë's* first mother ... and her only hope."

CHAPTER EIGHT

Molderëin

Clea raised her hand, shielding her eyes from the sun as she leaned back to look at the towers reaching for the sky. She hadn't seen the Towers of Molderëin since she was a little girl. Her father insisted on taking each of his children on a journey to the homeland, where they could learn the traditions of the Molderëinian people.

Brecken remembered this country, being older when they left, but Clea had been newly born—a weeping infant in their mother's arms when they left the city to join Vihaan Sundragon's kingdom. He'd taught her everything she needed to know about the streets and people. Clea never thought she would come back here without the supervision of one of her brothers. She felt strange, having nearly her entire household around her, yet feeling so alone. Clea leaned in, stroking Copper's neck as the animal murmured and stomped, unsettled by the unusual horns bellowing inside the city walls.

The iron gates stood one-hundred feet tall, twisting intricately like vines. The streets were unevenly laid with cobblestone, homes molded from the very rocks of the mountains. Clea's cheeks puffed as she released a long breath, tugging on the tie at her cloak. Rheatha reached up, snatching the cloak before it could fall onto the dusty road. Clea smiled, unbuttoning her long coat, handing it down to the woman as well. Rheatha smiled, patting her hand before turning to put Clea's things in the back of the wagon.

She'd forgotten how far away Winter's touch was from Molderëin—the heat of being so close to the southern mountains nearly overwhelming. Clouds rumbled overhead, yet there was no sign of the violent storm sweeping the north. There was nothing about Molderëin Clea could honestly say she liked, but it didn't help the last time she visited here, her father was almost killed and she nearly abducted by one of the city's notorious sorcerers. Her father discovered Clea was special that day. There was magic in her blood, pumping stronger than in any of his other children.

Clea motioned for her company to follow, riding through as the gates squealed on their hinges, the wary guards watching her through narrowly squinted eyes as she passed. The one thing about Molderëinians was they all looked alike. At least, Clea thought so.

With their long, black hair and matching dark eyes—skin so easily touched by the sun to darken them. These were features that set her and her siblings apart from the people in the north. Here, she blended in. There could be no doubt in anyone's mind she was of Molderëin.

Curling her fingers tighter around the reins, she let Copper move forward of his own accord, hooves clomping loudly on the nearly empty street. Morgren rode up alongside her, his hand resting tentatively on his sword as he watched the few people who walked the streets. The rest of Molderëin wouldn't waken for another hour at least, when the sun had risen fully in the sky. Clea never understood how the people could remain in their beds for so long. She woke the moment the first rays of morning touched her window.

The deeper into the city they went, the quieter it became. Shadows fell upon her company as the homes rose higher in accordance to the mountain they'd been carved from. The grey stones glittered in the sunlight, their ridges and crevices smoothed to perfection like onyx stones.

Straight ahead stood the Towers of the King, where the Lord Ruler Rhoydaen Molten sat upon the throne of Molderëin. Brecken always said the Molten descendants were left the duty of protecting the country and the people until the true king of Molderëin returned. Years had passed since the last king had come from his home and declared himself. None of the common people knew who was of the royal blood, only a Molten descendant would know for certain. Only they knew the true name of the ones who possess the royal blood.

Clea shook her head, remembering the stories her father used to tell her. Molderëin was a place to be feared, the savagery of the men something the north had never seen before. The Lord Ruler didn't begrudge them their violent ways. He did nothing to stop them and it had been so since the previous king disappeared, his heirs not to step forward for what could be hundreds of years.

Ruling Molderëin would be difficult for any man, and the royals of this strange land were given the choice to walk away if they wished—to not shoulder the responsibility if they didn't want to. Not many left Molderëin, but some had traveled, as Clea's father had, to the north where they could live the rest of their lives in peace. Clea sometimes wondered if the royal blood of Molderëin had done the same. Gone far away to the Shadow Lands even, just to escape the violence of their own country.

The city was nothing like any in the north. Quiet now, she knew when the people stepped from their homes there would be chaos. This was a city without laws—where people did as they wished, no matter how heinous their desires. Clea could trust no one, as Morgren told her constantly the closer they came to the city walls. Any one of the men or women she passed on the streets could possess the dark powers of the southern sorcerers, ready to manipulate her mind and bind her, selling her as a slave. That was how slaves were made in Molderëin—at least from within the city.

Outside the city walls, in the small country villages, men and women were forcefully taken from their homes by the *Glárdëon*. They were a society of men, some of the many savages who gathered together to take free people into slavery. *Glárdëon* meant 'thieves' in the almost forgotten language of Molderëinians—a proper name for the men who took free souls into their possession with such ease.

Clea breathed deeply, calming her racing heart. Since the incident in the woods, she'd been unable to calm down. Morgren had been right—using so much magic had weakened her and dulled her senses. Yet the closer she came to Molderëin, the clearer her purpose became. She knew what she had to find, but attempting to take possession of what she needed would draw the attention of every sorcerer in the city, bringing unwanted attention to her and her company.

Rheatha and Izeana still bearing the mark of slavery on their wrists wouldn't help matters either. The brand was why Clea ordered them to wear their long sleeves, knowing any Molderëinian had the right to take them from her the moment they saw the mark. Her companions walked freely, without the chains around their ankles the slaves in Molderëin were forced to wear. An insult to Molderëinian tradition was to see a man or woman with the mark free of chains. Rheatha and Izeana understood the risk of returning, but they came all the same.

Morgren inched closer to her, his dapple grey gelding pumping his head and snorting. The city was much too quiet for the horses. They were used to lively, noisy cities. This place felt strange to them, with so little noise and interaction with others. It only heightened the uneasy feeling they'd had since leaving the woods and taking to the roads at a breakneck pace. Their animals weren't used to such urgency, and the shadows of the mountains were disturbing to any pure heart.

After living her entire life near woodlands, Clea didn't think she could ever become used to the mountains. They were dark and oppressive, an enemy if ever she saw one. Despite the heat emanating from the rocks, there was no warmth, nothing welcoming about the glittering onyx reaching for the sky. Clea breathed deeply, reaching for her hip without looking to touch her sword. She gently patted the hilt, reassured the weapon was still there.

"It's quiet," Clea murmured. "Almost too quiet."

"They rise when the sun has fully entered the sky," Morgren answered, telling her something she already knew. "It is how they see the shadows and keep them at bay."

"Shadows?" Clea frowned.

"There are terrible things lurking in the shadows of Molderëin." Morgren tilted his head back, looking toward the top of the mountains. "The people came to know them and their strengths. They began to fear the distant mountains and would not enter those paths. Now they wait until the sun shines completely upon their city before they emerge from their homes."

"Is it like the darkness plaguing the Kliat Plains?" Clea tilted her head.

"Worse. Much more dangerous." Morgren's lip curled when he snarled, his fingers tightening around his sword. "We need to find lodgings."

"If no one has woken, we will not be able to find a place." Clea tugged on Copper's reins, bringing everyone in the company to a stop.

Glancing over her shoulder, she swallowed. Choosing to leave her small army of men outside the city walls had been difficult. Ryker was in charge of them, and he would keep them in line, but to be without the added protection within the city was beginning to grate on her. Morgren was perfectly capable of protecting her, but if these people became violent, she knew even her most experienced guard could not hold them at bay for long.

Morgren was watching her. She could feel his eyes boring into her as she looked back and forth. There was no sign of an inn—there wouldn't be one, not until they were further in. The center of the city would be the busiest area. Where the crowds gathered for the market and public fights.

Clea shuddered as she remembered being a small child, trying to hide behind her father's leg as two men fought to the death in the middle of the circle. Her father had pushed and shoved, trying to get her out of the thick of the crowd surrounding them before she saw the death blow. But he'd been too late. She saw everything and knew then that Molderëin, a once great city where men held high rank and women were given the greatest respect, had fallen. Her father's stories of his birth land had been just those, stories which would be told for generations but held no hope of a similar future. Even if the true king or queen of Molderëin stepped forward, it was too late to turn the hearts of the people, of that Clea was certain.

Rheatha appeared at her knee, patting Copper's side absently as her eyes roamed over the city. Her face had paled—her raspy breaths letting Clea know she was frightened. Reaching down, she took Rheatha's hand in her own, squeezing tightly. Izeana put her arm around Rheatha's waist and the two women held onto each other. They both understood what coming back to Molderëin meant, and they had done so for love of Clea.

Clea wished, more than anything, they had stayed behind in Quintaria, where they were safe. Letting them out of her sight while here would be the hardest thing Clea ever did, and Ryker would never forgive her if Izeana went missing, ending up in chains again. But Morgren wouldn't leave Clea's side, which meant Rheatha and Izeana would be left alone at the inn, to defend themselves as best they could if anyone saw their slave marks.

Clea gave Rheatha's hand another squeeze. "Everything will be all right, Rheatha."

"I know, little miss," Rheatha whispered. "I know this. All will be fine."

"There is an inn I know of." Morgren pointed. "Near the Towers of the King."

"So close to the center of the city? Is that wise?"

"It is the best place, close to the Tower where you need to be and clean. I can better protect you there where there are so many guards on the Tower to defend those of noble birth."

"I did not think they cared about noble blood here." Clea frowned.

"The Lord Ruler does his best to look out for traveling nobles," Morgren responded. "You clearly are of the nobility, Clea. You will be noticed."

"Creator's Night!" Clea raked her hand through her hair. "I didn't want to be noticed, Morgren!"

"You don't want Rheatha and Izeana to be noticed. They won't if they remain in the room, out of sight."

"We will be fine," Rheatha cooed at her knee.

"You cannot gain the trust of the Lord Ruler without a way in. Your noble birth is the way. Word will spread like fire in this city when the name Jandry passes your lips." Morgren grinned. "It has been—"

"Thirteen years, I know," Clea sighed heavily. "Thirteen years since a Jandry has passed through the gates of the city. Thirteen years since a Jandry fought on the streets of Molderëin. Thirteen years since—"

"Do not take this lightly, Clea." Morgren glared. "Your family holds great rank in this city, and the people will listen to you."

"I am not here for Molderëin, I'm here for my brother. Brecken sent me here on a mission. I did not come to win the trust of the people or the Lord Ruler. Brecken said I would know what to do when I came here. Though nothing is clear yet, there is great magic in these stones and I will find what little magic of summer has been left here." Clea's chest swelled and she squeezed her heels into Copper's sides.

Morgren rode ahead of her, leading her toward the inn he'd spoken of. She watched as the shadow of the Towers fell upon her company the closer they came, the sun reaching above the tallest peak. Clea arched her neck back, looking to the battlements circling the four towers, connected by stone bridges between each. Her brow furrowed when she spotted movement, her magic swirling and warming in the center of her chest.

Clea's vision cleared, and she saw the man, his hair black as midnight falling to his shoulders, held back by two small braids and dark green eyes, a color as uncommon among Molderëinians as Lathan's blues were. His skin was darkened by sunlight and his chest bared to the waist where his thick brown leather belt supported the weight of his wide-curved sword.

In that moment, he seemed to look directly at her, into the very depths of her soul. Clea gasped, releasing her magic. Once again, he was a mere speck on the bridge between the first two towers. Gooseflesh rose on her arms and she shivered, suppressing the heaviness falling over her. Rubbing her chest to alleviate the pain of using her magic, she urged Copper to walk alongside Morgren and didn't look back at the towers.

Deep, pain-filled moans echoed down the halls of the Towers of the King. Grange Molten followed the sounds down the spiraling stairs, the image of the small traveling party still fresh in his mind. Long ago, Grange discovered his gift, and his mother had helped him hide his power from his father. She'd insisted the man who raised him could never know there was magic in his soul—that he had abilities which far surpassed those of a normal being. But when Grange looked down, when he laid his gaze upon the raven-haired woman, he felt something he never had before. They seemed to look into each other's souls. Like she could see him, as clearly as though he stood beside her.

His chest tightened, every fiber within him fighting against what he had to do next. Bringing this news to his father would not be easy. Thirteen years had passed since they'd seen the face of their future. His father had spent all of those years in denial, refusing to believe the world was preparing to turn. Rhoydaen Molten avoided the truth since he'd taken over the city as Lord Ruler. Grange was raised to believe the Creator had given them this place. They'd been granted this responsibility because they were meant to rule over the people until the end of time. But everyone always spoke of the one who would come to liberate those in chains. The one who would come in search of the summer flower, but who would change Molderëin forever.

Grange shuddered, quickening down the steps, his boots echoing against the walls. He'd grown up in these halls, listening to the stories of the king who'd disappeared—the one who would return. But then the prophecies had changed, and his father's heart became as hard as the stones these towers were made of. His rule had grown weak, his resolve to rid Molderëin of its savage ways diminishing. He allowed the violence to rule the streets, and for many years now the people had prayed for a savior. Rhoydaen was deaf to their pleas, and Grange had been unable to act without his father's permission.

His lip curled in a snarl as he reached the bottom of the stairs, striding down the narrow hall before taking the south stairs to the throne room. The moans grew louder, and he knew his father was at work. If he kept going like this, he would kill the woman. She would not want to live anyway, even if they were able to release her. His father had held her for so many years, Grange was certain her people believed her to be dead. None other in the city knew his father had her. If they did, there would be a riot. She was of the Mountain and should be there, not here. The one thing the people of Molderëin held to; the one law they didn't break.

Except my father. Grange's skin warmed as he tried to suppress his anger. He couldn't control what his father, the Lord Ruler of Molderëin did. Rhoydaen did as he pleased, and the news Grange was bringing him would not be well received, he was certain. A scream suddenly shattered the moans. Grange sprinted forward, lunging at the doors to the throne room.

They shrieked and scraped against the floor as they swung open. Grange skidded to a halt, his breath stolen from his lungs when his eyes fell upon the woman of the Mountain. He'd seen her many times before. She was the secret his father kept—the secret Grange was forced to keep. Her hair was tinted the color of the dragon skin covering the entire right half of her face. A crooked line curved down the center of her face, separating the amethyst scales from the smooth, creamy human skin which embodied the rest of her.

Her pale white eyes were haunted as he looked into them, crystal tears staining her cheeks as her father circled her, a bloody whip dragging behind him. Then his eyes focused, staring unblinking at the scar marring her beautiful dragon skin. His father had tried to cut it off, many years ago, for the price it would bring at the Molderëin market. But the skin was unyielding, refusing to be removed. Grange could still hear the woman's screams as his father hacked at her, to no avail.

He stormed forward, grabbing his father's wrist when he raised the whip again.

"Enough!" Grange bellowed, the slap of his palm on his father's skin as sharp as the crack of the whip itself. "What has she done to deserve this?"

"You dare touch the Lord Ruler?" Rhoydaen growled, his dark eyes rolling with thunderclouds.

"I dare touch my father!" Grange shoved him, and he stumbled on the hem of his robe, nearly falling before he regained his composure.

"She would not See for me!" He tossed the whip, the thin leather hissing on the floor, sliding to the other side of the room.

Grange circled the trembling woman, wincing as her blood dripped into a small puddle at her feet, the back of her dress torn to shreds where his father's weapon had cut right through to her skin. Her back also bore the mark of her birth, the dragon skin covering nearly half and disappearing beneath her dress. He came around, her chains rattling as she shifted, refusing to fall down even though he knew she was weak.

"Nadilla!" he called.

The slave scurried from her corner, the chains around her ankles clattering. Nadilla kept her head bowed, never raising her eyes to his.

"Take Kalea back to her rooms and send for the physician to tend her wounds," he ordered. Grange touched Kalea's face, and she grimaced, squeezing her eyes closed. "Forgive him."

Looking up at him, another tear slipped from her eye. "Forgiveness can only be given to one who asks. I am a free woman of the Mountain, and your father has put me in chains. This, I cannot forgive."

Nadilla grabbed Kalea's arm, and she groaned, stumbling against the woman's side as Nadilla rushed her from the throne room. Before they stepped through the doors, she turned again, looking him the eye.

"You have taken hope from my people. Only one other remains like me, and her life is endangered every day in the northern lands. Is this your wish, Grange Molten? To destroy my race?"

"Silence!" Nadilla hissed, kicking the woman's ankle. She did not react, numb now to all pain. "You will not speak to the Lord Ruler's son this way!"

Grange opened his mouth to respond, but Nadilla dragged the woman out before he could speak. Turning, he glowered at his father.

"Whipping her will not bring the Sight!" He paced, flexing his fingers around the hilt of his sword. "She only grows stronger in her resolve to resist you when you hurt her."

"Perhaps." Rhoydaen slumped down on the throne, his hands limp in his lap as he stared up at the ceiling.

"I did not come to interfere," Grange sighed, turning to face him. "I came with news."

"What news?" his father mumbled.

"The heir has come." Grange held his breath.

Slowly his father lowered his head, meeting Grange's gaze with a cold stare. "What did you say?"

"She rides upon a red horse and bears the Sword of Kings."

"Your eyes have tricked you!" Rhoydaen stood, his fists trembling at his sides.

"My eyes do not deceive me, my lord, I assure you. The world is making its turn. I have seen the heir, just as prophecy spoke of her. A woman whose company wears no chains and the sword of *Kläerjaen* rests at her side. She has come, father. Only the Creator—or the Abyss—could stop her now."

CHAPTER NINE

The Outskirts of Kaldon

Adlae lowered the scope from her eye, turning to hand it back to Klade. His horse shifted beneath him, feeling the coolness of her breath as she exhaled. Kaldon was the second largest city in Nfaros, only slightly smaller than Sunkai itself. She most certainly could not take it, not with so few men. But there were those inside the city walls she had to see. Those whose loyalty she needed to secure. After losing Navaria and Krow, Adlae knew she'd need reinforcements; someone to stand at her side as her Second. Krow had respectfully declined the honor because of Navaria's weakening heart in these northern lands. Glaydin was a good protector, but Adlae needed someone who knew her, someone who could speak to her and trust her completely. Someone who had grown up with her.

Jabon. We need Jabon. She bit her lip, shuddering when Winter's voice vibrated inside her heart.

Her thoughts turned to Navaria's proclamation before they left. She'd pulled her aside and told her they had to go, they had to fulfill their mission here to find the *Almaër Dominje* before they returned to the Mountains. Adlae rubbed her arms, even though she knew rubbing wouldn't do any good. She couldn't even warm herself. But Navaria's words had chilled her even more than was normal, and they'd struck fear in Adlae's soul.

This is your destiny, listen well and heed my words. You must take the road to the Gracian Wood. You must take the road to the Tower of the Dead. There you will seek out the Winter Queens of the past and the mortal Kings of old. There you must seek the Shadows, and dance. For only they hold the answers. Dance with the Shadows, Adlae Sundragon, and discover your fate.

Instead of following Navaria's direction, Adlae had continued on her course. She could not venture so near Sunkai, not with so few men to stand behind her. If it was true, and the Shadows were coming, then she would find them soon enough. But she could not come so close to her enemy without a larger army, and Jabon Malaki had the men she needed.

You have not seen Jabon in years, Adlae. You cannot be sure he will swear loyalty to you. This is a risk.

"A risk we must take," Adlae whispered. "Mirae has built her army among the Woodlanders. They will follow her, and I cannot wait to see if she will come to me. Jabon is just the start. If Kaldon swears to me, then others will follow. Men and women will come from the villages to stand with us."

Your sister loves you. She will come.

Adlae covered her necklace with her hand. "Blessed sun, I hope you're right."

"Your Majesty," Klade interrupted her reverie. "Do we move in?"

Adlae turned to him, shifting her staff from one arm to the other. "No. We cannot alert the people to your presence. I must go alone to Jabon Malaki's home. Once we have his support, then we can reveal ourselves to the people of Kaldon."

"Is that wise?" His eyes narrowed on the walls of the city, hands tightening around the reins, bringing his horse to attention. "Will you not be easily recognized?"

"Not if I leave this behind." Adlae turned, carefully leaning her staff against one of the trees. "No one must lay a hand on this. This weapon was born of a magic few understand and will bring harm to those it doesn't recognize."

"I will guard it." Klade slid down from his horse.

"Allow me to accompany you, Your Highness." Glaydin came to her side, stepping in Klade's path. The distrust for her new follower was clear in his eyes. Adlae couldn't help but smile.

Perhaps it was a habit of his, to mistrust anyone new who entered his life. She knew this place was strange to him, this cold land where children frolicked in the snow, and their parents relished the cool breezes. She touched his face—his skin scorched her fingers, sending bolts of fire up her arm. This wasn't the sweet warmth of human flesh, but a fiery magic that burned and pained her. Fascinated her. She stayed strong, looking directly into his eyes.

Adlae shook her head. "You must stay here, my friend."

"You will not be safe."

"I never am."

You should let him come. You do not know what Jabon Malaki will do when he sees you.

"No." Adlae bowed her head, muttering. "I must do this alone. If Navaria was right, and I must face the Shadows, then I will need Jabon. He will listen only to me, I am sure. Only I can win his loyalty, and I will not succeed with an armed guard at my back."

"Your Majesty." Glaydin tilted his head, curiously. "Are you all right?"

"I'm fine." Adlae reached back, pulling her hood up over her head to hide her hair. "I will return shortly. No matter what happens, do not move against the city. If I do not return before the moon reaches its peak, then you must move on. You will follow the path through the woods in search of my sister, Mirae Sundragon."

"Lady Adlae—" She held up her hand, silencing Klade.

"Are my orders clear?" Her brow arched irritably.

Klade bowed at the waist, and Glaydin pressed a fist to his heart. Adlae nodded as she backed away toward the border of the woods.

"I will return. Keep a watch on the walls, and do not fear. Creator be with you."

"Be careful, my Queen," Glaydin whispered.

Adlae spun away, gliding swiftly through the forest toward the walls of Kaldon.

Kaldon was nothing like she remembered. The steep dipping of the stony hills and narrow back stairs leading to High Town were rough and cold. There was nothing welcoming about the city—nothing warm. When her father ruled the land, Kaldon had been a simple city, never looking to compete with Sunkai, never hoping to grow as large—even larger—than the Mother City. There had been love for Sunkai then because they had a king they could respect. One they trusted. Now Kaldon was falling into decay, she could feel it in her bones, her magic growing weary beneath the weight of the changes the city had undergone.

Adlae's bare feet chafed on the stone, her heart thumping uneasily against her chest. Perhaps she should have brought Glaydin, but the presence of such a big, unusual man in this city would certainly have been noticed. She knew Glaydin wanted to come with her, but she couldn't take the risk. Jabon might have perceived him as a threat, and facing him again for the first time in years by herself was a better choice.

He wouldn't know her, not really. He wouldn't see her for the girl she was, he would only see the Winter Queen. But if the truth had spread across Nfaros as Klade's soldiers said, then he would know she was truly Adlae Sundragon, despite the Winter Queen's mask.

Sighing, she tilted her head back, looking at the Ruler's palace. She shook her head, seeing the greed in the height and splendor of the mansion, while the people's homes were failing; crumbling and weak.

There is nothing you can do for the city now. Do not dwell on it. All this will change when the true heir sits upon the throne.

"I know."

No, you don't. You should not have come here. You should have gone to seek out the Shadows, as Navaria said. They will descend upon the people if you do not meet them! Winter's anxiety shuddered Adlae's heart.

"You know why I came here."

Yes, your heart is weak. You believe Jabon Malaki will fall into your hands, loyal to a fault. But how do you know for certain? How do you know his heart holds true for you?

"Because I know Jabon. I knew his father, and that kind of love doesn't change. Their hearts have always belonged to the Sundragon. They have only been biding their time."

You have such faith for one who has stood beside the usurper with a sword in his hand for five years. I wish my heart was as trusting.

"Please, do not worry," Adlae paused, slipping into one of the alleys. "These steps will take us to the Manor. Are you prepared to help, if I am in need of you?"

You should have let Glaydin come.

"Too late for that." Adlae tugged her hood farther over her forehead. "Are you prepared?"

I am prepared. Winter's voice quieted.

Adlae sprinted up the stairs, her hands grazing the walls as they grew narrower the farther up she went. The city was unusually quiet, and she couldn't help feeling it was because of the increased number of guards on the walls. The people shrunk in fear of their Ruler, when they were supposed to love him. Roderick had changed the whole of Nfaros, and Adlae's heart ached for the country.

Stepping quickly along the curve of the steps, Adlae reached the top, pausing when she saw the iron gates rising high to encircle the Manor. Such a long time had passed since she'd seen this place—so long since she'd stepped foot inside this home. The Malaki's had always been close to her family, so Tyrese Malaki's decision to support Roderick Kael had shocked them all. Jabon had said nothing, merely bided his time and did what he had to. Adlae never knew for certain if he truly had any loyalty to Roderick.

You are here now, Adlae Sundragon, why do you hesitate?

"Do not take a tone with me," Adlae hissed. "There are ways of getting into the Manor without being detected. I cannot alert his guard."

Forgive me. But if you know the way, then why do you stand here staring?

"I haven't seen him in five years." Adlae shivered. "He won't recognize me. He'll know me, but he won't see *me*. He won't see who I was in my face."

He is not meant to see this. If he cannot still love you without the face you once had, then he is not who you thought he was. He is not worthy to stand at your side.

"I cannot begrudge him his changed feelings. It would be wrong."

It would be wrong if your appearance mattered so much. If he cannot see the beauty the Creator has bestowed upon you, then he is a fool. Now do not wait any longer, there are guards approaching.

Adlae rubbed her chest, trying to relieve the pain in the center of her heart before she shuffled forward. Taking a deep breath, Adlae slipped into the shadows, her back pressed to the gate as she moved along toward the back. She remembered being a child here, accompanying her father on his trips to Kaldon to visit the Malaki's. Jabon had shown her the secret way in and out of the Manor.

There was a small door in the gate, invisible to any eye that didn't know it existed. Made by children, for children, so they could sneak in and out without their parents knowing. She had gotten into all kinds of mischief with Jabon Malaki and his sister Gelsey when she was little. Sometimes, Adlae wished for those days back, when the most difficult thing in her life was facing her father because she'd snuck out to play in the Ruler's fountains with Gelsey.

Shaking her head, Adlae crouched, running her fingers over the cold iron to the latch. A smile tilted her lips as she tugged, the lock screeching a protest after so many years of disuse. Adlae laid flat on her belly, bending her neck forward as she scooted through, the tight space squeezing her hips as she wiggled through, her cloak pulling against the small hole. Once through, Adlae turned, tugging the little door closed once more. She watched it disappear, mixing with the rest of the gates.

Now you are within the walls, what do you intend to do? Climb through a window?

Adlae grinned, looking up at the light shining through Jabon's library window. "Yes. That's precisely what I intend."

Jabon leaned his elbows on his desk, face pressed to his palms. He hadn't seen Afra since the night she disappeared, and his heart was worried. Ever since his sister Gelsey disappeared into the Night Wood over a year ago, he'd become very protective of Afra. Now, seemingly, she had abandoned him too.

Grumbling under his breath, he sat back, his neck arched as he stared up into the shadows on the ceiling. There was no telling where she'd gone, or why. But it had been a long time since Afra had performed a Passing, and he couldn't help worrying she was lying on the ground somewhere, too weak to rise because of the magic overwhelming her. A sinking feeling in the pit of his stomach told him this would be the first of many Passings for his sister by law.

A breeze brought him around, brow furrowing. He'd been certain he closed the window. Sighing, Jabon pushed himself out of his chair, marching over to pull the window closed and click the lock into place. He stared down at the city, the streets beginning to grow quiet as the sun made its slow descent on the horizon. He rubbed his hands together, a sudden chill filling the room, unlike anything he'd felt so far during this swift and harsh winter. His heart lifted with the thought it grew colder because Adlae was moving closer to Kaldon.

The rumors were vague, but he knew the Winter Queen was moving north, and if she'd already left the Gracian Wood, she had to be close to Kaldon by now. There'd been no sightings of her in Quintaria, at least his spies hadn't seen anything. Jabon pinched the bridge of his nose, attempting to shake off his unease. But the feeling wouldn't go, just as the sudden gust of cold wind wouldn't go away.

The dawn had come and gone, and the king received no reply from Malaki Manor. He would not send his armies to the man—he would not fight beside him against the Sundragon. His silence would be all the answer Roderick would need, and Jabon knew the usurper would come before long to take Kaldon by force.

"Such worry." He stilled at the sweet voice echoing in his chambers. "You will create lines on your face. Then no woman will have you."

Jabon spun, his breath ragged, steaming, in front of his face from the cold her presence released. Slowly, she stepped from the shadows, carefully pulling back her hood from her head. Jabon swallowed the lump in his throat, his heart sinking. There she stood, her white hair roped over her shoulder and icy blue eyes blinking at him curiously. A smile tilted her pale lips and, for a moment, he thought he recognized her. But as much as his heart wanted to, he knew there was nothing about her he knew—nothing about her he understood anymore.

"Your Majesty." Jabon bowed quickly at the waist, his fist pressed to his heart.

"I never required a bow from you before, I do not require one now," she said. The voice was Adlae's, and if he closed his eyes, he could see her. Her beautiful green eyes and her long, wavy red hair.

He rose again, lowering his fist to his side. "You are a queen now. *The* Queen."

"And you are still my friend, are you not?" She stepped closer, and Jabon stiffened, his eyes narrowing as he searched her face.

"I no longer see my friend in your face," he rasped. "I see a stranger."

"Yet my soul remains the same." Adlae pressed a hand to her heart. "You know why I have come here, Jabon Malaki. I see the truth in your eyes."

"You have come with a question." Jabon turned, never taking his eyes from her as she circled his desk, running her pale fingers along the edge of the glimmering wood. "The same question Roderick Kael has asked me."

Adlae froze beside his desk, blinking slowly. His breath caught in awe as flurries floated from her lashes with every bat of her eyelids, each flake clinging to his desk. Her magic glowed all around her, flowing strong throughout the room so even he could feel the power.

"What answer did you give the false king?" Adlae looked up at him from beneath her lashes.

"I gave him my silence." Jabon stepped forward, leaning against the desk as he looked deeply into blue eyes he didn't recognize. "I gave him no answer."

"Which is answer enough." Adlae began circling the desk again, her fingertips leaving traces of ice along the surface. "There are nearly five-thousand men waiting for me in the Aulend. Though a great army, they are not nearly enough to face the Mother City. I have the loyalty of Jandry blood on my side, but even they are scattered to the wind, out of my reach."

"There are eight-thousand men in my barracks." Jabon followed her, a grin tilting his mouth. "I believe thirteen thousand would be sufficient to overwhelm Roderick, to keep him from entering the Gracian."

"Are you standing for the Sundragon, Jabon Malaki?" She looked up at him from beneath her shuttered lashes, and his breath caught.

In this moment, she wasn't the Winter Queen. In this single moment, he saw Adlae, her sweet smile and lilting voice. Her beautiful, flushed skin and the glitter in her eye she reserved only for him. For a moment, he saw the woman he'd grown up with. The woman his heart ached for.

The woman I love. Jabon trembled.

"I have always stood for the Sundragon," he rasped, reaching across to snatch her cold fingers in his hand before she could get away. "I will *always* stand by your side."

Her shoulders squared, her chin lifting. "And I by yours. Forever and to death. Welcome back to the Circle of the Sundragon, Jabon Malaki. We have waited long for you."

CHAPTER TEN

The Night Wood

Damari's hand tightened around the hilt of her sword, eyes darting back and forth. The strange magic stirred within her again, scorching her heart. Something was close. Something horrible was close, and she couldn't see them. The ache behind her eyes grew—the hammers ramming into her temples until she thought her head would shatter into pieces. Noelle fidgeted against Damari's chest, rubbing her fists on her face sleepily. Damari stroked the child's hair, wishing she calmed as easily as Noelle did with one gentle touch.

Another gust of wind nearly took her hood from her head, the icy draft melting away from the heat radiating off her skin. Subtly, Damari reached for her sword. Whatever was coming, it was of the Abyss. Damari didn't know how she knew, she simply did, and she wouldn't take a chance. Not with her little charge wrapped warm and safe against her heart. Winter's vengeance was felt throughout the land, the storm fiercer than any Damari lived through in the years before her brother took the throne.

If there was any doubt the Winter Queen really was Adlae Sundragon before, there was none now. Her rage could be felt in every whisper of wind, in every icicle crackling overhead. Every frozen flake falling from the sky in a gust declared her anger at the usurper. This winter was not a blessing, but a curse.

A low rumble vibrated through the woods. The trees themselves began to tremble as Damari tugged on the reins, bringing her horse to a full stop. Noelle lifted her head.

"What's that?" she asked. Raising her hand, she pointed her little finger straight ahead of them.

Damari couldn't breathe. The black cloud was rolling toward them; tumbling with dark figures she'd once thought only existed in children's stories. There were far too many of them. Too many for her to fight.

What else can I do? Damari grabbed Noelle around the waist, lifting her as she jumped down from the saddle.

Noelle began to weep, clinging to the front of Damari's dress as she set her down behind a tree.

"Listen to me, darling," Damari said, cupping Noelle's round cheeks between her palms. "If you hear me tell you to run, then you must run. Run as fast as you can. We've entered the Night Wood now, Noelle. The Eventide Sisters will hear you and come for you. But you must run and you must not look back. Do you understand?"

Noelle nodded vigorously. Then she looked up at Damari, her emerald eyes pooling with tears.

"B-But ... you ..."

Damari smiled, in awe over how much wisdom a child as small as Noelle had. There was knowledge behind her eyes—a knowledge of something dark no child as young as four years should have.

She knows this is my end. Damari pulled the girl close, taking a moment to breathe in the fresh scent of her hair and infusing her warmth into her so she might survive the cold, at least for a little while.

Then she stood, rounding the tree without a backward glance.

"Remember," she said, reaching for her sword. "When I tell you to run, you must run."

"Yes, Mama Damari," Noelle answered.

Damari's hand curled around the hilt of her sword ... and froze there. Something rose within her—a furnace of fire boiling in her belly and veins. Without knowing exactly what she was doing, Damari lifted her hands from her sword, palms facing each other. A white spark glinted between her palms, sputtering before it lit. A low rumble reverberated in the center of her hands, forming and rolling into a pure white ball of fire.

Damari's body shuddered with the euphoria of the magic, her skin prickling, and suddenly, she gasped. Her skin was beginning to shimmer like small diamonds, fairer than it had ever been. But as quickly as it did, the glow faded back to smooth, milky white. Then, with a thrust of her arms, she sent the flame out.

The Wraith Spawn shrieked when the white fire touched their cloud, evaporating the darkness in one swift glare of light. Damari stumbled back, shielding her own eyes from the brightness with her arm. They were silenced ... but only for a moment. When Damari recovered herself, she moved forward, watching their distorted figures rising slowly from the ground, no longer covered by the Abyss's cloud. Their yellows eyes glared at her. Damari drew her sword.

"Run, Noelle!" she shouted. "Go now!"

Damari rushed forward, racing toward her fate ... then came to a skidding halt. A bolt of ice shot from the sky, piercing one of the Wraith Spawn in the chest. The creature grunted, looking up before bursting into ash. Damari's eyes popped, and she looked up, watching as streaks of white light flew down from the sky, the tiniest figures she'd ever seen creating a battle of ice and snow upon the Abyss's creatures.

A frozen whisper touched her ear. Damari turned her head. The little fairy smiled at her, hovering over her shoulder. The tiny woman's white hair piled atop her head in a mass of waves and her eyes were bluer than the winter sky. Iridescent wings batted furiously behind her. After a moment taken to smile warmly at Damari, she faced the dark creatures, raising her glittering hand.

Frostlings! Damari's breath returned, filling her lungs with a hiss.

"Protect the *Almaër Dominje*!" the fairy shouted. "Protect the Mountain Mother!"

She watched the little Frostling charge in a streak of light, leaving a trail of snow dust behind her.

The Wraith Spawn shrieked, their long claws searching for their attackers. But the Frostlings were too small and too quick for them. She never thought Frostlings would fight in battle, but she supposed every creature of light would take up the fight against the Abyss.

"Go to the little one, Damari," the Frostling's voice echoed in the air.

Noelle! Damari spun, returning to the tree.

Noelle hadn't gotten far, just a few feet before she'd stumbled in the thick layer of snow on the ground. Damari picked her up, cradling her near her heart. She went for their horse, grabbing at the reins as the animal stomped and whinnied frantically.

"It's all right!" Damari said as soothingly as she could. "Please calm down ... please ..." Her eyes brimmed.

A soft *whoosh* passed her ear. Damari spun, clutching Noelle close. The Wraith Spawn hovered over her, his claw raised for the kill ... and out of his chest protruded a man-made arrow. Damari's chest rose and fell rapidly in terror. The creature's black, bald head glistened under the sunlight, long crooked fangs protruding from bleeding lips and his murky yellow eyes stared at her.

One moment he was there, the next Damari was choking on the dust of his death. The white-feathered arrow lay on the ground, soaked in black blood.

She turned, her heart leaping into her throat.

"Lathan!" she sobbed. "Maxx!"

The Jandry brothers charged, Lathan with sword in hand and Maxx allowing his horse its head as he fitted another arrow to his bow. He loosed another into the chaos behind her, the streak of Frostling light parting to allow the brothers to finish what was left of the Wraith Spawn.

Silence enveloped the woods as the last of the Wraith Spawn fell, their shrieks fading on the wind as a cloud of black dust rose away from the battle site. Damari stood motionless for a moment, still holding onto Noelle with a firm grip as she looked about. The Frostlings were circling Lathan and Maxx as the brothers cleaned their weapons before sheathing them. Noelle raised her head.

"Uncle Lathan! Uncle Maxx!" she squealed, wiggling furiously in Damari's arms.

Damari set the child down, allowing her to run to her uncles. Lathan caught up the little girl first, nuzzling his face in her hair. He bent slightly, shoulders shuddering with suppressed tears. Damari had no such control, openly crying. She turned away when Lathan looked at her, handing his niece over to Maxx.

In four long strides he was before her, gathering her in his strong arms. Damari melted in them, burying herself against the solid chest of the man she'd longed for her whole life.

"Thank you," Lathan said hoarsely. Damari opened her eyes, looking up without raising her head at the Frostling floating in the air above them. "Thank you for saving them."

"Our light is for all rulers who possess a pure heart," the Frostling replied, smiling down at them. "The *Almaër Dominje* has much work to do, and your little niece has many years ahead of her. No evil will touch her again."

"Blessed Creator," Damari wept. "I pray that's so!"

"We must leave you now," the Frostling said. "Our task is not complete, and there are others in the Night Wood who are in need of our light."

"Go with the Creator," Maxx murmured next to them.

"You also," the Frostling answered.

In a flash of snow flurries, she rose above the trees with her followers and disappeared into the bright sky. Damari turned her face against Lathan's coat, squeezing her eyes closed.

"I prayed you would come," she whispered. "I wanted you to come. I needed you!"

"And I am here." Lathan placed his big hand against the back of her head, forcing her neck back. She looked up at him, shivering under the rough feel of his palms on her cheeks. "You are unharmed?"

"Yes." Damari nodded.

"How did the Frostlings lower the Wraith Spawn shield?" Maxx asked, his arms still wrapped around Noelle. She rested comfortably on his hip, her big eyes still watching the sky where the Frostlings vanished. "I didn't think they had fire magic."

Damari's cheeks flamed. "They ... they don't."

Both men looked at her.

"I do," she whispered. "I dropped the shield."

Lathan took a step back, his brow creasing slightly with confusion. Suddenly, Noelle lowered her gaze.

"Mama Damari?" she whimpered. "I'm getting cold."

Damari reached out. Noelle wiggled out of Maxx's hold and into her arms.

"Do the magic?" Noelle requested. "Please?"

Damari smiled and turned her back on the brothers. She couldn't bear to look at them right now. Not with what she was about to reveal.

"Can you bring some kindling?" she asked them over her shoulder.

Damari heard them shuffling about, one gathering the horses while another searched for sticks among the snow. She used the heel of her boot to create a small circle in the snow, kicking the fresh powder aside until she could see the dirt beneath. Lathan appeared a moment later, dropping a pile of sticks into the hole she'd made.

"Can you hold her please?" Damari whispered.

Lathan stared at her as he took Noelle onto his hip, his blue eyes intense with the need for answers.

He might as well know. A lump formed in her throat. *I cannot keep it a secret.*

Pulling in a long breath of crisp air, she raised her hands, palms facing each other. The fire sparked to life, faster than the last few times. Damari smiled, watching the white globe of flames roll and crackle between her hands. The power was becoming more a part of her every time she sought it—the magic swirling like hot liquid in her belly. With a gentle twitch of her hands, she sent the flames down on the sticks. They ignited, snapping and hissing.

Noelle giggled, kicking her legs until Lathan set her down so she could hold her hands near the white fire. Damari raised her eyes hesitantly to see his reaction. The stunned expression on Lathan's usually stoic face raised gooseflesh on her arms.

"It happened after we left the city," she explained quietly. "I didn't know. It was sudden, as if some sort of survival instinct—my need to keep Noelle alive in the winter storm—brought the magic to life inside me."

Lathan merely nodded, his lips pressed together firmly. Maxx appeared at her side, resting his hand on her shoulder. Damari looked at him.

"This is a gift, Damari," Maxx assured her. "Don't be ashamed of it."

"I'm not," she answered, her gaze shifting back to his older brother. "I'm trying to understand, that's all."

"This changes everything," Lathan declared, raking a hand through his hair. She noticed he'd removed the braided cord normally tied around his temples—a blue and yellow cord marking him the second son of his family as was tradition in Molderëin.

He must've removed it so others wouldn't take notice of him when they left the city. Damari bit her lip.

"Why does it change things?" she asked, her heart rocketing frantically against her ribs. "I'm still Damari Kael of Nfaros."

"Yes, you are." Lathan's eyes softened, but only for a moment. "Yet, you're not. I'll return shortly."

She opened her mouth to say something, but he'd already walked away, weaving between the trees and out of sight. Maxx squeezed her shoulder.

"I'll talk to him," he said. "He doesn't mean what you think he means. But ... he should be the one to tell you."

"Tell me what?" Damari grabbed his wrist. "Oh, Maxx, please! Tell me."

"I can't." Maxx touched her cheek lightly with his finger. "Don't worry, Damari. Stay with Noelle. I'll bring him back."

He slipped away from her, jogging into the forest after his brother. Damari sat down beside Noelle, hugging her knees.

What's changed? Why do things have to change? A tear rolled down her cheek, and when it fell on the snow, a whisper of steam rose from the ground.

Damari stared at the steam, barely feeling Noelle cuddle against her side to fall asleep. The heat of her own tears was impossible, yet the fact remained they could melt ice. She no longer felt even a little of the cold—not even while sitting a foot deep in snow.

Things *had* changed. But where did she go from here?

Lathan stopped when he was some distance from the campfire, resting a hand against a tree. He breathed deeply, the cold air making his breath steam before his face. Navaria's words echoed in his ears, and he trembled, closing his eyes tight.

You must find Damari Kael. You must find our Almaër Dominje. With each hour that passes her power grows stronger and she begins to change. She will tell you this herself when you find her ...

Almaër Dominje. That's what Navaria had called her. An ancient name Lathan didn't understand but which rang with power and strength. Lathan's hand curled against the rough bark of the tree. He'd hoped Navaria was wrong. He'd hoped Damari would be as she'd always been, without the weight of an unknown future hanging over her shoulders.

Yet aren't all our futures unknown at present? Lathan exhaled heavily, tilting his head back.

"You have to tell her."

Lathan spun, glaring at his brother. Maxx stood, legs spread and arms crossed. Thunderclouds rolled across his brother's face, clear anger at Lathan sizzling in the space between them.

"Has she not been through enough?" Lathan growled.

"What will happen to her if you do not tell her? What will happen if you ignore Navaria's instruction and bring her with us to the Winter Queen?" Maxx took a step closer. "She'll die, Lathan. With no knowledge of her power, with no help from someone like Navaria ... she will die!"

Lathan grabbed his brother by the collar dragging him forward. "Cease!"

Maxx took hold of Lathan's arms. "You love her!"

Lathan let go, spinning away. He tangled his hands in his hair, taking in deep breaths. Maxx placed a cautious hand on his shoulder.

"You know what you have to do, brother," Maxx whispered, hoarsely. "I will take Noelle and find the Eventide Sisters. She will be safest among them, and they will protect her. She has Sundragon blood, and they have declared for Adlae. Once I know she's safe, I will go in search of Adlae myself."

Lathan bobbed his head slowly, his stomach knotting.

"You must take Damari to Draedin, and if Navaria is no longer there, you will continue to the Mountains."

"You truly believe Noelle will be safe from Raphaela if she's with the Eventide Sisters?" Lathan asked.

"Yes. The Eventide woman I am bound to may have been cold as ice, but she spoke truth when she said they were going to fight for Adlae. Besides, the Frostling said evil will not touch Noelle again. I cannot take the child into the Winter Queen's camp where she will be surrounded by soldiers preparing to fight Roderick. I won't."

"No. You're right, that is no place for her." Lathan turned around, facing his brother. "I will tell Damari. She and I will go to Draedin."

"Merchant ships dock outside of Sunkai, near the border of the Aulend to bring trade to Quintaria faster. You can buy passage from there and avoid the city," Maxx suggested.

"Yes," Lathan said, his mouth dry.

Without another word, he brushed passed Maxx. He heard the snow crunching behind him, his brother following close on his heels as they returned to the camp. The fire was still bright and strong. The pure white of the flames reminding him of how Damari changed in an instant.

Lathan crouched beside her. She'd fallen asleep, the hood of her cloak pulled up and her body limp against the nearest tree. Noelle was curled in her lap, round cheeks rosy not with cold but with warmth. Warmth even Lathan could feel radiating off of Damari's body. Her fair skin fairly shimmered in the sunlight. Lathan frowned. There was something about her skin—as if it was shifting from glittering white diamonds back to smooth pearly white.

He rested his hand on her head, smoothing his thumb along her hairline. Damari shifted, her eyes fluttering open. She stared at him in silence, uncertainty lighting her sapphire eyes.

"I need to speak with you," he said quietly.

Damari nodded. Lathan swiftly lifted Noelle out of Damari's arms, turning to hand her over to Maxx. The child didn't even stir, settling comfortably in her uncle's arms. Maxx brought her to the fire, offering an encouraging nod over his shoulder at Lathan.

"Is everything all right?" Damari asked as Lathan took her hand, pulling her gently to her feet.

He kept a firm hold of her fingers, walking a short distance away from the fire. The further they walked from the fire magic, the colder the air became, reminding him how fierce the winter storm was.

And this is only the beginning. Lathan shuddered.

"Damari," he said, turning to face her. He clasped both her hands in his, holding them against his chest. "Did you meet a woman named Navaria?"

Her eyes widened. "Did you?"

Lathan nodded, pressing his lips together tightly.

"She … she came to me in the Blood Keep gardens one night. She told me …" Damari's voice trailed away.

"She told you you are the *Almaër Dominje*," Lathan finished for her. "I know. She told me the same."

Damari tried to step back, but he held firmly to her, keeping her close.

"I don't know what it means!" Damari exclaimed, her beautiful eyes brimming. "I don't know what any of this means!"

"Navaria's guard, Krow, was fatally wounded. She saved his life, but she needed to flee with him to the Mountain Lands," Lathan continued, his voice a low, comforting rumble. "She told me to bring you to Draedin, and if they are not still there, on to the Mountains. They need you and you need them."

"But … but the Winter Queen!"

"The Winter Queen is gathering her armies. If we are to help her, we must know what your magic means."

101

"I can't leave Noelle! I promised Brae! We need to get her out—"

"Brae is dead."

Damari stepped back. This time, he let her go. Her face paled another shade—shoulders shaking beneath the weight of what he'd just revealed. Lathan stared at her as she attempted to understand what he'd told her.

"D-Dead?" Damari stuttered. "She … she's … no! She can't be!"

"I saw it myself," Lathan whispered. "Raphaela had her executed. I couldn't stop her … and Brecken! Brecken is now Raphaela's prisoner, and I don't know …"

Damari rushed forward, wrapping her arms around his waist. Lathan put his around her, one hand on the back of her head, pressing her firmly to his chest. They stood in silence, comforting each other the only way they knew how.

"Maxx will take Noelle to the Eventide Sisters," Lathan murmured gently against her hair. "She will be safe among them as they've declared for the Sundragon. Then, he will go on and find Adlae."

Damari nodded. Then, she tilted her head back, looking into his eyes.

"Lathan, I'm so afraid!" A tear rolled down her cheek.

Lathan caught the drop on the tip of his finger. The small, crystal bead was strangely hot—even her tears a reflection of the magic pulsing through her body.

"I know, love," Lathan answered. "You're going to be all right. We're all going to be all right."

"Do you truly believe that?"

Lathan stared at her for a moment in silence. He moved his hands over her hair, trailing his fingertips down her temples and cheeks. She closed her eyes, leaning into his touch. He'd longed to touch her like this for years. To hold her—cherish her. Just days ago, a future with her seemed so impossible. She'd been made a Princess of Nfaros. They did not marry lieutenants in the king's army.

But now … Lathan breathed deeply, his chest expanding.

Now, with the return of Adlae Sundragon, anything seemed possible.

"Yes," he finally answered her. "I do, Damari. I really do."

CHAPTER ELEVEN

Somewhere Between Land and Sky ...

The Place Between was beautiful. A land of shadow and light which only a Passer could understand. A land only a Passer could bear to enter. This was not a place for the living. This was not a place for any who hadn't felt the Creator's touch—who had not been given a power bestowed directly from the Creator's command. Afra Malaki knew this from the moment she'd entered the Place Between. This was where she guided the souls. This was where she directed them into the Creator's keeping.

If only I could have done so for Brae ... Afra sighed. She knew Brae had been lifted by the Creator himself, protected from the Abyss's clutches, yet guilt gnawed at her heart for not being there for her. Her sister by law was peaceful now, which was all that mattered in the end.

She floated through the Place Between, waiting for the next command. The Creator would take her wherever she needed to be. Whether at Adlae Sundragon's side, or back to Kaldon, she did not know. So she waited—her body adrift in the Place Between. Her heart full of the peace that came with being so close to the Creator.

There were not many Passers left. The Abyss did its best to grab hold of a dying soul and drag it from the Creator's light. Afra had hidden for some time, afraid the Abyss would come for her, as it had come for so many other Passers before her. Yet the Creator's light never wavered in her soul, and the cry of the dying could no longer be ignored. War was coming, and many would need the gentle Passing only Afra could offer.

A soft urging turned Afra from her present course. She closed her eyes, allowing the will of the Creator to weave through her soul—guiding her physical body out of the Place Between. A moment later, her feet landed on cold stone. Afra frowned, opening her eyes.

Darkness surrounded her, blinding her. Blinking rapidly, she tried to adjust to the dimness of the room.

Where am I? she wondered as a chill breeze swept through, echoing against the walls.

Trust me, my child. The Creator's answer filled her heart.

Afra stepped forward, lifting her gaze to the ceiling. The darkness was beginning to clear; her eyes adjusting to the blackened room. A frown creased her brow. She was in a dungeon; empty chains hanging from the walls and a domed ceiling offering no windows of light.

Why am I here? Her heart began to pound. A sinking feeling twisted her stomach. A low moan made Afra spin around. She gasped, tears rushing to her eyes when she saw him.

Brecken hung chained to the wall, his legs limp beneath him and his bare chest covered in bruises and cuts. Blood was drying where it had dripped from the wounds.

"No!" Afra cried, tilting her head toward the ceiling. "I won't! I won't Pass my own brother!"

Go to him, my child. The Creator said.

Afra burst into tears, covering her face with her hands. How could He ask this of her? How could she do this?

"Afra?" Brecken's voice whispered across the space between them. "Is it you?"

Afra dropped her hands, stumbling forward. She clasped him, burying her face against the thick curve of his neck and crossed her arms over his back.

"I'm here," she sobbed. "I'm here, brother."

"Have you come to Pass me?" he asked.

Afra cried harder, gasping for air. Then, she felt *His* touch. The Creator was present, hovering over her like a warm cloud in the middle of winter. Afra closed her eyes and reached out for Brecken's soul.

She sprang back, her eyes widening.

"You ... you are not dying," she murmured.

Brecken looked up at her lazily, an exhausted grin tilting his mouth. "Really? I feel like I am."

"Don't tease, Brecken!" Afra moved forward again, resting her hand on the center of his chest. An elated laugh slipped from her lips. "Your heart is strong!"

Brecken leaned his head back against the wall. "Then I don't understand ... what are you doing here?"

"Don't you see?" Afra smiled, tears of relief now sliding down her cheeks. She took his bruised face gently between her palms. "I am not here to Pass you. I'm here to rescue you!"

"How? There are guards everywhere."

"How did I get in, brother?"

Brecken opened his eyes again, and Afra arched an eyebrow.

"The Place Between?" he asked, breathlessly.

She dipped her head yes.

"But ... I cannot! I am not a Passer!"

"If He wills it, then you can. You must." Afra waved her hands over the chains.

Brecken's wrists fell away from the binds, and he stumbled. She caught him, bracing him beneath his arms. He found his footing, still leaning heavily into her.

How long since he's eaten? How horribly Raphaela must've tortured him! Afra cringed when she felt the dark magic covering him like a thin layer of dust on his skin. Raphaela Kael was certainly lost forever to use dark magic on a man she claimed to love.

"What's going on in there?" one of the guards shouted from the other side.

"Hold onto me, Brecken," Afra said, glaring at the dungeon door when the lock clicked and keys jangled. "Don't let go."

Brecken's grip tightened around her shoulders. "Hurry, sister."

Afra closed her eyes, the peace of the Creator rushing through her like a forceful river. Then, they rose, floating high above toward the Place Between. Brecken's breath grew shallow with sudden fear, but she held tighter to him, turning her face until her forehead touched his temple. The touch of her seemed to calm him, his heart slowing down from its frantic pounding.

"We're here," she whispered. Afra opened her eyes and smiled. "Open your eyes, Brecken. Look upon the Creator's Realm."

She watched him, waiting until his eyes opened. Brecken's breath caught, his eyes widening in wonder as he breathed in the air. A silver glow surrounded them, glittering under a pure white sky.

"The air is ripe with His power," Afra whispered. "And His love and mercy flows through the realm. Yet this is only the Place Between."

"How is this possible? How am I not dead?" Brecken asked.

"Your task is not complete," Afra answered. "You are not meant for this place, Brecken."

"Did Brae come here?" Brecken asked suddenly, his gaze lowering. "Was she lost here?"

"No," Afra replied, her voice thick. "No, Brae did not come here. Brae was lifted by the Creator Himself and brought directly to His realm."

Brecken nodded. "For that, I am thankful. She is at peace."

"Yes, my darling. She is at peace." Afra hugged him, stroking his hair softly. "We must leave here, Brecken. He has found a place for us."

Brecken responded with a low groan, pressing his chin on her shoulder. Afra supported him with what strength she had as the Creator guided them down out of the Place Between.

A haze of black and red flickered beneath his eyelids as he came to. He could hear the spitting of the fire—felt the warmth of the flames even as he sat in something cold and wet. For a moment, he thought he was dreaming. He had to be dreaming. Surely he was still chained to the wall in Raphaela's dungeon, waiting for her to return to offer more dark magic torture.

Brecken turned his head, the back of his scalp scraping against something rough. Then he felt something warm pressed to his lips. Steam rushed up into his face, the scent of freshly brewed mint tea filled his nostrils.

"Drink, brother," her distant, beautiful voice filled his ears. "The tea will help, my darling."

Brecken reached out blindly, grabbing hold of her arm. He was too tired to open his eyes; too exhausted to look at her.

"You're real," he murmured.

"Yes."

"It's really you. It's really Afra ..."

"Yes, love. It's Afra. I'm here. You're safe now."

Brecken nodded and parted his lips. The warm liquid swam on his tongue, sliding smoothly down his throat to warm his gut. Ever so slowly, he began to open his eyes. The light of midday assaulted him, and he moaned, squeezing his eyes closed once again. He felt Afra nursing his wounds, her hands moving like a gentle wind over him as she brought healing to his body.

When he was ready, Brecken opened his eyes again. The light didn't hurt so much now. He squinted, watching her image clear before him. Afra had returned to the fire. The supplies were a mystery—something the Creator must've provided when He dropped them in the woods. Brecken placed a hand over his bruised chest, wincing at the touch of the bandage Afra had applied.

"They'll heal quickly," Afra said, drawing his gaze.

She was draped in thick robes to keep warm, hands bare, and her thick, dark brown hair roped in an intricate braid down her back. She stared at him with wide, brown eyes glittering like melted chocolate in the sunlight. Brecken sighed. Afra had always been considered the plain one in their family with her sharp cheekbones, thin mouth, and slightly crooked nose. But she'd won the heart of Brax Malaki, known in his time to be the handsomest man in Nfaros. No maiden in the land had ever forgiven her for earning his love, but Afra's happiness could not be stemmed with a few jealous looks.

Then she lost him. Oh, how much she lost the day he died! Brecken swallowed the lump in his throat.

"I've missed you," he said, choking on the words.

Afra's eyes flooded. "I missed you too. Oh Brecken! I'm so sorry! I should've been there for Brae!"

"No." Brecken shook his head. "No, sister. Raphaela would've killed you on sight."

Afra ducked her head.

"Do not be ashamed, Afra Malaki," Brecken ordered sternly. "You've nothing to be ashamed of. I wasn't there when she needed me either."

Afra sniffled, using her sleeve to dab at the corners of her eyes. She stood up, moving to crouch in front of him.

"Do you feel your strength returning? We can't stay here long. We need to find a Circle."

Brecken frowned, looking about. The snow was thick, but not as thick as it would be in a forest further north, like the Night Wood.

"Where are we?" he asked.

"Judging by the trees," Afra said, placing her hand on the trunk he sat against. "I'd say the Pilvaa."

Brecken sat up straighter. *Mirae!*

"The Pilvaa ... you're certain?"

Afra nodded hesitantly.

"Mirae is here." He struggled to rise, but Afra placed her hands on his shoulders restraining him. "We have to find her! We must join her!"

"Yes, as is the Creator's intention," Afra confirmed, kindly. "But you must also rest and heal, brother. If Mirae Sundragon doesn't find us first, then we will find her. It is the Creator's will, love."

Brecken exhaled loudly, surrendering when Afra pushed him softly back into the rough tree trunk. The need to get to Mirae and tell her all that happened was great. The need to join her in the fight against Roderick and Raphaela even greater still.

Then his thoughts turned. His heart ramming into his ribs and his body trembling as he saw behind his closed lids a little girl. Hair as red as blood and eyes as green as her mother's.

"Noelle ..." Brecken breathed.

"Safe," Afra replied. Brecken opened his eyes. "Damari Kael got her out of the city before Brae ..." Afra shuddered. "She got her out before everything happened. Lathan and Maxx are searching for them, and they will find them."

Brecken nodded. "They'll keep her safe. Thank the Creator she was no longer in the city walls when her mother was killed."

"Yes."

"Damari Kael ..." he muttered. "Who'd have thought?"

"Indeed." Afra turned so she was sitting beside him. "Damari Kael surprises those who believe they know her best at every turn. Her part to play in the coming days is great."

"How much does the Creator tell you?" Brecken asked. "Do you know the outcome of all of this?"

"No one knows, Brecken. No mortal, anyway." Afra squeezed his hand. "I always prayed you would come to love Brae with your whole heart. I never dreamed when you finally did, you would lose her."

Brecken's eyes stung and he looked away, staring off into the woods. "It is done. I must set my mind on things to come. To my daughter's future."

"Yes. But it does not mean you must forget Brae."

"I'll never forget her. I was unable to save her, and I will carry that knowledge with me for the rest of my life, Afra." Brecken's lip curled in a snarl. "And when the time is right, I will put my sword straight through Raphaela Kael's heart and gain my vengeance. Blood is repaid with blood."

"Brecken ..." Afra whispered, her voice weak. "Brae would not want you to take such a dark path. Vengeance does not belong to us, and if she did not know this in life, she knows it now."

"Yet, I am still of this life. Because I did not stand for her, because I did not believe her, she is dead. I gave my loyalty to a usurper and a murderer. I am paying now and I will not rest until I kill everyone who took so much from my Brae, including her life."

Brecken's heart lifted with anticipation—his blood rushing like a raging river.

"No, sister. This is my time now. Raphaela Kael will be sorry she ever laid eyes on me."

Snow flurries swirled all around as Mirae walked quietly through the woods with Ahmet. Her Third murmured to himself as they scouted the forest, pausing to cut pieces of bark off different trees or bend to pluck a winter blossom from the ground. Mirae would observe with little interest when she was forced to stop with him, watching him tuck his samples away in the little book he carried everywhere. Most likely, they would return to camp and Ahmet would disrupt Astra's newlywed life to ask her what they were, what they were for, and if they possessed any magical properties.

And most likely, she would tell them they are all just bark and flowers, nothing magical about them simply because they grow in the Pilvaa. Mirae smiled, shaking her head.

Despite his passion for all things magical, Ahmet truly did make a good Third in Command. Once he had a sword in his hand, no one would ever suspect he was a scholar at heart.

"We should move on, Ahmet," Mirae urged as patiently as she could. "We're nearly through with our sweep. I believe this will be a good place to rest for the night."

"Strange," Ahmet mumbled, still crouched to the ground. "No darkness. No black magic ... this is the Pilvaa! *Something* should've tried to kill us by now!"

"You sound disappointed," Mirae said, barely hiding her amusement.

"Not disappointed. Concerned. If the darkness is quiet ... that can't be good. They're waiting for something. Just ask Astra."

Ahmet stood, tucking away his book in the front pocket of his coat. He wiped his hands on his trousers. Then his nose wrinkled and he tilted his head up a bit, sniffing the air.

"Do you smell smoke?" he asked.

Mirae closed her eyes, breathing in deeply as she searched for whatever he was smelling. Then the scent came to her, a soft whiff of smoke filling her nostrils.

"A fire," Mirae agreed. "Coming from the south."

"Not one of ours. We're north, behind us." Ahmet gestured over his shoulder. "This is ahead of us."

Mirae turned slightly, looking in the direction of the scent. "Should we see who it is?"

"Your decision, Your Majesty," Ahmet replied.

Mirae hesitated, pondering. If they were enemies, she should know so she could get her people away as fast as possible. But she also risked them finding her and her people if she went close enough to get a decent look.

Or perhaps they are Woodlanders in need. This storm will turn fierce soon enough and they will not survive alone ... Mirae tugged her sword loose with a low hiss.

"Let's go," she murmured.

Ahmet nodded, fixing an arrow to his bow as they moved silently through the woods, the way Jaeger taught her. In the throes of the start of the greatest storm Nfaros had seen in years, moving quietly was difficult. A thin layer of ice crackled beneath her boots unless she stepped carefully, the flurries drifting down from overhead creating a light powder over the frozen earth. Mirae shivered, using her free hand to draw her cloak closer against her chest.

The smell of the fire grew stronger, guiding her and Ahmet in the right direction. Faintly, she heard the sticks crackling as the flames consumed them. Mirae picked up her pace, Ahmet keeping up with her as they came to a small clearing. She ducked behind one of the trees, Ahmet a few feet away behind another.

"I see a woman!" Ahmet said quietly. "There's a tent, but I think she's alone ..."

Mirae turned her head carefully, looking over her shoulder. She nearly dropped her sword. The woman she saw was covered warmly in thick black robes, her hands bare as she held them out to the fire. She was humming softly, an old tune Mirae recognized from childhood. She knew the frame of the woman, recognizing the slight form beneath the robes and the shimmering brown braid falling behind her back, nearly to her waist.

Then she turned her head, and Mirae caught her breath.

"Afra?" she called, stepping out from behind the tree. She ignored Ahmet's whispers for her to come back, moving forward instead. "Afra Malaki?"

Afra stood up calmly, turning to Mirae as if she'd been expecting her. The woman rested her hands against her skirts, staring at Mirae with round, chocolate-colored eyes. She was standing between Mirae and the tent. For a moment, Mirae thought she looked more like a guard than a lone woman.

Ahmet rushed to her side, huffing and puffing. He glared down at her, but Mirae paid no attention to his disapproval. She took another cautious step, and Afra tensed.

"Hello, Mirae," Afra greeted cautiously. "I knew you'd find us, eventually."

"Us?" Mirae repeated, her heart pounding. "Noelle! Is Noelle with you? Did she get out? Oh please let me see her! I've never met—"

"No," Afra whispered. "Noelle is safe, but she's not with me."

"Then ... who?"

Someone moved in the tent, a rustle of blankets and ripple of the tent flaps alerting her.

"Please sheath your sword, Mirae," Afra requested. "I need to know you won't do anything ... rash."

"Who's with you, Afra?" Mirae wondered.

Afra lowered her gaze to Mirae's weapon. Slowly, she began to slide the blade into its sheath.

"My lady, no!" Ahmet growled at her side.

"Enough, Ahmet," Mirae snapped. "I have known Afra Malaki since we were children. I trust her with my life, as should you. Do you not recognize a Passer when you see one?"

Ahmet's eyes widened, and his head turned sharply back to Afra, who cringed. He lowered his bow.

"How did you know, Mirae?" Afra wondered.

"I have been hiding all these years, Afra. It doesn't mean I wasn't listening." Mirae crossed her arms over her chest. "There now, my sword is put away. Who is with you?"

Afra turned her head, barely looking over her shoulder.

"Come out now," she ordered. "I ... I think it's all right."

The tent flap flew back with a *whoosh*.

Mirae stilled, watching. Brecken sauntered forward like a mountain cat assessing his prey. Despite the cold, he was shirtless, bandages wrapped neatly across his torso and chest. He didn't appear bothered by the winter wind rushing through the forest. His black hair had grown, hanging low over his ears, his dark eyes brooding and broad shoulders beautifully laced with years of hard-worked muscle rippling with every step he took. His physique had only seemed to improve, in spite of the past days of torture she knew he must've endured in Roderick's dungeons. There was a slight pallor to his skin, and his ribs were more defined beneath his strong torso, but those were the only indications of his ordeal.

Besides the bandages covering Creator knows what. How severe are the wounds? Mirae's heart went into her throat. Because, even though she tried to deny it, she cared a great deal more for Brecken than she would ever admit.

Afra still stood between them, a tiny wall of defense for her brother. Mirae didn't think Afra could do much for Brecken if it came down to a conflict. But then, she didn't know the extent of the woman's power.

"You have no reason to trust me," Brecken said, breaking the tense silence.

Mirae looked directly into his eyes, no longer seeing Afra between them.

"Yet, you're asking me to," Mirae replied.

"Yes. I am." Brecken took another step forward and Afra shifted nervously on the balls of her feet. "They killed my Brae. *Our* Brae. I have no love for the Kael king or his sister. Whatever loyalty I had died, even before my wife was taken from me. I just didn't realize until that moment."

Mirae's eyes brimmed to overflowing. "You really loved her, didn't you?"

Brecken trembled, closing his eyes. His thick brow furrowed and his hands clenched at his sides.

"Loving your sister kept me alive," Brecken whispered. "Loving her saved me in more ways than she ever knew. I *had* to love her."

"And she loved you, too." Mirae reached for her necklace, encompassing the dragon in her palm. "I felt her love for you through our link."

"I'm sorry, Mirae." Brecken gasped, his chest heaving. "I'm sorry I couldn't save her."

Mirae closed the distance between them, throwing her arms around his neck. Brecken lifted her right off her feet, holding her just as tight—his strong arms wrapped all the way around her waist.

"My lady!" Ahmet hissed in warning.

Mirae didn't care. What he thought of Brecken didn't matter. Only what she thought.

"I do trust you," she said as Brecken lowered her to her feet. She looked up at him. "I shouldn't, but I do. You let me live that day on the Kliat, and I know you didn't just spare me for Brae's sake."

Brecken bowed his head. Mirae placed her fingers beneath his chin, forcing him to look at her.

"Will you join me, Brecken? Will you captain my army? Will you help me find Adlae, the *true* Sundragon?"

Brecken fell to one knee and kissed her knuckles.

"I will," he whispered. "I swear, before the Creator Himself, I will be your humble servant, your fierce captain. I give my sword to the true Sundragon, Queen Adlae, and pledge my loyalty to you, the Queen of the Woodlands. May the Creator strike me dead if I betray either of you."

A tear slipped down her cheek and she smiled.

"Then rise, Captain Jandry of the Woodland Armies. We have work to do."

CHAPTER TWELVE

Molderëin

A roar rose in the air, reaching through the open window of Clea's room. She stroked her blade with a stone, guiding the smooth surface along the crescent curve of the steel until it reached the tip. Then she started over. The Tower Gate Inn stood under the shadow of the four Towers themselves. Built directly from the nearest mountain, its black stone walls and rough rock floors were cold and unwelcoming. Each door was made of thick oak, brought across the sea from the north of Nfaros. They were heavy, with three locks lined from ceiling to floor on each for the safety of guests.

How low Molderëin has fallen! How much worse the city must be since my father brought me here all those years ago … Clea sighed.

The city erupted in chaos not long after Morgren found them a room at the inn. She had to admit, the almost instant brawling which accompanied the rise of the sun had sent a rush of adrenaline through her. But her excitement for danger did not reach so far as to tempt her down onto the streets.

The weight in her chest thickened, and Clea paused mid-swipe on the sword. She closed her eyes, breathing in—pushing out the weakness wanting to overwhelm her body. The power she'd used in the woods against the Black Ones still covered her like a shroud. She had not used so much of her strength in a long time, and Morgren was right. She'd been foolish to wipe out an entire army of evil by herself.

Clea sighed and resumed sharpening her sword. Molderëin was everything she expected, yet completely unexpected at the same time. There was a darkness here she hadn't expected. Darker than the usual savagery—even darker than she'd remembered as a child. Her one visit here with her father had imprinted an image on her mind not easily shaken, making her wish she'd seen the city through Brecken's eyes. Before her family left, Molderëin was a different place. A better place.

How does one explain that? How much could one family—particularly a poor one like mine with little nobility in our blood—influence an entire city? We certainly don't have much sway in the north. Clea puffed her cheeks.

Izeana sat down beside her carefully, the mattress dipping beneath their combined weight.

"When will you venture outside?" she asked.

Clea looked at her, offering a small smile. "When Morgren returns. You've nothing to fear, Izeana. As long as you remain in the room and keep your long sleeves on, you will be safe."

Izeana nodded, though her bony shoulders trembled. Clea put her arm around the girl, rubbing her arm comfortingly.

"I won't let anything happen to you," Clea whispered. "I need the Summer Flower. It will anchor my power so I may seek out the fate Brecken told me I would find here. He said I could save us all, Izeana. I intend to see this through, no matter what comes. But if I don't find the Summer Flower …"

"You will weaken," Rheatha said from across the room. Clea and Izeana both looked at her where she stood before the window, staring down at the rumbling streets below. "Your magic was born in summer, not winter. Only the Summer Flower can restore your power to you, along with your strength. Only the flower can help your magic withstand the frozen wind of winter."

Clea nodded. "You see, Izeana. Once I have the flower, I can truly keep you and Rheatha safe."

"How do you know it's in the Towers?" Rheatha asked, spinning to face her. "How will you gain entrance?"

"Morgren and I will work together to gain entrance. You needn't trouble your heart with our methods, Rheatha." Clea slid her sword back into its sheath, putting the weapon aside. "Morgren should be back any moment."

She stood, walking over to stand beside Rheatha at the window. Her thoughts turned to her men, watching and waiting from a distance. She could only pray Ryker was keeping them quiet and out of sight. They didn't want to let her go alone, but if the city saw them upon her entrance they would think her a threat to them.

If Morgren is right, and all it will take is my name to get me within the Towers, then I will have the Summer Flower soon enough.

Clea rested her hand against the window, rubbing her thumb on the smooth glass. She hated small spaces. Being locked in never sat well with her, even if it meant her safety. As a child, her brothers and sister couldn't hold her back. They did their best to restrain her, especially when their parents required her to be a little lady, but they all loved her too much to hold her back from being who she was.

A knock resounded on the door. Clea frowned, turning around. Rheatha and Izeana both looked at each other, then at her.

"M-Morgren would n-not knock," Izeana stuttered, and Rheatha went to her, holding her close.

Clea crossed the room in two strides, yanking her sword out before going to the door. She paused halfway there, air catching in her throat. She could feel the pulse from the other side of the door. The magic was stifling—the being beyond the door pulling as much into himself as possible in preparation for her to reveal herself. Clea looked over her shoulder at them.

"Into the corner," she instructed, pointing with her sword. "Get down, darlings."

Rheatha guided the softly weeping Izeana to the corner, and they both curled up, holding each other. Clea clutched her sword tighter and closed her eyes.

"What strength I have left," she whispered. "Give it me now, my Lord. Fill me with the power only You bestow on the gifted. Protect us."

Clea groaned, the power filling her more painful than ever before. Once she felt the pulse rushing through her, flushing out and replacing the pain with the sweetest tingle, she opened the door.

The sorcerer screeched, his fiery eyes glistening in round red orbs and his yellowed teeth dripping with saliva. Clea shouted, thrusting her sword and catching him in the arm. He jerked back, raising ashen hands with claw-like nails toward her. Dark magic erupted from them in a burst of fire and smoke. Clea threw down her sword and raised her own palms, a light like none she'd ever possessed bursting forth from them.

The light gleamed off the sorcerer's bald head, turning his ashen skin to a sickening green. The color reminded her of the sorcerer who'd attempted to kidnap her straight from her father's arms all those years ago. Something inside her had bloomed that day. Something inside her exploded, and her tiny little hand had burned a hole right through the sorcerer's sleeve. Clea could feel the same power blooming in her heart now—deep and hot, burning like no magic she'd ever felt before.

With a cry, she thrust her hands forward. The light hit the sorcerer in the chest, and he shrieked, the sound echoing down the halls. He spun, his red robes billowing as he raced down the stairs away from her. Clea picked up her sword.

"Stay here!" she shouted before slamming the door behind her.

The power in her blood would not be tamed. She had to see the end of the sorcerer, or he'd return. He'd wait for her to be weak, for the magic to drain out of her until she couldn't fight him.

Clea stumbled down the stairs, holding her sword high as she chased the shrieking sorcerer from the inn. People gasped and shouted, racing after her as she chased evil itself out onto the streets. Crowds parted for them—women screamed. Men cheered. Clea didn't care as the sorcerer came to a skidding halt in the middle of the street, too surrounded by people looking for a good show to get away.

He spun back, his red eyes glaring at her. Then, they focused on her sword and whatever his intent was before disappeared. He was stunned, raising a finger to point.

"*Kläerjaen!*" he exclaimed, his guttural voice sending ice down her back. "You hold the *Kläerjaen!*"

Clea frowned, her eye catching the markings on the side of her sword. The people were murmuring; the streets quieter than they'd ever been before. Clea swung the hilt of the sword between her fingers, the blade *whooshing* in the air. The sorcerer scowled, shuffling back away from her.

"Cut off his head!" someone yelled suddenly. "Use the *Kläerjaen!* Prove you are the Heir!"

Clea's heart raced, her magic beginning to fade beneath the confusion muddling her mind. The *Kläerjaen?* That was impossible!

The Sword of Kings was lost years ago … Clea gripped the hilt of her sword tighter.

The sorcerer began to walk, and she moved in the other direction, each of them walking the wide circle the people had created around them. Clea had never been in one on one combat before. Any fight she'd had had been with her siblings, or using her magic against the Abyss, as she had in the woods. This was different. This could end with her killing another being with her own hands.

"Stab him through!" another person shouted.

"Cut him!"

"Kill him!"

"Do *something!*"

Their cries grew louder, and she began to drown in them. With a shout, she raised the weapon to the sky. A bolt of lightning came down, connecting with the blade. Clea's face glowed as she watched the strike brighten the blade, but not burn it. The markings lit, golden and showering the streets with color.

Her voice grew to a shrill pitch, rising above the fearful cries of the people.

"SILENCE! YOU WILL BE SILENT!"

The lightning pulled back, leaving her blade aglow. The entire city had gone quiet. The sorcerer cowered on the ground, his palms flat and his forehead against the cobblestones as he whimpered. Clea's chest heaved, every breath painful as she looked around. The people were staring, some of them holding onto loved ones, others with mouths agape. They all looked the same—none of them looked to be of the nobility. They wore simple robes of dark color, despite the heat of Molderëin. Their skin was leathery from so much exposure to the sun, dark hair glistening.

Clea rested the blunt of her blade in the other hand and stepped closer to the sorcerer, not quite closing the distance between them.

"You will leave here," she hissed and he looked up at her, his face stricken with terror. "You will leave this city and never return. You will never again touch that which is pure, else the Creator strike you down. With this I show you mercy, but let this also be your lesson."

With a swift swing, she cut off his ear. The sorcerer wailed, clutching the side of his head. Blood dripped between his fingers.

"GO."

He leaped to his feet, pushing through the crowd. The sorcerer ran like a madman, arms flailing and legs trembling all the way down the street out of sight.

"It's her!" a woman gasped.

Clea turned, finding the tall woman in the crowd. Her hair was raised on her head in a pile of intricate braids and she wore a thin black dress, the neckline scooped low and a brown rope tied around her waist as a belt. She stepped apart from the crowd, not nearly as afraid of Clea as the rest of them seemed to be.

"She is the one! The one who bears the *Kläerjaen!* The one whose company bears no chains!"

Clea turned full circle, watching the people whisper amongst themselves. It dawned on her she was surrounded; none of her own company in sight. Morgren still trying to gain entrance to the Towers and Rheatha and Izeana ...

Rheatha and Izeana defenseless in our rooms! Clea gasped, spinning toward the inn.

She crashed into a broad chest and stumbled back. Her eyes widened. The man from the Towers stood before her, the one who'd seemed to be directly before her until she released her magic. His green eyes glowed down at her and his black hair was let completely loose now, falling against his temples in shining waves.

Before she could slip away, he grabbed her wrist, raising her arm above her head so her sword pointed to the sky.

"People of Molderëin!" he shouted, his voice a deep, pleasing sound. "The Heir has come home!"

Clea struggled, but he held firm. The people dropped to their knees, bending until their foreheads touched the cobblestones. Clea looked around in awe, her heart thundering.

What's happening?

The man let go of her wrist and bent on one knee before her. "I, Grange Molten, declare for you, the Heir. What is your name?"

Clea stared, unblinking.

Grange Molten looked up at her expectantly, his mouth thinning the longer she remained silent.

"I don't know who you think I am," she hissed suddenly, keeping her voice low so the people wouldn't hear. "But I am not the Heir!"

"You are the one prophecy spoke of. The woman with raven hair from the north whose company bears no chains and by whose side rests the *Kläerjaen.*" Grange's brow arched. "I knew the moment your magic touched me, for the same magic flows in my veins."

Clea's breath caught. She bit her lip.

"Your name, my lady," he urged, eyes darting to the people who still lay prone on the streets before her.

"Clea Jandry."

His emerald eyes lit with recognition on her surname and he rose.

"Of the Jandrys of old?" he asked.

Clea dipped her head yes. Grange rested his hand on the hilt of his sword.

"To think they were the royals all the time …" he shook his head. "Now your name need not be a secret. Now, our royals may rule the way others do in the north. Molderëin's time of savagery and secrecy has come to an end with your arrival."

"I don't understand …"

"People!" Grange shouted, ignoring her. "I give you Clea Jandry, Heir to the Throne of Molderëin!"

The people rose, a low cheer growing to an ear-splitting roar. Clea's head spun, her knees growing weak beneath her.

"Clea!" Morgren's voice boomed above the rest and she spun, her hair swinging.

"Morgren!" Clea broke free from the hold Grange had on her as her guard shoved his way through the crowd. She landed in his arms, nearly dropping her sword. "What's happening?"

"I thought you knew, little one," Morgren said into her hair. "This is what I feared. This is why I did not want you to return here."

"Brecken didn't say a word to me! We … we can't be royalty! If we were, then Brecken would be the Heir, would he not?"

"Not here, Clea!" Morgren grabbed her by the arms. "At least act as if you know who you are and what you are meant to do!"

"But—"

"Silence!"

Clea reared back. Never in her life had she seen such fury in Morgren's eyes. He schooled his features quickly, looking over her head.

"Grange Molten," he growled. "The Heir would like entrance to the Towers, if you please. Her company is to be brought forth untouched from the inn."

"Of course, Morgren Lanfira," Grange replied, bowing slightly at the waist.

"You've met?" Clea asked, hoarsely.

"Whether we've met is of no consequence," Morgren assured her. "Go inside, Clea. I would speak to the Lord Ruler's son."

"But Morgren—!"

"Inside!" he yelled, pointing to the inn. "Gather Rheatha and Izeana. I want you out of sight, now!"

Clea stared at him, her frustration bubbling into anger. Her face pinched, her brow curving inward toward the bridge of her nose. Tilting her nose into the air she spun, stomping back into the inn. As soon as she was out of Morgren's sight, she ran, tripping her way up the stairs.

The Heir of Molderëin ... it's impossible! Simply impossible! Oh Brecken, why didn't you tell me? Why didn't you warn me?

Clea burst into tears.

"Are you responsible for this?"

Grange met Morgren's cold stare impassively. What the man thought of him didn't matter. It was enough he'd declared the Heir himself, something his father would despise him for.

When he'd seen her come racing out of the inn with the sorcerer, he knew now was the time. He knew if he didn't get to her quickly, the mob would overwhelm her. There were some in Molderëin who did not wish for the Heir's coming, though most desired her arrival with all their hearts. To redeem their country would be a hard, bloody task. But it was what the people wished for nonetheless.

To be restored to glory. To be a great country once more, not a savage place of darkness. She has already brought life back to the city.

"The Heir declared herself the moment she stepped onto our streets with the *Kläerjaen*," Grange answered calmly.

Morgren raked a hand through his hair, turning away as the people began to disperse. Grange couldn't remember when the city had ever been so quiet. The public fights had ceased, leaving blood pooling in the streets and trash cluttering the gutters. The people were returning to their homes to watch and wait; to see what the Heir would do.

"The Heir requires the Summer Flower," Morgren said, abruptly changing the subject. "Does it remain protected in the North Tower?"

"Yes," Grange answered, cautiously. "All that dwells in the Towers belongs to the Heir now. But the Summer Flower … is my father's most prized discovery."

"You will deny the Heir her only request?" Morgren moved forward, nearly coming nose to nose with Grange.

"I will hear the Heir's desires from her own lips and see them fulfilled," Grange said, spitting at Morgren's feet. "She needs no one to speak for her!"

Morgren glared at him. "If you hurt Clea …"

"She has come to save us. Why would I harm her?"

"Your father is a tyrant!"

"Let me handle my father, old man!" Grange shoved Morgren away, curling his lip in an animal-like growl. "Mind your place. There has always been a Molten in the Towers and there always will be, even with the Heir. I will sit at her right hand, as tradition dictates. I will see her will done in all of Molderëin and you will not stop me."

"If Rhoydaen lays a hand on her—"

"The Heir will see all evil things from this city. She has proven that today!"

Morgren smirked. "How tragic for a son to believe his own father is evil."

Grange cringed. "I have had years to learn this, Morgren. Do not judge me by the man who gave me life. We are nothing alike."

Grange turned, marching away before Morgren could respond. His heart had gone wild; racing out of control. Seeing her, being so close to her … he'd learned how powerful she truly was in those few moments. Her beauty matched no one else's. Her clear Molderëinian features somehow standing apart from all other women he'd met. She was fairer—flawless. Perhaps from her exposure to the north. Perhaps her magic.

All he knew was she could drown a man in her eyes. He was drawn to her like no other, and already, she'd cast a spell which required no magic over the whole city. He saw it in the eyes of the people. He felt it in his own heart. There was no doubt she was the Heir of their people, come to rescue them from the evil which ruled their city for far too long. They were all lost to her. Completely in her power.

Grange looked up at the Towers, his insides twisting.

Now to control my father …

Clea clutched Rheatha and Izeana's hands in her own, staring up at the Towers of the King. They were darker up close—more intimidating. They rose in onyx stone spirals toward the sky, carved to a sharp point at the top. The stone bridges connecting them curved and dipped in perfect arches, chipped from age and years of battle. Coming closer, she realized the battlements themselves were crumbling, little repairs having been done. Years had passed since anyone fought to obtain Molderëin. The Lord Ruler clearly thought keeping the battlements strong was not worth the effort.

A harsh, hot wind blew from behind her, urging her forward through the gates. They groaned and scraped against the ground, stone dust puffing from beneath as they opened wide to allow her entrance. Clea stepped through, keeping Rheatha and Izeana close to her sides. Morgren walked behind them, a solid wall of soldier with the same scowl he'd had for hours twisting his features. Clea had noticed Rheatha sparing glances over her shoulder at the Captain of the Guard, but Morgren hadn't even offered her a soothing glance. If Morgren was too distracted not to take notice of Rheatha's concern, then their situation had to be precarious.

Clea tilted her head up, each of her steps growing stronger as she crossed the wide, circular courtyard. Convincing Morgren they had to do this had been horrible. Never before had she used her authority over her Captain this way. But if it meant getting closer to the Summer Flower, she was willing to do whatever these Molderëinians believed she was meant to do.

Whatever Brecken failed to tell me I was meant to do. Clea frowned. She'd have to have a talk with her big brother ... if she ever saw him again, that is.

Grange Molten was waiting for her at the top of the ramp to the first tower, his hair glistening beneath the sun and neatly brushed against his neck. He looked much the way he had the first time she'd seen him on the towers. Sun-bronzed chest bared, wide belt around his hips and dark trousers. His hair was held back from his temples by two small braids and his unusual eyes gleamed.

Clea bit her lip. She had to admit he was handsome. Despite the similar features of all Molderëinians, he didn't remind her of her brothers as she always imagined men of this land would. He was different somehow and she saw honesty in his eyes.

When she approached, he bowed low at the waist.

"Welcome, Your Majesty," he murmured, his voice a deep rumble in the air between them.

"Please don't do that," she replied, gesturing for him to rise and he looked up. "I don't like it."

Grange frowned, confused. He turned, raising his arm in a gesture for her to precede him inside. Clea stepped across the threshold into the tower, reaching for the tie of her cloak. She tugged on the strings, letting Rheatha remove the garment from her shoulders as she tilted her head back. The first tower opened to a wide foyer, dark blue draperies falling from the high ceilings and a spiraling stone staircase rising from the center of the round room.

"This will lead to the throne room," Grange explained, coming to her side. "The rest of the towers are for the Meetings of the Masters and your personal quarters. They are being prepared now."

Izeana stepped away from him nervously, keeping her eyes on the ground and her hands folded in white-knuckled fists before her. Clea's breath came harder—a struggle.

There is honesty in his eyes. He won't hurt my girls. Clea forced a smile.

"I'd like to see the rest of the tower," she murmured.

"Certainly." Grange moved forward.

Clea started to follow when Morgren grabbed her arm, yanking her back. He pressed his mouth to her ear.

"Do not be dazzled by him," Morgren warned. "Grange Molten may be a better man than his father, but he has his own reasons for wanting you on the throne. Remember, Clea. Molderëinians cannot be trusted."

Clea tugged herself loose from his grasp. "You so soon forget I am Molderëinian."

"Raised as a northern lady," he reminded her. "You are different. You are only seventeen, Clea. You are young and vulnerable. I do not want—"

"Enough!" Clea held up her hand, her sharp command making Grange look over his shoulder. She calmed herself, eyeing Morgren angrily. "We will discuss this later, in private."

Morgren tightened his lips, but nodded. Clea walked away, her heart growing weary of Morgren's suspicious nature. She followed Grange, lifting her skirts to her ankles as she began to climb the stairs. She knew already Grange had these towers memorized. The way he moved within them—the same way she moved about in her home in Quintaria.

He was probably born in these towers ... Clea's throat began to close. If he was born here, then surely he wouldn't want to relinquish his home so easily. Surely, this had to be painful for him, leading her inside.

Yet he did not act like a man who was about to have everything he'd ever known taken away from him. Clea took a deep breath.

I don't want this. I never wanted this! How could Brecken not explain to me what I was meant to do here? She frowned.

Having the armies of Molderëin at her disposal would be a great asset for the Sundragon. If Clea could bring them north to fight for Adlae, then surely being here and taking this responsibility was worth a little difficulty. But if she couldn't ...

Then my purpose here will have come to an end. I will not sit on a stone throne in the South while my family fights for the Winter Queen in the North. Clea's chest tightened.

They reached another foyer, this one much smaller. To the left more stairs and to the right a narrow hall. Grange guided her down the hall before stopping in front of a pair of doors. He glanced back at her, grinning before he shoved the man-sized stone bricks. They flew back, opening to a throne room like none Clea had ever seen before.

Opening in a wide circle, the room followed the path of the round tower with three thick columns of rough silver stone rising to either side of the aisle. There were no royal rugs or tapestries, only barred windows making the throne room look more a dungeon than a royal hall. At the far end of the room, raised slightly on a platform, sat the throne. The back curved, the stone perfectly carved into a huge chair with a semi-circle of symbols ingrained across the top, just above the head of its occupant.

Clea swallowed when her eyes met the man's sitting on the throne. He could only be the Lord Ruler, Rhoydaen Molten. His silvering hair lay in stringy waves to his shoulders, the thin, golden circlet of the Lord Ruler perfectly fitted round his temples. His skin was leathery and dark from sun exposure, his eyes so black she thought she would fall into them and perish.

Clea Jandry was not one to cower, though. Straightening her back and tilting her head up, she marched down the long aisle toward the throne. The Lord Ruler seemed taken aback by her confidence, but he recovered quickly, an ugly scowl twisting his aging features. He was draped in so much fur, Clea wondered he hadn't melted under the hot sun of Molderëin.

Her magic seemed stronger here, alerting her the Summer Flower had to be close. Clea rested her hand over her heart, trying to calm its pounding. She stopped a few feet in front of the throne, watching Rhoydaen stand, sweeping his cloak behind him before he stepped down off the platform.

"So this is the Heir." He sneered. "I expected ... more."

Clea felt Morgren tense at her side, reaching for his sword. She placed her hand on his wrist.

"As did I, Rhoydaen Molten," Clea answered, tipping her head up. "I've heard so many tales of you, but seeing you in person truly disappoints."

Rhoydaen stormed forward, but she held firm, reaching for the *Kläerjaen*. He hesitated when he saw her hand touch the sword, thunderclouds rolling in his eyes.

"If I were you," Clea said, breathlessly. "I would not present yourself in such a threatening manner to the one who bears the *Kläerjaen*."

Rhoydaen smirked, his entire face twisting, making him ugly. Clea slowly slid her fingers from the hilt of the sword. She saw Grange move a little closer to her from the corner of her eye, as if he too feared his father's actions. What sort of relationship did they have, that his son should fear his own father? Clea couldn't imagined such a thing. Her own father had been her hero until the day he died.

"You," Rhoydaen spat, leaning forward, "do not even know what it means to carry that sword. You are a stupid, insignificant little girl who doesn't deserve this great country!"

Well, if he's going to be cruel about it ...

"Great? You call this country great?" Clea shouted, striding forward. Morgren rushed after her, reaching for her arm which she skillfully avoided. "You have *destroyed* this country! You and all who came before you allowed this city to fall into the savage ways of old! You have no right to call yourself Lord Ruler and even less right to call yourself a king."

"Why you little—!"

"Enough!" Grange bellowed, springing in front of her.

His sword glittered at his side, the blade slowly rising to point at his father. Clea peeked over his shoulder, more irritated than anything that he'd interfered.

"She is the Heir, father," Grange said, lowering his voice. "We are at her command now."

Rhoydaen growled like an animal. "Perhaps you are, boy. But all I see is a little girl with a large sword. She'll never survive this country."

"I am a pure Molderëinian, Rhoydaen Molten. If the Creator wills I sit upon the throne of Molderëin, then there is nothing you can do to stop me."

Rhoydaen took another step forward. Morgren appeared at her side, hovering at her back. His tension flowed between them and a trickle of sweat rolled down the back of her neck. She breathed in and out slowly, meeting Rhoydaen's glare head-on.

"Think what you want, little girl," he sneered. "This is my throne. I have powers at my disposal you can't possibly imagine. Things you never even knew existed."

"Perhaps," Clea whispered. "But you don't know me, my lord. You've no idea what I am capable of."

Rhoydaen spat, the spittle moistening her cheek as she jerked away. Morgren lunged, but she stayed him with a soft hand to his arm. The Lord Ruler brushed passed them, his thundering footsteps echoing on the walls until he disappeared.

Grange stepped in front of her and she looked up into his deep green eyes. "I will see you safely to your rooms in a moment so you may begin preparations for the coronation."

Coronation? Clea swallowed the sudden lump in her throat.

"First, may I have your leave to see my father keeps out of trouble?"

"Of course." She dipped her head.

Grange bowed low before hurrying around her. Clea turned away from the throne, hugging her arms against her ribs as she faced her Captain of the Guard. Morgren's smile was hardly sincere, the hardness in his gaze seething through her down to her toes.

"This is dangerous, Clea," Morgren said, his shoulders rising and falling with raspy breaths. "We should find the Summer Flower and go."

"There may be more for us here than the Flower, Morgren," Clea replied.

She stepped around him carefully, staring at the open doors to the throne room where Grange had disappeared. A nervous breath tapered her lungs.

"Molderëin has one of the greatest armies in Nfaros, and if I am truly the Heir, then I intend to pledge that army to Adlae Sundragon. My brother said I could save us all … and that's exactly what I intend to do."

CHAPTER THIRTEEN

Kaldon

Adlae skimmed her finger over the top of her staff slowly, staring up at the large Manor house. With each circle of her finger, the snowfall thickened. With each exhale, the wind strengthened. The hood of her cloak fluttered against her hairline, resting softly on the delicate skin of her forehead. Thornlay Neverly's mansion stood at the very center of High Town, surrounded by battlements, the towers beyond made of tan stone. They seemed to hover over her, attempting to intimidate her with the guards dressed in black armor patrolling the battlements and the towers casting dark shadows across the streets.

Behind her, Jabon's armies stirred. Their spears clattered on the stone every time they shifted their feet, armor tinkling. Glaydin stood a few feet to her left, arms behind his back and steady glare on the battlements. To her right ... Jabon. Her Jabon. The man who'd held a piece of her heart since she was fifteen years old. Seeing him again had been more painful than she'd cared to admit, and there'd been a quiet relief when she returned to the comforting presence of Glaydin afterward.

Why do you look upon the Manor? Thornlay Neverly will not come out, Winter said, irritation ripe.

"I know," Adlae replied quietly, the pad of her finger rubbing the perfectly smooth globe of her staff. "He is outnumbered and a coward. With Brecken and Jabon's armies at our backs, he would not dare stand against us."

Then what are we doing here?

"Waiting." Adlae's chest rose with a deep inhale. "I do not know where we are meant to go from here. Thornlay Neverly may have not declared for me, but the rest of Kaldon has. We will leave him in his Manor to cower. The Creator does not intend for us to stay here. We will be trapped if we attempt to keep the city. Roderick will come as soon as he hears."

Indeed. You and any who wish to follow you must leave.

"Yes. Kaldon will be abandoned by nightfall if those loyal to me are wise to flee Roderick Kael's wrath."

Look to your captains, Adlae Sundragon. Your True Heart approaches.

Adlae turned sharply, and Jabon came to a sudden halt. She tried to soften her face with a smile, but she knew smiling did little good. More than anything, she wanted him to see her warm, green eyes again, not the cold blue ones they were now. She wanted to show him she was still the same, even though she was a creature of ice now. Even though she couldn't feel mortal warmth anymore, only the scorching burn of a creature of magic like Glaydin. Yet despite the pain of seeing him as she was now, Winter was right. Jabon was still her True Heart.

Always and forever. Her eyes brimmed and she looked away quickly so he wouldn't see.

"Do you remember the first time we stood here together?" Jabon asked, his voice low near her ear.

Adlae grinned. "Yes. Heston Yourk was the ruler of Kaldon then. Eight years ago now."

"You were beautiful that day," Jabon commented, inching a little closer to her. "You are beautiful today."

Adlae bowed her head. "And you were very handsome for a lanky eighteen year old. I was so thrilled when you asked my father for the privilege of escorting me to the Manor. Who'd have thought only three years later we'd be at war and then divided? Who would have imagined we'd be here now, conquering Kaldon, you a nobleman and me a queen?"

"Indeed." Jabon cleared his throat. "How would you like us to proceed, Your Majesty?"

Adlae looked up at him, her heart sinking.

You've reminded him of how you are divided still by the laws of the country. You see in his eyes his sadness.

Adlae shook Winter's voice from her mind, hardening herself once more. She turned her back on Jabon, stepping closer to Glaydin. He was frowning, his eyes shifting back and forth between her and Jabon curiously. There was a spark in them she didn't recognize. The sharpness of his unusual eyes—one green as emerald stones and the other bluer than the Nfaros Sea—sent a strange sensation down her spine. Clearly, something about Jabon troubled the man, though Adlae couldn't imagine what.

"We will not rise against Thornlay Neverly. Unlike the usurper, I am merciful." Adlae looked up at the battlements, a scowl twisting her face. "The Creator calls me to the forest."

Glaydin bowed low. "As you wish, My Queen."

He turned, shouting orders. The rest of his men spread out, walking among the lines of men standing tall and straight, prepared to march down from High Town. She knew they did not understand this sort of formation. The Mountain People were not violent by nature. They served and protected each other. They did not have armies. They created armies from the people when they were forced to.

You bear so much knowledge. Your father taught you well. Winter's smile touched her soul.

"What are you doing?" Jabon hissed, coming to her side as she placidly watched the army turn to begin their march. "This is your chance to take all of Kaldon!"

"To what purpose?" Adlae quirked her brow at him.

"What do you mean?" Jabon growled. "You are trying to take back this kingdom, Adlae! Why not start with the second strongest city?"

"And who will hold this strong city?" Adlae asked. "I cannot stop my march to hold one city, Jabon. I must move on, and we cannot afford to leave a force large enough to protect Kaldon from Roderick's hold. Everyone who is loyal must seek refuge elsewhere or stay and risk Roderick's fury. I will not take the Manor and lay trapped within, waiting for my enemy to come. There are things I must do. Prophecies which have been foretold."

Jabon frowned, eyes blazing. "But to let Kaldon slip through your fingers ..."

"Once Roderick Kael is defeated, Kaldon will be mine. Leaving now will not matter when the war is won."

Adlae snapped her staff to the ground and flecks of ice shot across the cobblestones, crackling and shattering into pieces. Soon, Kaldon would be covered in layers of snow. The storm was growing stronger, resounding through her like an echoing gong. Calling on all the power the Creator had ever given her to cover the land—halfway across the Nfaros Sea—in ice and snow. Soon, the ships wouldn't be able to leave the docks, the ice would be too thick. Trade in Sunkai would slow down.

Soon, there will be no more travelers. Your allies to the south may not be able to reach you ... Winter's worry mirrored her own.

"We will be fine," Adlae whispered. "Even without them, we will be fine."

"I know," Jabon answered her. "I simply hate to leave the city to Roderick, that is all."

She smiled a little, realizing he thought she was still speaking to him. Adlae looked up at him. "Roderick doesn't truly care for Kaldon. He will come to show his strength and then move on. I am the target."

"Yes." Jabon clasped his hands behind his back, his thick brow curving in a deep frown. "Your own allies are scattered to the winds, Adlae. No one knows where any of the Jandrys are and as for your sister ... she disappeared into the Pilvaa nearly three weeks ago."

"Mirae will find me when she's ready," Adlae replied firmly. "They will all find me when it's time."

Damari Kael will find us. She will remain true. Winter concurred, a flutter of concern shuddering through Adlae. **Where is the young princess now? Where is the one who denied her own family in the name of the Sundragon? And where is your niece?**

Adlae quickened her pace, walking ahead of Jabon so he wouldn't hear her.

"I don't know," she rasped, tears nearly choking her. "I just don't know. But I cannot worry about them now. The world is turning and if Navaria's prophecy is to be believed, then the shadows of old are coming with a message. I must prepare."

She slipped between the lines of men, catching sight of Glaydin up ahead holding Starlight's reins firmly as he glared at Jabon's soldiers marching by. Adlae frowned.

"I will have to talk to him," she murmured.

He loves you.

"Don't be ridiculous. He hardly knows me."

He resents Jabon and his armies because he sees how you feel about the nobleman. Glaydin, Son of the Haven Star, loves you, Adlae Sundragon.

"Even if that is true—which I don't believe it is—it is the least of my concerns." Adlae looked up, the dark clouds rolling across the sky coming ever closer to the city. She pointed with her staff, her heart beating ever faster. "That is our concern. We are out of time, Winter. We need to leave."

The Shadows? Winter asked.

"Yes."

Adlae came alongside Glaydin, reaching to gently pet Starlight. Glaydin leaned over her, glaring at her.

"I do not like him," he muttered.

"Yes, you've made your feelings quite clear, Glaydin." Adlae shook her head, tapping her staff impatiently on the ground.

"How can you trust him? He did not fight for you when the Kael King took your father's throne!" Glaydin snarled, his lip curling.

"I have known Jabon Malaki longer than I've known you, Glaydin," Adlae replied. She looked up at him, a small smile touching her lips when he frowned in contemplation. Glaydin took a small step back, his broad chest rising and falling with a deep breath. "Eight years, to be exact. He will not betray me."

"For five of those eight years you were apart," Glaydin reminded her as she prepared to mount Starlight. "I did not see him make a vow to you. I did not see him kneel before you and swear his sword to you as I did."

"He did so to me and me alone." Adlae swung lightly onto Starlight's back, readjusting her skirts and her staff before she looked down at him.

Glaydin stood taller than any man she'd ever seen—almost two feet taller than herself—and he was the perfect specimen for a guard. He was broad and scarred—a washboard torso firm and callused from years of servitude in the name of his rulers. He seemed not to feel the frozen wind of her storm, walking as he had done from the moment he stepped off the ship.

Shirtless. Adlae swallowed, raising her gaze from his naked chest to his copper tinted hair and captivating eyes.

"Please let my trust in him be enough, Glaydin," she said, her voice lowering to nearly a whisper. "Jabon Malaki is a good man and I …"

Glaydin waited, staring at her with an intensity that set her heart to racing. She reached down, hesitating only a moment before she placed her hand on his cheek. His skin was aflame, burning her fingers, sending shots of fire up her arm. Adlae ignored the pain, keeping her hand steady. Glaydin tilted his head slightly, leaning into the touch.

"Trust *me* Glaydin," she whispered. "Please, my friend. I've entrusted you with my life … trust me with yours."

Glaydin raised his hand, his fingers brushing her wrist. "Always."

He turned abruptly, shouting for his men as he strode over to the other horses. Adlae sighed, picking up the reins.

You still believe he does not love you? Winter taunted, her voice sending shivers down Adlae's back.

"He cares for me because I am his queen. That is all." Adlae turned Starlight sharply and the animal whinnied, stomping her feet in protest.

"Did you say something, Adlae?"

Her head snapped to the left, Jabon suddenly beside her atop his own horse, a beautiful dapple gray stallion. The animal swung his head impatiently and stomped his foot, irritating Starlight who answered with a light shriek, dancing to the side.

"No," Adlae answered quickly, gripping her staff tighter. Ice crawled from her fingertips, traveling along the length of the rod as her nerves were stretched thin.

"Did you see?" Jabon pointed to the dark cloud creeping closer to the city. "Is it the Abyss?"

"No." Adlae gripped the reins tighter. "No, that's not the Abyss. That's something so much more than the Abyss."

She felt Jabon staring at her, but ignored him, digging her heels into Starlight's sides. They bolted forward, running head-long toward the cloud.

Here come the Shadows, Adlae Sundragon. Are you ready to face the dead?

Falshire
The Capital of Draedin

Navaria lifted herself onto her elbow, staring down at Krow. He was sleeping peacefully, his chest rising and falling, small puffs of air escaping through his parted lips. She smiled, stroking the smooth, shaven side of his head. Her back itched, the magic she'd used to hasten their arrival in Draedin still tingling within her. So rarely did her people have to use the part of them they kept hidden.

But Damari will change all that when she comes. Navaria sighed, bending over to kiss Krow softly on the lips.

He moved beneath her, his hand rising to slide across her waist and pull her deeply against him.

"Wife," he rumbled against her lips, and she grinned. "You refuse to let me get any sleep."

Navaria raised her head, resting her palm against his cheek. "Husband, I am merely giving you every reason to show how quickly your strength is returning."

Krow's eyes softened, his fingers tracing her dragon skin. "I am still mad at you."

Her eyes sparkled. "Really? You didn't seem so last night when we were wed."

"You gave up your mortal soul so you could save me. I do not take that lightly, Navaria."

"You would have done the same for me. I love you, Krow. You are my True Heart. You have been my True Heart since I was a child."

"Even when you were bound to ... him?" Krow winced, turning his face. She turned him back, forcing him to look at her.

"It was my sacred duty to wed him, Krow. You and I both knew this. He had a mortal soul, as did I. He was kind to me. But that did not mean I forgot you. I never did and when you became my *Chalqüin* after he was gone ... I knew it was only a matter of time, no matter how I feared our immortal future." Navaria stroked his face, smiling. "You have been over three hundred years on this earth, my love. I have lived nearly two hundred. The Creator would not have given us such long lives if he did not intend great things. Even with a mortal soul, I lived long, as our people before me. Though none with such resilience, if I say so myself."

Krow tangled his hand in her hair, pulling her down to kiss her fiercely. Navaria sighed, wrapping herself around him. She settled beside him, curling into the curve of his body perfectly. They fit together and only the Creator could have formed them thus.

"Will you tell her when she comes?" he asked, staring into her eyes. "Will you tell her, her destiny?"

Navaria nodded, unable to speak.

"And ... and will you tell her who you truly are?"

Tears sprung suddenly to her eyes and she looked away, staring across the small room they'd taken at the inn.

"How?" she wept softly, trembling.

Krow stroked her waist, holding her warmly to comfort her. Navaria pressed her forehead on his shoulder.

"How do I tell her, Krow?"

"Navaria, you must."

She looked into his eyes, tears overflowing down her cheeks.

"How do I tell her I bore her in my belly? How do I tell Damari Kael she is my child … and I gave her away?"

CHAPTER FOURTEEN

The Border of the Aulend Forest

Damari's teeth chattered. She clutched her golden eagle necklace in both palms, drawing from the warmth the amulet offered. The stronger the storm became, the harder for her necklace to fight the cold. Despite the roiling heat burning in her belly, her body was weakening. Something wasn't right and—though she'd never imagined she would—she couldn't wait to board the ship.

The further away from the storm I am, the stronger I will be. Damari closed her eyes tight. She didn't know how she knew, she simply did.

Lathan looked over his shoulder where he stood on the ramp of the merchant ship, concern etched in his stony face. Damari tried a reassuring smile, ending in a grimace when another chill wrapped itself around her, trying to steal her heat. She pulled her cloak tighter around herself, attempting to trap whatever heat she had left. She watched as Lathan exchanged money with the captain and then came striding back down the ramp to her. The moment he reached her, he wrapped his big arms around her. Damari sunk into his body heat, his presence sending the cold flying from her body like a gust of summer wind.

Damari sighed, resting her cheek against the thick material of his coat, sinking her hands between his cloak and coat to warm them. Lathan stroked her hair.

"Are you all right?" he asked hoarsely.

Damari nodded, her throat too sore to answer. He kept a firm arm around her shoulders and guided her up the ramp. Damari gripped his waist, looking wide-eyed at the men aboard the merchant ship—they rarely took passengers so Lathan had to use a lot of persuasion—most of which was a fat purse—to gain them passage to Draedin.

Especially now that a war is on. Damari trembled, holding Lathan's waist tighter.

"The captain agreed to give us a cabin below deck," he announced, glaring at any man who looked her over. "We'll be safe from winter's wind down there."

"Good," Damari whispered. "T-That's g-g-good."

Lathan rubbed her arm, offering her a little more warmth as he led her to the narrow door leading below deck. The hinges creaked, and Damari turned, firmly gripping his hand as she lowered herself onto the first rung of the ladder. She kept a hold on him until she was low enough to wrap her fingers around the ladder itself. Damari jumped the last two rungs to the floor and turned. Below deck opened to a wide room, a single door to the right and another ladder peeking up from a second level down.

Lathan appeared a moment later, cupping her elbow in his palm. "This way."

Damari followed him to the door to the right that opened with ease, the hinges recently oiled as they didn't make a sound. The cabin was small but comfortable with an oval, multi-colored Quintarian weaved rug in the center of the room, two cots pushed together to the right and a porthole straight ahead. The quarters would do very nicely for their—hopefully—uneventful trip to Draedin. She stepped to the center of the room and turned.

"I think this will do," she murmured, feeling warm already, shielded now from the harsh air outside.

"Yes." Lathan cleared his throat loudly, eyeing her cautiously as he closed the door behind him. "There's one more thing, Damari."

"What?" She tilted her head, amusement bubbling in her chest at how nervous he suddenly was.

Lathan rubbed his palms together, avoiding her gaze as he observed the simple room. Damari untied the string of her cloak, tossing it across two cots.

"The captain ..." he mumbled the rest, head slightly bowed.

"What?" Damari leaned forward, her brow pinching the bridge of her nose. "I can't hear you, Lathan."

He cleared his throat and coughed. "The captain ... thinks we're married."

Damari's eyes widened and her hand lifted to her throat. "Married?"

"Yes." Lathan finally looked at her, his face stoic but his eyes darting with a worried spark. "I thought it would be best if we traveled as newlyweds. No one will be looking for an elated couple from Draedin, returning home to their loving families."

"But ... but I don't look anything like a Draedinian!"

"I do, and I can pass you off as one. Your features aren't common in Draedin, but it's your manner that matters most. People won't question us."

"But Lathan ..." Damari's eyes flashed to the cots and a heat that had nothing to do with her newly discovered magic rose in her cheeks. "We're *not* married. We are not even *close* to being married. You've never even ..." She bit her lip, cutting off the words.

Kissed me. He's never even kissed me. Damari closed her eyes and turned her back on him.

She thought he was going to kiss her in the woods. When he told her he'd take her to Draedin, she thought he might kiss her. When he didn't, her last ounce of hope had been swept away. She was different now, he didn't want her. Maybe he never had, even when he thought she was normal. Yet the way he looked at her ... she was so confused!

"Damari," he breathed into her hair and she gasped, having not realized he'd come closer.

Her breath caught when he spun her around. Lathan wrapped his arms around her waist, pulling her flush against him. Damari's heart raced out of control as he raised her up onto the tips of her toes, tilted his head, and gently brushed his mouth on hers. Her eyes fluttered closed, knees trembling. He raised one hand to her cheek, tilting her head and she allowed him, too frozen to stop him as he molded their lips together deeply—kissing her the way she'd always wanted him to.

When his lips eased from hers, feathered the corner of her mouth with a relieved sigh, Damari's heart sank. He was more than everything she'd ever wanted and yet, they were still divided by reality.

She licked her lips, her eyes still closed.

"There," he said, voice uneven. "Now that's out of the way, let me make a pledge to you."

"A … pledge?" she whispered, still dazed.

Lathan's forehead touched hers. "This is my promise to you, Damari, one I have been wanting to make for years. From the moment I saw you as a child in your big heavy coat and those beautiful eyes that swallowed me up every time you looked my way, I knew it was always going to be you. You were the one. When all of this is over, when we've won, I am going to marry you. I will honor you, cherish you, and, from this moment on, keep my distance until you're ready to be mine forever."

Damari cooed softly, halting the sound by biting her lip. She opened her eyes to look into his. Lathan was grinning, his beautiful ocean blue eyes swirling with a love she'd only dreamed of.

"And if I'm ready now?" she whispered.

Lathan's grin wavered with uncertainty. "You want the captain to marry us? The captain who believes we're already married and hence gave his men orders to stay away from you? The *mercenary* captain who is no better than a pirate and won't hesitate to kill me to get to you as soon as he knows we're not really wed?"

Damari's throat closed. "Oh."

Lathan chuckled. "I'm not sure pretending guarantees my survival, but it's a start and we are only five days from Draedin."

"So we should remain imprisoned in this room for five days to be safe. Just the two of us … alone." Damari raised a brow and rested her hands on his arms, pushing subtly to put a little more distance between them.

Lathan's eyes lit, his mouth curving in a smirk that fluttered her stomach. He crossed his arms as she continued to back away until she was directly beneath the porthole.

"I'll put my cot on the other side of the room," he said, his eyes raking over her unashamedly. "May I suggest we sleep in our clothes?"

"Yes," Damari choked out and coughed, her throat dry as dust. "I believe that would be wise, Lieutenant Jandry."

Lathan swept his arm and bowed dramatically. "Your wish is my command, Princess Damari."

She giggled, watching him grab ahold of the end of one of the cots, dragging it across the rug to the other side of the cabin. The ship dipped and swayed, the thundering of boots overhead announcing the captain was ordering their departure. Damari turned, rising on tiptoe to peek out the porthole. For miles all she could see was ocean, rising and falling with gentle waves. The storm hadn't touched the sea yet. In a few days, a hidden port like this would be covered in ice, making it impossible for a weak little ship like this to break through. Only a ship of war could break the Winter Queen's ice.

Or a magic hotter than the sun. Damari swallowed the eagle pendant with her palm.

Lathan's breath tickled her hair and she lowered herself from the porthole, leaning back into his strong chest. He wrapped his arms around her, rocking her gently.

"Everything's going to be all right, Damari," he whispered. "*You* are going to be all right."

"I know." She sighed, sinking deeply against him. "But ..." she hesitated, tears springing to her eyes. Lathan held her a little tighter. "But what if we're too late? What if I discover this magic too late to help Adlae?"

"That won't happen." Lathan turned her around, grasping her shoulders. "The Creator wouldn't awaken this magic in you now only to have you sit by and do nothing. You are meant for something, Damari. Something greater than anyone ever imagined. We are going to find Navaria, and when we have the answers we need, we will return to Adlae Sundragon and help her win the throne. I promise you."

Damari put her arms around his waist and buried her face in his chest. She smiled.

"As long as you're with me," she whispered, her heart settling for the first time in days. "I know we can do anything."

Lathan's grip strengthened around her and she smiled. Turning, she looked up at the porthole, feeling the shift of the ship as they began to depart. The wind picked up, whistling against the thick glass of the round window and she smiled.

We're coming, Navaria.

"Damari! Damari wake up!" Lathan's strong hand shaking her shoulder forced her from sleep. Damari moaned, raising her head.

The ship pitched violently and she gasped, sitting up. "What's happening?"

"Storm." Lathan grit his teeth, raising his arms to the low ceiling for support. The ship rocked again and Damari fell back, slamming into the wall. "We lost the mainsail."

Her eyes widened, and she slid carefully off of the cot, her bare feet splashing into ankle deep water. Shouts echoed overhead along with the frantic pounding of feet; claps of thunder trembling the wooden frame of the ship.

"T-They've sailed through w-worse right?" Damari asked, reaching out to him. She grasped a handful of his shirt, balancing herself against his solid body.

"This is a winter storm, Damari," Lathan groused, grabbing her around her shoulders to pull her as close as possible. "These sailors haven't seen a winter storm on the sea in over five years."

The ship rolled violently to the left and Damari fell full force into Lathan with a shriek, throwing her arms around his waist and hanging on. His breath quickened, the water sloshing around their ankles rising higher.

"We have to get out of here!"

"Won't it be worse on deck?" Damari gasped as he took her hand, dragging her toward the door.

"We could die if we stay here. Up there we'll at least have a—"

His sentence was swallowed by another roar of thunder. The ship pitched, sending Damari and Lathan flying toward the porthole. Damari screamed as they were rammed back into the wall, falling end over end as the vessel rolled onto its side. Water sloshed up, pouring through as they were upended and landed on what once was the ceiling.

Damari gasped, water weighing heavy in her hair as she tried to regain herself, lying now in foot-deep salty sea. Lathan growled, shaking the drops from his hair as he stood up. The water was rising rapidly now, up to her knees.

"What do we do?" she shouted above the roar of the raging sea. "Lathan! Where do we go?"

He stared at her, his chest rising and falling. The water reached her waist now and she pushed through, throwing her arms around his neck. Lathan wrapped her up in his, lifting her off her feet.

"It doesn't end here!" She sobbed as the strength of the water lifted them both off their feet, floating them toward the boards above their heads.

"I'm sorry, love," Lathan whispered.

He thrust his hand into her hair, pulling her head back. He crushed her lips beneath his in a desperate kiss that stole her breath. She broke it on a sob, burying her face in his neck. The water was freezing, seeping into her swiftly, attempting to steal her warmth.

Damari raised her head.

My heat. She gasped, pushing out of Lathan's arms, kicking fiercely to keep her head above water.

"What are you doing?" Lathan asked, pumping his arms in the water.

"We are not dying here, Lathan Jandry."

Damari raised her hand above the water, her fingers touching the ceiling. She closed her eyes, drawing on the heat boiling in her belly. The magic rose swiftly at her call, tingling up her arm, into her fingertips. Then she heard the crackle that was becoming so familiar. A smile stretched her mouth when she saw the white flames gather into a small ball above her palm. With a cry, she tossed the fire.

The flames burst through the wood, burning it away in an instant and glowing pure white overhead. Lathan didn't waste a moment, grabbing her by the wrist and yanking her up, one hand braced on the newly made hole. They climbed into the lower deck, the water not having touched there yet. Damari sent up another ball of flame, this one evaporating the bottom of the ship. Lathan lifted her up and the wind immediately knocked her down. She landed with a thud, pain slicing through her body as she started to slide toward the ocean.

Lathan grabbed her wrist, yanking her back up and onto her feet. They stood on the slick wooden surface, slowly sinking. Rain pounded her, stinging her eyes and weighing her hair ever heavier. The vessel was descending faster now. Lathan pulled her with him along what was left of the ship. He hesitated only a moment at the edge, looking at her. Damari nodded once and together, they vaulted into the sea.

Damari went under, the water soaking into her skirts, weighing her down. She struggled furiously against the pull of the ship and the enraged thrust of the ocean itself, reaching for the surface.

A strong arm circled her waist, pulling her up, up, up to the surface until they broke. Damari gasped when her head rose above the water, gulping in as much air as she could. Lathan dragged her away as the last glimpse of the ship disappeared beneath the water. Debris floated all around them, but she saw no sign of any other survivors. Lathan pulled her along, grabbing hold of a thick wooden plank, floating on the choppy waves. They both shuddered as they wrapped their arms around the wood, winter's touch on the water reaching into their bodies.

"W-What do w-we d-do n-n-now?" Damari stuttered around her chattering teeth.

"We pray the Creator," Lathan replied, his teeth clenched in an attempt to keep his voice steady, "sends us a ... passing ship."

Damari nodded, her eyelids growing heavy. She rested her cheek on the rough wooden plank, a piece of the ship she'd been sleeping on moments ago. Three days aboard ship with beautiful weather, not a hint of darkness on the horizon. Three of the best days Damari ever spent, walking the deck hand-in-hand with Lathan, no longer needing to hide how she felt about him. No longer needing to hide at all. For those three days, she'd been free.

Only two days away from Draedin and this happens ... Damari trembled, her cheek beginning to stick to the plank from the cold.

"I don't want to die, Lathan," she whispered.

He moved closer to her, the water splashing her arm as he put his around her. He kissed her head.

"You won't. I promise, Damari. We're going to get through this."

Damari turned toward him, her forehead brushing his throat. She only wished she believed him.

Lathan saw the doubt gleaming in Damari's eyes. He hugged her tighter, the water numbing him from chest to toes. He ground his teeth together to keep her from seeing how cold he really was. In a few minutes, they'd both want to sleep. If they did, then their lives would be over quickly.

He rubbed her arm hard. The storm still raged overhead, sending pelts of rain down on them, the waves picking up again to toss them about on the raging sea. If even the sea so far from the shores of Sunkai were feeling winter's storm, then this truly was the harshest storm any Winter Queen had ever brought to Nfaros. For all he knew, they would arrive and discover Falshire, the Capital of Draedin, drowned in snow.

If we somehow survive this. If the Creator blesses us with another ship before it's too late. Lathan shook his head. There was no chance of that, no matter how he wanted Damari to hope.

Damari groaned, the pain-filled sound rising above the growl of the storm. Lathan frowned, looking down at her.

"What's wrong?" he asked, placing his hand on the back of her head.

"I don't know," she moaned, her eyes squeezed shut and her hands clenched. "It ... it hurts!"

"It's just the cold," he said soothingly, massaging her shoulder. "You're going numb ..."

"No!" Damari shook her head. "No, not the cold ... the *heat!*"

Lathan frowned, drawing his hand away slowly. Damari shrieked and bit her lip, a drop of blood sliding down her chin. He noticed then, how red her skin had become, as if she was burning up. Her breath quickened, her head thrown back so her neck arched at a sharp angle.

"Damari, whatever you're doing, stop!"

"Lathan!" Damari snapped. "If I could, I would!"

She turned to him, opening her eyes. Lathan's breath whooshed out of him, staring into her eyes. Her beautiful, blue eyes, and dark pupils thinned to horizontal lines like ...

Like dragon eyes. Lathan shook his head, drawing away subtly.

Damari moaned again, shutting her eyes as her head tossed from side to side. Then her back arched. She screamed, the sound rising above the roar of the wind and rain. Lathan lunged toward her, but she brushed him off.

"No I ... I can do this ... I have to ..." Damari's fingernails dug into the plank.

She began to shake, a muffled scream rumbling from her throat. Lathan's eyes perused her, pausing on her back. The material, glued to her body from the water, was shifting. Pushing, rolling, as if there was something beneath her skin attempting to escape. Lathan shook his head.

What is happening? His own breath quickened, the heat of his trepidation shutting out the chill of the sea.

The dress ripped open in the back and Damari released another piercing scream as her skin rounded behind her, stretching until it was nearly transparent, followed by a gut-wrenching *rip* that split her back open on either side of her spine.

Damari slouched against the board and Lathan stared in wonder. Out of the gashes rose two wings, as white as Damari's skin but sparkling like marble. They sloped down and then sharply up, spanning the width of his

147

arm and the length of his body. They folded, then unfurled as if testing their movement, and then, she shot into the air.

Lathan gasped, nearly going under as he lost his hold on the plank, watching her twirl into the air and then spread her wings wide. The span of the wings was overwhelming, larger than Damari herself. With every pump, they shimmered, the rain splattering over them and sending drops flying in all directions. They sloped and rose to points on top and bottom, arching delicately out of Damari's back.

Dragon wings. Lathan shook his head, disbelieving.

When she looked at him, he couldn't breathe. Her eyes were glistening, their color brighter than ever before and the horizontal lines of her pupils glared at him. Damari dove and before he could protest, she caught him, lifting him out of the water and shooting through the air toward Draedin.

Lathan clung to her, watching the water flash by faster than any ship could've carried them. Faster than a horse could run.

How is this possible? Lathan gripped her arm tighter, his legs flailing beneath him as she carried him with an unwavering grip. Where did her strength come from?

They picked up speed, the sea a mere blur beneath them. Not even the rain seemed to hinder her. Then, they'd passed the storm. The sea turned from an angry black to a soft, deep blue, the sun peeking out of the sky as they left the rain clouds behind. Before he could stop it, a laugh slipped from his lips. Lathan couldn't take his eyes off the earth below. His heart especially picked up when the sea gave way to land.

Draedin. He looked up, but Damari wasn't watching him, her gaze intent on what was ahead. She flew high above the docks, out of sight of people, most of whom wouldn't even be looking for a creature such as her. The dipped suddenly toward a forest just beyond the city.

The trees came closer as she began to lower them to the ground, searching until she found a small clearing. She rested him on his feet gently before scurrying away, her back to him and shoulders hunched. Lathan rubbed the last of the raindrops from his hair, his clothes still soaked through and chilly, but drying quickly.

"Damari—"

"Don't!" she cried and his eyes widened. Her wings were folded against her back, the tips touching the ground by her heels. Her dress was completely ruined, the back lying in shreds down her spine and shoulders;

the skirt barely hanging on. Her shoulders trembled. "I ... I'm hideous. I know I am!"

Lathan stepped up behind her cautiously. His fingers skimmed the hard edge of her wing and she shuddered, letting him know she could feel them as she felt any other part of her body. He gripped her shoulder, forcing her to face him. Damari kept her head down, shielding her eyes from his sight. Gently, he placed his finger beneath her chin and forced her to look at him. The horizontal lines of her pupils caught him off guard again, but he hid his momentary shock and instead delved deeper, seeing the woman he loved behind the magic she possessed.

"No, my love," he whispered, bending close to kiss her nose. "You are the most beautiful woman in the world."

Damari's eyes flooded and she clutched him, falling against his chest. "I'm so scared, Lathan! The fire magic was one thing but this ..."

"Hush. I know, sweetheart, I know." He awkwardly attempted to put his arms around her, her wings getting in the way.

Damari grunted, and he watched in awe as the wings began to retract. They slid easily beneath her skin until her back was smooth and silky once more, leaving faint scarring where the wings released from her body. When she looked up at him, her eyes were normal again and Lathan sighed.

"How did you do that?"

"I don't know. They just ... came to me. Perhaps our dire situation forced them out of me but ..." Damari touched his face, her hand hot on his wet skin. "I am grateful."

"As am I." Lathan clasped his hands at the small of her back, holding her firmly. "Falshire isn't far from here. If the Creator blesses us, Navaria and Krow will still be there."

Damari licked her lips. "And if they're not?"

"Then we go on to the mountains. You are changing, Damari, and you need them ..." Lathan's throat clogged for a moment.

She needs them more than she needs me. He shuddered, trying to put the thought from his mind. What sort of man was he, that he couldn't save his own beloved from what was happening to her? He didn't understand the changes any more than she did—he couldn't shield her from this and the knowledge was killing him.

Lathan shook his head, pushing those thoughts aside.

"You're right," Damari whispered. "We should get to Falshire before anything else happens."

"Nothing else is going to happen. Trust me, Damari." Lathan took her hand, turning in the general direction of Falshire. Damari hesitated.

"Lathan ... my dress ..."

He looked down, heat scalding his face when he saw how the garment was practically falling off of her, the wings having shredded the laces in the back. He removed his coat, still weighed down by water and wrapped it around her.

"That will have to do," he muttered. "We'll find you something once we reach the city."

Damari nodded and took his hand again. "I love you, Lathan."

Lathan looked into her eyes, seeing the fear and uncertainty lurking in them. The need for him to say the words back gleamed in her eyes so strongly her craving tore his heart apart. He leaned in, pressing his lips to her forehead.

"I love you, too."

Damari breathed easier once he said the words, her long exhale making him grin. Gently, he tugged her through the woods, keeping her close to his side. The storm had taken everything but his dagger, leaving him with very little to defend her with if he needed to. His eyes narrowed, brow furrowing deeply.

Blessed Creator, let them still be there. Let us find Navaria and Krow before the sunset ...

CHAPTER FIFTEEN

The Caravan Road

To the West to the East, to the castle for the feast! We sing, we dance, we'll put you in a trance … Winter sang in Adlae's head, a rhythmic thump accompanying the spirit's voice.

Adlae flexed her fingers around her staff, glaring up at the mass of shadows circling overhead. The moment she'd approached the clouds, they retreated from Kaldon. So, she followed—convinced the cloud would lead her where she needed to go.

Winter was singing a traditional caravan song, one Adlae hadn't heard since she was a little girl. A proper song, considering they were riding the Caravan Road, the wide dirt path creating a brown streak across the plains from Kaldon to the Gracian Wood. The Caravan Road was the widest thoroughfare north of Sunkai, perfect for the entertainers who traveled with their large wagons and animal cages, bringing laughter to the cities they passed through.

Now, the road swarmed with her soldiers, not a caravan in sight. Watching from the Ice Mountains all these years, Adlae had seen the failure of the caravans. Roderick's rule had diminished the people's joy in every way; even stealing business from the traveling entertainers Vihaan Sundragon had supported and loved.

Adlae could still see his smiling face when the caravans came to Sunkai. She could still hear the deep rumble of her father's laughter—a sound so far away now her heart broke again. There had been no laughter in the last year she spent with her family when Roderick Kael began his campaign to take the throne out from under Nfaros's rightful ruler.

Starlight shifted nervously, stomping her feet with the desire to move faster as Jabon brought his horse alongside her. Adlae peeked at him from the corner of her eye. His dark brown hair, thick and wavy, but trimmed neatly at the nape of his neck, went wild in the morning breeze. Eyes that melted her heart on more than one occasion, tight now with worry. She knew he didn't understand why they were following the shadows instead of heading for Sunkai, or at least toward the Pilvaa where Mirae was last seen.

He doesn't understand the prophecy given by Navaria Lightmaker. Winter murmured and then, as suddenly as she'd paused, she continued her song.

"I don't like this, Adlae," Jabon said, voicing his thoughts.

"I know, Jabon," she replied softly. "How do you think of me?"

He frowned. "What do you mean?"

"Do you think of me as I was? The same eighteen-year-old girl who ran from Sunkai five years ago? The same girl who danced with no one except you at her father's last ball, and who begged you never to lose hope when looking to our future?"

Jabon's Adam's apple dipped when he swallowed. "I will always think of you that way. You are still the same woman."

"Yes ... and no." Adlae looked ahead, fixing her gaze on the shadows as they rolled closer to the forest beyond. "I am also a creature of magic now, Jabon. What dwells in that shadow is for me and exists because of me. They have a message."

"Who, Adlae? All I see is darkness and to anyone with eyes it looks ..." Jabon shuddered.

"Like the Abyss?" Adlae finished for him.

He nodded, his mouth pressed tightly to a thin line.

"Perhaps it is. Yet, it is still meant for *me*. I do not expect you to understand."

"Good. Because I don't. I don't understand why you, the future and hope of our country, would risk your life by pursuing that ... thing."

He pulled the reins sharply, ordering his animal around. He galloped down the line, checking on the men. Adlae sighed. She didn't truly expect more from him. No one would simply accept her certainty. Even the soldiers were uneasy the closer they drew to the woods. But Adlae knew the moment they reached the forest, the shadows would stop. She knew where they were taking her.

The Tower of the Dead ... Winter trembled.

"Yes, the Tower of the Dead," Adlae repeated in a whisper. "Why else would the shadows lead me to the woods? I am meant to find something there."

They put your father's body to rest there. They ... they would have sent your sister Brae there also, instead of honoring them in the King's Crypt.

"Yes, Roderick and Raphaela would do such a thing."

Winter's hesitation buzzed in Adlae's head, and she frowned, the continuing *thump-thump* in her temples making her dizzy.

I am buried there, Adlae Sundragon. As well as every Winter Queen who came before. Nameless tombs where our earthly bodies rot.

"Yes," Adlae whispered. "I'm sorry, Winter. I can't imagine ..."

The knowledge does not pain me. Only ... frightens me. The shadow could contain anything, whether good or evil even I do not know. The Creator has been silent these past days, Adlae Sundragon.

"He may yet speak to us after tonight. If we reach the forest by nightfall, I will know what the Shadows want from me."

Are you truly prepared?

Adlae didn't answer, staring instead at the large expanse before her. She wished she could ride ahead of the army, but she knew Glaydin and Jabon would never allow her to. The moment they reached the border of the woods would be hard enough, attempting to explain to them why they couldn't follow her into the darkness. They'd want to keep her safe, not understanding their lives would be in jeopardy, not hers. Whatever was held within the shadows, Adlae knew she could handle.

Her fingers tightened around her staff, the frozen pole crackling and chipping. Her staff seemed to constantly be growing, lengthening and strengthening under the weight of the magic in her heart. She raised her gaze again, her soft exhale sending a mist of white from between her lips.

Everything was covered in white. The road and fields drowned in a thickening layer with each snowflake falling from the sky. The storm was calm today at her command, making her journey a bit easier. Adlae tilted her head toward the sky. Thick clouds rolled overhead, stray spots of blue sky peeking out from between them. Nightfall would approach quickly now, making her need for haste all the more urgent.

"Creator bless us," Adlae whispered. "Hasten our steps."

She reached for her necklace, a sting of tears touching her eyes. Adlae would give anything to feel Brae's presence right now. To feel her sister's soothing, calming nature wash through her as it used to. Those feelings couldn't be replaced by anything; not even Mirae's strength could fill the void she now felt.

Look ahead, Adlae. Brae would wish for your success. Look to the Shadows now, Winter urged her.

Adlae looked up, her breath catching. The Shadows had stopped their journey, roiling and rumbling above the treetops. Just beneath, she could see the very top of the Tower of the Dead. The cylindrical stone structure stood at the very heart of the unnamed forest between the Night Wood and the Pilvaa. This was where the disgraced royalty were sent to rot—a tower Adlae had despised all her life, and yet, fate had brought her here.

Clucking softly, she encouraged Starlight ahead, cantering up the line until she led the army. They quickened their pace at her urging, keeping up with Starlight's excited gait. Just beyond the border of the woods, Adlae signaled for a halt.

She slipped down off of Starlight, stepping in front of the animal. She stroked the mare's nose softly, leaning in to press a soft kiss on her forehead.

"This is as far as you can go, my friend," Adlae whispered. "I must tread this path alone."

Never alone, Adlae Sundragon, Winter reminded her. She smiled.

"Why are we stopping?" Jabon asked, drawing his horse to a halt before her.

Glaydin rode up on her other side, barely sparing Jabon a glance before frowning down at her.

"I do not wish the army to enter the forest," Adlae replied quietly, refusing to look at either of them. "The woods are a dangerous place in these days."

"Fine." Jabon dismounted and Glaydin followed suit hastily. "Glaydin and I will accompany you into the woods for your protection."

Adlae turned her back, taking a few steps away from Starlight. Then she spun back around. Both men stared at her, pausing as they took in her suddenly tense stance, the square of her shoulders and the lift of her chin. Adlae breathed deeply.

"I cannot risk either of you," she said, gripping her staff firmly. "You must stay with the army. If I do not return by tomorrow's sunset, then you must pursue Mirae into the Pilvaa."

Jabon and Glaydin shared a glance. "Stop talking nonsense, Adlae," Jabon said, shaking his head. "We're coming with you!"

"No," Adlae whispered. "You're not."

She raised the staff high in both hands and brought it down with a thundering *crack*. Jabon and Glaydin fell back with the force of the magic. A thick wall of ice formed from the bottom of her staff, crackling and rising, encircling the entire army, following the border of the woods before cutting across the road. Snow dust flew, the wall breaking through the thick layer covering the ground, rising nearly as tall as the trees behind her.

"No!" Jabon shouted, his voice muffed by the wall as he flung himself at it, slamming the solid ice with his fist. "Lower it, Adlae! Don't do this!"

"As queen, my duty is to protect you," Adlae replied. She rested her hand on the ice where his fist still pressed against it on the other side. Slowly, he unfurled his fingers, their palms facing each other as they tried to reach through the impenetrable wall she'd created.

"I'm not losing you again," he said hoarsely.

"You won't."

"My Queen," Glaydin murmured and she looked at him. His shoulders were hunched, hands clenched into fists at his sides. "You must have protection in the woods. A creature of magic who can assist you ..."

"No, Glaydin." Adlae shook her head. "You swore your loyalty to me. Trust me now and obey my command. These Shadows are not meant for you. Only for me, and only I can look upon them."

"Adlae, this is madness!" Jabon punched the wall again. "Please ... don't ..."

"The wall will keep you safe. No evil can touch you." Adlae stepped back, her hand sliding away from the slick slab of ice between her and the two men whose love for her plainly shone in their eyes.

I was right, Winter said smugly. **I told you how Glaydin felt! Look into his eyes now and tell me I was wrong.**

"You were not wrong," Adlae mumbled. "But we must think of other things now."

"Adlae ..." Jabon pleaded. "I beg you not to go in there alone."

"Your Majesty, I must agree with Captain Malaki," Glaydin said. "Lower the wall."

"I do what I must to be certain you will live. If I do not return, find my sister. Join her and fight for her. That is my wish. Creator's Blessing, I will return to you before the sun sets tomorrow."

"Adlae!" Jabon roared.

She ignored him, turning her back. Adlae breathed deeply, pushing the sound of their protests from her as she walked away.

I am here, my friend. We will do this together, Winter whispered.

Adlae held her head high and stepped on the forest path.

Jabon walked down the line of tents, the orange glow of the setting sun reflecting off the pure white snow beneath his feet. He tugged his cloak further over his shoulders, gaze straying toward the woods for the thousandth time. Glaydin still stood before the wall, unmoving, hand to the hilt of his sword and gaze focused.

After an hour of failing to break the wall and pursue Adlae, Jabon finally turned to his men. They'd begun erecting the tents, building fires with whatever supplies they had and putting the camp cook to work on supper. Best to keep warm food in their bellies and hot fires to warm themselves by. A contented army was a patient one and less likely to panic being trapped as they were.

How could you do this, Adlae? Jabon breathed deeply, sidestepping around one of the campfires where a group was gathered, sitting in a circle scarfing down fresh stew and sharing stories.

He approached the wall, coming to a stop. The ice was as clear as glass, giving him a flawless view of the trees. One could almost imagine the wall wasn't there, offering the illusion he could step right through it.

"You should eat," Jabon suggested. "I'll keep watch for her now."

Glaydin turned his head slightly, eyeing Jabon from head to foot before his penetrating gaze returned to the woods.

"My queen is in danger," he mumbled. "I am contented here."

Jabon clasped his hands behind his back, legs spread and shoulders hunched. They stood in silence for a moment, the wind whistling around the walls. The snowfall had stopped, leaving them only with a frozen breeze and a darkening sky. Jabon cleared his throat.

"Have I done something to offend you, Glaydin?" he asked. "You seem angered by my presence here."

Glaydin turned to him slowly, and Jabon did the same. The mountain man was taller than him, which irritated him to a certain degree. Jabon put the thought aside, meeting Glaydin's stare with his own.

"You loved her when she was a girl," Glaydin said.

Jabon froze, his heart thundering. "I love her still."

"You love a memory, Jabon Malaki," Glaydin replied, taking a small step forward. "She is not the girl you loved."

"And you know who she is?" Jabon hissed, his shoulders shaking with bottled anger. "You who have known her for mere days? I've known her for eight years!"

"Three," Glaydin replied. "Five of those eight years she was gone from your sight. She is a creature of magic now, and a creature of magic should not be with a mortal."

Jabon scowled. "Fine. You disapprove. Adlae and I do not need your approval to love each other."

"No, you do not." Glaydin turned away, staring at the wall once more. "But I tell you now, Jabon Malaki ... you are wrong for her."

"Where you are right for her?" Jabon asked.

A muscle in Glaydin's cheek trembled, his jaw grinding. "I never saw her true face and I love her. I would love her without the mask of Winter shrouding her. I would love her from across a distant sea, through fire and water. Though magic stood between us I would love her. I would love her, even after the madness of her power took her mind, and she no longer knew me."

Glaydin took a breath. Jabon's mouth was dry as dust, unable to form words as he watched the stone-like man tremble, his eyes closed as the power of truth in his words ratcheted through him.

"I would love her from the mortal earth to the Creator's Realm. Even if I am not her True Heart, I will love her." Glaydin looked at him, clasping their gazes in an unrelenting stare. "Is that how you love her, Jabon Malaki? Do you love her for what she is now ... or for what she once was?"

Jabon's brow furrowed. "I love every part of her. Even the part that's different."

Glaydin's eyes glistened with doubt. "I am glad to hear it, Malaki. But the part of her you say is different, you will never understand. I do. Only a creature of magic could truly love her for everything she is."

Jabon snarled. "I will hear no more of this."

He stormed away, heart pounding out of control. The doubt lurking in his heart battled the passion planted there for Adlae. What if Glaydin was right?

What if I can never truly love her the way I should? She has changed ... Jabon banished the thought, striding toward his tent, nearest the wall. The sun was nearly set now, the shadows above the forest growing darker. Fiercer in their intensity.

The night was going to be long.

A whisper floated across the soft winter breeze, rustling Adlae's cloak as she moved deeper into the woods. Darkness settled over her the moment she'd walked among the trees. Adlae gripped her staff a little tighter. The air in the forest grew thicker the closer she drew to the Tower of the Dead. A dense fog coiled and whispered around her ankles; swirling with each step she took.

This is a dark place, Adlae Sundragon. Winter shuddered.

"How many have ever ventured to the Tower of the Dead when their intentions were pure, Winter?" Adlae whispered in return. "Darkness surrounds this place because the Abyss feeds off the deaths of good men, buried in dishonor and false condemnation."

There is something else. The air is thick with the presence of the dead and the shadows circle overhead ... Winter's urging caused Adlae to tilt her head back. She stared at the blackened sky, her heart racing out of control when she saw strange figures swirling and flying throughout the clouds. Shaking her head, she returned her gaze to the path before her; stepping unsteadily on the pebbled pathway toward the tower.

A giggle echoed in the forest. Adlae spun, her eyes widening when she saw a young girl—no older than ten years—run past a few feet away. She wore the garb of a woodlander—a thick woolen skirt and loose white blouse. Her hair nearly reached her knees, dark brown and silky. Another giggle erupted when she rushed behind a tree, then peeked around it directly at Adlae.

"You're looking for the kings and queens of old," the child said, her voice clear and distinct. The accent akin to a child of Sunkai.

What is she doing out here alone? Winter wondered.

"I can take you to them," the girl announced. "Would you like me to?"

Adlae took a hesitant step forward. "Where are your parents, child?"

The little girl smiled. "I have no parents. They are long dead." She stepped around the tree slowly, gesturing behind her at the tower. "I live there now. Will you come and see?"

Adlae's fingers tightened around her staff. "I don't understand ..."

"You will." The little girl smiled gently. "My name is Akaria. You are the Winter Queen."

Adlae nodded, her mouth too dry to form words. There was something about the child ... she could not put it into words. Only that there was a peacefulness about her and an almost unearthly quality that tugged at Adlae's subconscious.

"Then you must come. They are expecting you." Akaria closed the distance between them and softly took Adlae's hand, leading her deeper into the forest toward the Tower.

"How long have you been out here, Akaria?" she asked.

"In this place, time has no meaning," Akaria replied. "We live by moments. We live by the stars."

"We?"

Akaria grinned. "You will see."

The child is familiar. Do you feel it? Winter asked frantically. **This could be a trap of the Abyss, Adlae Sundragon!**

Adlae pushed Winter's fear from her, holding onto Akaria's hand. If this was a trick, then the child was a victim of the Abyss, and she would not leave her. No matter where she was leading her, Akaria was an innocent who deserved saving.

"There," Akaria murmured. "There is the Tower of the Dead."

Adlae looked where the child pointed. Her hand slipped from Akaria's when she took another step, staring up at the tall, dark tower looming just beyond the rusty iron gates surrounding it. When she looked back, Akaria's sweet smile had faded. The sparkle in her eyes gone.

"Akaria?" Adlae whispered.

"Feel in your heart who I am, Adlae Sundragon," Akaria intoned, her voice growing stronger, louder. "Feel ... who we all are."

A whisper breathed passed her ear, and Adlae gasped, spinning. They appeared with the wind, rising in ethereal beauty from the ground. Women of all coloring and sizes. Some young, some old. Some Draedinian in appearance, others Quintarian. All transparent and floating in a beautiful swirl of white magic. Adlae looked to Akaria again.

"You ... you cannot be ..."

Akaria smiled. "I am Akaria Moonlight, Daughter of the Shadow Lands and sixty-fifth Winter Queen of Nfaros. I lived two-hundred years upon the earth until the Abyss came for me, and I was forced to pass the privilege to another. I was dead three-hundred years before you were ever born."

"You are a child!"

"Do you question the will of the Creator? He recognizes no age for the honor of bearing such beauty. I was chosen for a reason. Though I never aged, my soul grew old within me, and I am proud." Akaria tilted her head up. "But you did not come here to listen to our pasts."

"She has come for another purpose," a new voice murmured and Adlae turned.

The phantom of another Winter Queen moved forward, her raven hair falling in thick braids around her shoulders and dark eyes piercing. "She wishes to learn what is to come. For we are the shadows who called her here."

"You have a message for me," Adlae said, breathlessly. "I am ready."

"Are you?" the woman asked. "Truly?"

"Yes." Adlae straightened her shoulders, chin tilted up. "Tell me."

"First, there is one with a message of his own."

The woman stepped aside, gesturing behind her. Adlae squinted in the silver cloud swirling and roiling toward her. Then, his image appeared. Adlae gasped, falling to her knees. His silvery hair was just as she remembered, and his pale gray eyes seemed to shine with more love than on the day she'd last seen him.

"Adlae ..." he whispered.

A tear rolled down her cheek.

"Father?"

CHAPTER SIXTEEN

The Pilvaa Forest

"If we attack from the south we have no tactical advantage against Kael's guards!"

"We don't need the benefit. Righteousness is filled with men and women who have sworn against the sword. The few guards who are there, I trained. They wouldn't dare raise their weapons to me."

"Who made you captain over us all?"

"Your queen did."

"Your Majesty, please!"

Mirae raised her head from sharpening her dagger. Brecken's breath caught for the hundredth time when he looked at her. Even with her red hair shorn—the ends barely brushing her shoulders—her resemblance to Brae was stunning. She looked over him and Jaeger with impassive emerald green eyes, as if she could care less if he and Jaeger came to blows.

"Did you truly make this man captain of our armies?" Jaeger hissed, scowling at Brecken with disgust. "This man who—"

"Who spared my life?" Mirae interjected.

Jaeger's teeth clicked shut, but his snarl didn't disappear.

"Brecken swore an oath to me, Jaeger Senne. He knows the consequences of breaking his vow." Mirae slid her dagger into its sheath, the blade hissing softly in the otherwise quiet tent. "If he says we should attack the tower from the south, then we shall. I trust him."

"I don't!" Jaeger sputtered.

"Then you needn't stand at the front line with us, Jaeger. These few days Brecken has stood beside us and walked amongst us. He has shown kindness, loyalty, and courage for the fight. If you still doubt him then so be it. But know I have no doubt in my heart at all." Mirae reached for her necklace, the one that mirrored the chain Brae used to wear. "Brae would want this, Jaeger. She loved this man, and that is good enough for me."

"I did not raise you into a queen for you to make such foolish mistakes!" Jaeger spat.

Mirae sprang to her feet, hand on the hilt of her dagger. "And I did not name you my Second so you might challenge every decision I make!" Mirae's slight shoulders rose with a deep inhale. "Now go find Griyer. I would speak to Captain Jandry alone."

Jaeger barely bowed, his head merely jerking forward slightly before he stormed from the tent. He allowed a gust of icy air past when he departed, and Brecken shivered.

"He only wishes to protect me," Mirae whispered, staring where Jaeger had disappeared. "You did, after all, attempt to kill me."

Brecken's lips tightened. "I never meant to carry out those orders. I just didn't know until we were on the battlefield."

"I know." Mirae sighed, turning back to the maps. She laid her small hands on the table, bending over the yellowed pages. "You truly believe attacking the south side of the battlement is the wisest choice?"

"The few soldiers posted at Righteousness will be expecting us from the north. If we circle the path of the woods and come upon them from the south, we will have an advantage. Over half your forces will be inside the walls before the guards are even alerted to our presence."

"Our forces," Mirae muttered.

"I'm sorry?"

"*Our* forces, Brecken. You and Afra are a part of us now. There will be no more separation in terms." Mirae arched a delicate brow and looked up at him through her thick eyelashes. "Understood, my captain?"

A strange rush skittered over the surface of his skin when she addressed him. Brecken shook it off and dipped his head.

"Yes, my Queen."

"Adlae is our queen," Mirae replied. "I am merely the queen of a kingdom which has never been properly founded."

"The Woodlands have always been free. It is an honor they would fall under the authority of anyone, Mirae." Brecken's hand inched toward hers, but he stopped himself short of touching her.

"I will release them of the obligation and myself of the title as soon as Adlae is crowned."

"And if they do not wish to relinquish their queen?"

Mirae smirked. "They will have no choice. I have fought these five long years for this moment. The moment when I would be restored to the Blood Keep. It is more than I could have hoped, to see my eldest sister there beside me. No matter how I love these Woodlanders and their ways, I must return to Sunkai."

Brecken nodded, clearing his throat softly. "Has there been any more word of Adlae?"

Mirae's hand lifted to her necklace again, enclosing it in her palm.

"None. Only what I feel. She is surrounded by darkness, but there is hope. I feel her hope like a fraying thread ... stretching ... tearing ... impossible to grasp, yet so close. She knows something terrible." Mirae bowed her head. "You must think me mad."

"Not at all," Brecken rasped. "I think you the wisest, strongest creature alive."

Mirae lifted her gaze, meeting his eyes. "Brae was the strongest person in this world ... and they took her from us."

"We will make them pay for that. *Adlae* will make them pay for Brae's death." Brecken stretched his fingers around the hilt of his sword. "With your permission, I will check on my sister."

Mirae nodded. "Of course. Please prepare the armies when you leave her. We should reach the Tower of Righteousness by tomorrow's sunset."

"As you wish." Brecken bowed at the waist.

He turned on his heel, marching out of the tent. A frozen wind assaulted him, stabbing his nose and cheeks with its intensity. His boots sunk, crunching in a mix of fresh powder and ice as he crossed the clearing. The Woodlanders set their tents up in a circle, clearing the snow as best they could to create an invisible wall of protection provided by their Tree Prophetess. Brecken moved among the people, ignoring the curious—and occasionally angry—glances he received.

Afra would most likely be keeping warm in her tent, away from the prying questions of the Woodlanders. It had taken mere moments for the Tree Prophetess to announce a Passer had walked into the camp. Afra had run for the cover of the tent Mirae provided as quickly as she could—surprisingly, with the help of one of the prophetess's guards. Brecken hadn't let it pass his notice how the one guard stared at his sister whenever she emerged from her solitude.

Cohdel. That's what the Tree Prophetess called him. Brecken snorted, recognizing it to be a name from the Shadow Lands. If the man's red hair was any indication, Brecken was correct about the silent guard's origins.

He reached the tent at the far end of the camp, ducking beneath the flap. Afra looked up the moment he entered, her hand moving in a constant motion where she gripped a spoon, stirring their stew.

"Elk," she announced. "One of the guards was kind enough to bring it. There weren't many vegetables still fresh, but I made do."

Brecken nodded, crouching beside the fire. "I want you to stay with the Tree Prophetess tomorrow."

"I can fight, Brecken."

"You've not picked up a sword in years, Afra. Not since your fourteenth birthday."

"The skill does not simply disappear, brother. I would like to stand beside you."

"You are a Passer. Your strength will be better served after the battle is won. Creator's Blessing, we will not need your gift."

Afra's wide eyes bored into him, forcing him to look at her. She didn't say a word, merely stared until his skin crawled.

"Don't look at me like that."

"Like what?"

"Like you know what I'm thinking."

Afra's lips formed a gentle smile. She reached across the space between them, taking hold of his hand. "I can't help it, Brecken. I do know what you're thinking and feeling. Your thoughts worry me."

"Afra—"

"You miss Brae. You miss Noelle. You're worried our brothers could not find her. But I know she lives, Brecken. I feel her life in my heart and if she were gone then ..." Afra stopped, pressing her lips tight.

Brecken closed his eyes. "The Creator would have sent you if the life was leaving my daughter."

Afra nodded mutely, gripping his hand tighter. "We have a long road ahead of us Brecken. The Creator has sent me to Mirae Sundragon for a reason. If I am to watch over her armies ... to Pass some of them if necessary ..."

"You've never Passed soldiers, Afra."

"Then this will be my greatest test. The Creator chose me for the Sundragon armies. He did not choose you to fight with them. If you wish to begin your own search for Noelle ..."

Brecken stood up, pulling his hand from hers. He paced across the tent, lifting the flap to look outside. A light snow had begun to fall, layering the icy ground in fresh powder. Women and children huddled close as they scurried to their tents.

Across the clearing, Mirae stood with a man and woman Brecken recognized to be Griyer and Lara. She smiled, a light laugh slipping between her red lips. The tip of her nose was pink with the cold, but she seemed untouched by winter otherwise, wrapped as she was in her heavy fur cloak. Until he'd seen her again, standing tall in front of him instead of cowering with uncertainty on the ground beneath the edge of his sword, he hadn't fully comprehended how grown up she was.

A wise woman now instead of the headstrong girl who fled Sunkai almost six years ago. Brecken sighed.

"I have thought about it," he murmured. "She is my flesh and blood. She is all of Brae I have left. But leaving Mirae now ..."

"Some would say the choice is an easy one. Noelle is your child."

"If the Creator did not mean for me to be here, right now, then I would not be. He would have guided me to Maxx and Lathan. Or perhaps directly to the place Damari Kael took Noelle. No, our brothers will find her. They will bring her to me."

"An army camp is not the place for her, Brecken. She will not understand. She is not like these Woodlander children who were born in tents beneath the trees."

"Perhaps not. But as you say ... she is my child." Brecken ducked out of the tent, stomping through the snow toward Mirae.

She turned her head, sensing his presence. Brecken paused a few feet away, their gazes locked in an unwavering stare. His breath stilled in his lungs; body stiff as he was struck once again by her eyes. So much like Brae's, yet so different. With a wave of her hand, Mirae sent Griyer and Lara away, offering him her full attention.

"Is there something I can help you with, captain?" she asked, folding her hands in front of her.

"I'd like to speak with your Tree Prophetess," Brecken announced, clenching his hands into fists at his sides.

Mirae frowned. "Oh …"

"Can she tell me where my daughter is?" Brecken stepped a little closer, lowering his voice. "Can she See for me?"

Mirae reached out, resting her hand over his tight fist. "She can try."

Brecken nodded, taking a steadying breath as he followed her across the camp. Mirae kept pace with him, standing close to his side. He noticed how she avoided the glances they received. Mostly glares directed at him from the Woodlanders. Brecken knew his transition to Mirae's side wouldn't be easy. Not after the recent battle on the Kliat. For all he knew, he'd killed the husbands of some of these women, the fathers or brothers of these families. Mere days ago, his sword had been stained with their blood. Now their queen had asked him to captain their army. It couldn't be easy for any of them. Trusting him certainly wasn't.

The two of them stopped near the edge of the camp, beneath the shade of the tallest tree. Astra and Braven's tent was small, enough to accommodate them and a small fire inside. At the flaps stood Cohdel, tall and straight; decked in full armor. The midafternoon sun glinted off the man's helmet, covering his hair beneath and his curious dark eyes observed as Brecken and Mirae came to a stop in front of him.

"How is she today, Cohdel?" Mirae asked softly.

"Strong," Cohdel replied. His eyes darted between the two of them. "Have you need of her Sight, Your Majesty?"

"We have. May I enter to see if she is willing?"

Cohdel nodded, reaching back to lift the tent flap. "As you wish."

Mirae ducked inside, gesturing behind her for him to wait. Brecken clasped his hands behind his back, staring back at Cohdel as they waited for a moment in silence. Then he took a breath.

"You've been watching my sister," he said.

Cohdel tilted his head. "Have I?"

Brecken scowled. "Afra is a delicate creature. She possesses a power few understand and her life has been … difficult, at best."

"I understand the ways of a creature of magic," Cohdel replied, wryly. "I would not hurt her for anything in the world."

"See that you don't."

"I do watch her. I watch her and I wonder about her. I have hope for her, Brecken Jandry." Cohdel leaned forward slightly. "Your sister has a pure heart, untouched by any evil and it shines within her. I have not seen such since I left my homeland and she ..."

Brecken waited, but Cohdel seemed unwilling to finish the sentence. He took a step forward.

"She what?" he hissed.

"She has no one to protect her."

"She has me." Brecken clenched his jaw, his fingers tightening around each other until they numbed.

"You are quite often with Queen Mirae, leaving your sister alone. There is great animosity for you among some of these people and their anger will spread to her. I have dedicated my life to protecting people like her." Cohdel shrugged a shoulder. "I do not expect you to understand the unspoken bonds between creatures of magic. But I feel your sister's pain, as real as anything else. Who will safeguard her, if you are off fighting the Woodland queen's battles?"

Brecken opened his mouth to reply when the tent flap lifted, and Mirae poked her head out.

"She's ready for you, Brecken."

He moved forward, bending to duck inside the tent when Cohdel gripped his arm. Brecken frowned, looking into the man's eyes.

"I understand people like your sister more than most, Brecken Jandry," Cohdel murmured. "Should the queen's plans go wrong when we reach the Tower of Righteousness, Afra's gift will be tried. If I were you, I'd stay close to her."

Brecken yanked his arm from Cohdel's hold and stepped into the tent. Mirae sat with Braven in front of the fire, shoulder to shoulder as they huddled near the warmth of the flames. Mirae nodded to the cot off to the side, gesturing for him to approach the strange woman sitting upon it.

Astra didn't look at him as he approached, her hands moving rapidly as she weaved three pieces of cloth into a braided cord. Her shiny black hair hung around her shoulders in tight waves, sable skin gleaming in the light of the fire in the otherwise darkened tent. Brecken crouched in front of her, but still she didn't look up.

"Can you tell me where my daughter is?" he whispered. "Can you tell me if she's safe?"

Astra hummed, the sound low and comforting, like a mother would to her child.

"Four years she is today, yes?" Astra asked.

Brecken closed his eyes. "Yes."

"Today is her birth date?" Mirae spoke up behind him, but he ignored her.

"Yes, she was born four years ago today," Brecken confirmed, keeping his focus on Astra.

"No snow on the day she came into this world," Astra muttered. "No snow. Cursed time, that."

Brecken shuddered, her voice grating his nerves.

"Can you tell me where she is *now*? I need to know she's safe. I need to know my brothers have her and are bringing her to me."

Astra finally looked up at him. His breath stilled at the sight of her silver eyes. Like round orbs in her head, glistening in the firelight. She raised one of her hands, palm up.

"Have you something of the child's?"

Brecken shook his head. "Only my own blood."

Astra tilted her head. "Her hair … your color or her mother's?"

"Her mother's." Brecken's voice lowered hoarsely, his chest tightening.

"Then blood we must take." Astra stuck her hand beneath the cot and returned with a thin blade. Taking his hand softly, she pricked one of his fingers, a dot of blood blooming. She dabbed the drop with her fingertip, staining her skin before drawing a circle with it in his palm. Astra bent over, her eyes beginning to glow brighter than before as she stared at the bloody circle in his hand.

"A man with a copper-hilted dagger holds her close," Astra murmured, her brow furrowing. "They travel the forests, seeking those of the Eventide for assistance. Seeking only those loyal to the true Sundragon."

"Maxx." Brecken released a breath of relief, looking over his shoulder at Mirae. "She's with Maxx! She's safe."

Mirae smiled, tears shimmering in her eyes.

"It is the other one I fear for," Astra's voice drew him back and he frowned. "The one without his family cord. The one who travels across the sea to the Mountain Lands with the Queen of the People of the Dragon. The *Almaër Dominjje*."

"Lathan … why would Lathan travel across the sea?" Brecken shook his head. "He wouldn't …" Words stopped on his tongue and he leaned closer. "Damari Kael. What happened to her?"

Astra looked straight into his eyes, clouds coiling in her own. "Damari Kael is the *Almaër Dominje* and her work has only just begun."

Falshire
The Capital of Draedin

The itch on her back wouldn't cease. Damari twisted her neck around, presenting her back to the mirror. The room Lathan had procured for them at the center of Falshire was small and warm, surprisingly comforting. She winced when she looked over her shoulder, staring at the pale scars. They were two inches wide on either side of her spine, trailing down to the small of her back, coming to a disconnected V at the end. Evidence of the wings she couldn't even feel while they were hidden beneath her skin. A part of her body she'd never known existed until she'd had dire need of them.

Shuddering, she pulled her dress up over her shoulders, doubling her arms behind her to do up the laces. Lathan had found her a decent gown— the first thing he'd done once they reached the city. A simple dress, dark blue with silver trim at the collar and cuffs, a slit in the skirt to show off her leg from knee to ankle. Where Draedinian wardrobe was concerned, this was the most modest outfit he could find, and Damari was grateful. The material was light, another thing to be thankful for as they would most likely be heading for the mountains soon.

Five days and he still hasn't found them. Damari breathed deeply, shuffling across the room to the window.

She took in the view of the mountains beyond, staring at the rise and fall of the peaks. As far as the eye could see there were black mountains, glinting under the light of an unrelenting summer sun. Reflections of copper and silver mixed with the dark stones, their dips and curves calling to her as no mountains ever had.

What is happening to me? Damari closed her eyes tight, threading her arms across her ribs. Her necklace burned hotter on her chest, reddening her fair skin. She'd slept like a baby their first night in Falshire while Lathan searched tirelessly for Navaria and Krow. Guilt gnawed at her when she'd woken to discover he'd had no rest, devoting every hour to searching Draedin's capital for the woman who could save Damari's life.

"I am the *Almaër Dominÿe's* first mother," Damari whispered. Lathan told her word for word what Navaria had said to him, explaining how the woman begged him to find Damari and bring her to the mountains. "What does that mean?"

She breathed in slowly, tightening her arms around her ribs. The sun was shifting toward the center of the sky and Lathan still wasn't back yet. He'd insisted she stay in her room and *rest*. Damari knew he was more afraid of her releasing her wings in the middle of the street, as her magic seemed to be proving unpredictable. The last thing they needed was her revealing one of the Mountain People's secrets.

Did my father know about this? Did Vihaan Sundragon know? Navaria told me my mother knew, so why did she never tell me? Damari closed her eyes, inhaling deeply. She pushed the questions into the back of her mind, knowing she would have her answers soon enough.

The magic bubbled in the center of her chest, a comforting warmth now compared to the fiery heat she experienced when she called to it. Her fingers grazed her eagle necklace and she frowned, wondering if she still had need of it this close to the hot mountains of the south. Navaria would be able to tell her. Navaria would have all the answers.

If we could just find her. Damari turned her back on the window, cutting herself off from the sight of the distant mountains.

A soft thump resounded outside the door. Damari froze, her fingers clenching around the pendant as she listened. The key rattled the lock and Damari breathed again when Lathan came marching through the door.

"Nothing?" she whispered.

Lathan's unrelenting frown answered her, worry crinkling the corners of his eyes and creasing his brow telling her without words that his search had once again been fruitless.

"They must have moved on," Damari sighed, patting her chest. The fire inside was overwhelming, urging her toward an unknown goal. "Navaria said we should meet her in the mountains if they were no longer in Draedin."

"Yes," Lathan grumbled. "I do not like the idea of traveling that road. The Mountain People aren't accustomed to strangers and if they do not give us the chance to explain …"

"Navaria knows we're coming." Damari returned to the window, staring at the slopes beyond.

A deep shadow spread across the sky, casting ghostly silhouettes on the stones. They danced over every dip and peak, seeming to settle on the tallest mountaintop at the very center of the Mountain Lands. A thousand daggers pierced her. The call of a language she'd never heard, a thousand hearts crying in unison, reaching into the very depths of her soul and stirring the fire within her. A tear slid down her cheek.

"Lathan," she rasped, gripping her eagle pendant until it broke the soft skin of her palm. Lathan's soothing presence came up behind her and she leaned back into his solid chest. "They *all* know we're coming."

Among the Shadows …

"I don't understand, Father. How are you here?"

"There are many things I cannot explain. So much power pulses in these woods, my daughter. There are so many things I wish to tell you! But you have come here for a reason, so please take heed. I have a message for you."

The shadows drifted all around her as Adlae took her father's hand.

CHAPTER SEVENTEEN

The Pilvaa Forest

"How did you know she spoke of Maxx?"

Afra turned slightly toward Mirae, watching how the young woman stared at Brecken. The air between the two of them shifted, thickening with the intensity of their eyes on one another. Afra had seen the connection the moment Mirae found them in the woods. Brecken didn't look at anyone the way he looked at Mirae Sundragon, and it troubled her. Having so recently lost Brae, the resemblance of the sisters had to be weighing on her brother's heart.

"The dagger," Brecken replied as they continued their slow walk through the camp. "Astra said there was a copper-hilted dagger. I gave such a dagger to Maxx when he made lieutenant."

Mirae nodded slowly. "The woods will be treacherous during this storm."

"Maxx will keep her safe," Afra interjected, drawing both their gazes. She tightened her hold on Brecken's arm as the three of them continued their leisurely walk through the camp. "He has been wandering the woods since he was a child. He knows every path, every magic stone. If anyone can get Noelle to safety, it's Maxx."

"Your brother was the first among you to reveal his true loyalty to me," Mirae commented, her mouth tilting in a small smile. "It's not that I don't trust him, I do. But Noelle is …" Mirae bowed her head.

Brecken reached out, resting his hand on the young woman's shoulder. "I know. She is a piece of her mother."

Afra looked away, her fingers flexing around Brecken's sleeve. The camp was alive. Woodlanders taking down their tents and hitching horses to the wagons in preparation for their departure to the Tower of Righteousness. She'd kept to the tent she'd been given as often as possible since her and Brecken's arrival among Mirae's people. The only one who'd come to her was the gentle giant who guarded the Lady Astra.

At least, to Afra he was a giant. She didn't think she'd ever seen a man like him before. The way he towered over people, his bright red hair glistening in the sunlight and the softness in his blue eyes. Strange, to see such a man among these small woodlanders. He was the sort she imagined marching the streets of a great city, or wildly roaming the darkness of the mountains.

Yet there was something comforting about him. Nothing Afra could explain and, after his third or fourth visit, she didn't want to. The sense he was something more than a mere man was overwhelming. Brecken covered her hand with his and she looked up, forcing a smile. Mirae had moved on, hurrying ahead to check the progress of the wagons.

"I worry about you sister," he murmured.

"Oh?" Afra rested her temple on his shoulder as they turned around, walking back the way they'd come.

"You've never seen a battlefield. You've never been called to so many souls before." He shuddered. "Promise me you will not Pass if you don't have to."

Afra frowned. "I will Pass all those the Creator calls, Brecken. Friend … and foe."

Brecken scowled. "He would not—"

"He would." Afra stopped walking, raising her head and forcing him to look in her eyes. "The Creator dwells in the hearts of many, even those you consider enemies. Do not forget, Brecken, not too long ago you stood beside the Kael king, his most beloved captain. The Creator did not abandon you and he will not abandon those who have given Him their hearts."

Brecken sighed. He leaned forward, pressing his lips to the center of her forehead.

"Get some rest, Afra."

He walked away before she could answer, stopping beside Griyer and Lara's wagon. Afra picked up her skirts in both hands, her boots crunching the snow as she left the camp circle. The Woodlanders watched her cautiously as she stepped from the safety of the circle, the curiosity in their eyes making her smile. They didn't understand her, and she couldn't blame when. When her gift first awakened in her, she didn't understand it either.

Afra tilted her head back, golden light streaming through the tree branches. A cold wind swept all around her, rustling her skirts. Behind her, she heard the Woodlanders maneuvering the wagons into a line, the last task before they were to depart. The horses were restless, despite the day being clear for the first time in over two weeks. Not one snowflake had fallen from the sky since last night, but the wind had intensified, whispering of another stage of the storm to come.

The crunch of icy snow beneath someone's feet caught Afra's attention. She lowered her gaze from the sky, staring now into the thick of the trees. The lightness of the steps told her it was a woman, most likely sent by Mirae to tell her they had to go. There was something about the center of the forest where she felt her power most strongly. The sweetest feeling, so pure and clear. Leaving was almost painful.

The heart of the forest could serve as her portal to The Place Between, if she so wished. All she had to do was draw the magic from within every tree. From every blade of grass, every leaf, and every flake of ice that fell from the sky. But she couldn't go there, not yet. The Creator had been clear.

My place is here until the next Passing. Afra exhaled slowly through slightly parted lips.

"You feel the magic of the woods deeply."

Afra gasped, spinning around. The woman tilted her head, a strand of her dark brown hair falling across her forehead. Afra had never seen her before, but she wore the thick woolen dress of a Woodlander and bore a quiver and bow on her back.

"I do," she replied softly.

"You are a strange creature of magic," the woman said. "I have never met a Passer before."

"We are an elusive people." Afra smiled.

"My name is Faël Eyres. I need you to come look at my husband's body."

Afra's breath caught. No one had made such a request of her in years. The belief of the people that she, a woman who could touch a soul, could sense a person's fate, leftover in the mortal body, ran rampant in cities like Kaldon. She'd not expected it here in the Woodlands, where there was a deeper understanding of the magic she possessed.

Her mind turned suddenly to Brax. What would her husband say about this? How would he advise her? Brax had never been a man of many words, but his simple wisdom had sustained and guided her into her adult life.

And he loved me. Creator knows why, but he did. Afra sighed.

"Why would you make this request of a Passer?" she asked. "If your husband has already passed, then there is nothing I can do."

"I need to know he feels the peace we are told of," Faël answered. "He was in so much pain. I just want to know it's over now and he is resting in the Creator's Realm. There was no Passer to take him when he went."

"There was no Passer when my husband died either." Afra placed her hand on the woman's arm. "I understand your pain ... but I cannot help you."

Faël frowned. "I do not understand."

"A Passer can only send the immortal soul to the Creator on a straight and peaceful path. Once the soul has left the body, it is not possible even for a Passer to know what has become of it, if they were not there to take them. I cannot ..." Afra's breath steamed in front of her face when she hesitated, watching the woman's face fill with anger. "There is only so much the Creator allows me to know. I am sorry."

Faël turned away looking into the woods.

"If you cannot help us," she hissed. "Then what good are you to any of us? What good could you and your brother possibly be here with our people?"

"Mistress Eyres, I—"

"Your brother is a murderer!"

Afra inhaled sharply, her insides roiling over the hatred she heard in Faël's voice. She'd hoped this wouldn't happen. She'd hoped if she stayed quiet and hidden in her tent, she would not have to face the bitterness that was growing in the camp toward Brecken.

"My brother is many things," Afra said softly. "But he is no murderer. Killing a man on the battlefield is not murder, Mistress Eyres, you know this."

"He doesn't belong here." Faël bared her teeth in a furious hiss. Afra stepped back, the woman's rage filling the air between them. "And neither do you."

Afra bowed her head, eyes stinging. "I am sorry you have suffered so. I am sorry this war has burdened you."

"You know nothing of my burdens! Do not pretend you know the depth of my pain, Passer."

"Then I say the same to you." Afra raised her head, meeting the woman's eyes. "Do not pretend you understand the pain my gift causes me. The pain of passing a human soul to another realm—of feeling the agony behind their death. I am not so untouched by this world because of my power. On the contrary ... the world is harsher because of this gift."

"I do not want to hear of your pain," Faël snapped. "Our queen made a mistake, letting you and your brother walk free amongst us. I am not the only one who thinks so. She will regret her decision."

Faël spun, racing back to the camp. Afra stumbled, leaning against one of the trees as tears slipped down her cheeks.

"Blessed Night," Afra breathed, resting her hand on her heart. "Please tell me what to do."

Trust me, my daughter. All is as it should be.

Afra closed her eyes, breathing in the clean air before forcing one foot in front of the other toward the wagons.

Between Shadow and Light ...

Adlae twirled, her fingers streaming through the thick shadows dancing all around her. A smile touched her lips when she saw Akaria spinning and skipping with the rest of the shadows, her eyes dark and misty.

"There will be blood with fire ..." his voice echoed in the air.

Adlae turned, looking back and forth. But she could not see him.

"There will be victory with sorrow ..."

"Father?" She raised her hands in front of her, stumbling through the shadows. They parted at the touch of her hands, swirling and fading.

The Tower of the Dead loomed before her. She stopped at the bottom step.

"Nfaros will be won with the blood of innocents."

Adlae slowly raised her head, looking up at Vihaan Sundragon standing at the top of the staircase. He held out his hand.

"Are you ready to learn your fate, Adlae Sundragon?"

CHAPTER EIGHTEEN

The Mountain Lands

Silver stones glistened in the sunlight, rising to jagged peaks higher and higher the farther they climbed. Damari had never seen a sky so clear. A perfect blue canvas with the southern sun glaring down upon the earth, settled at the apex of the sky. Not a cloud to be seen. Not a single one to gentle the sun's heat. Yet, she felt none of it. She couldn't remember the last time she'd felt so comfortable in her own skin.

Lathan grunted beside her, and she turned, her brow creasing worriedly. His skin glistened with sweat, a kerchief wrapped tight around his temples to absorb and keep the drops from falling into his eyes. His shirt clung to his body, completely soaked through. Yet he seemed glad, the reassuring smile he offered her and the excitement in his eyes completely opposite of the turmoil in her own heart.

Leaving Falshire after eight days of waiting and hoping had been difficult. Damari wished she and Lathan could just hide among the gentle folk of Draedin's capital. She wanted to curl up in a corner and never leave, determined to forget any of this ever happened. The warmth of the southern sun was enough to sustain her she was sure. But Lathan was the one who'd pressured her to carry on with Navaria's instructions.

He'd woken her suddenly on the ninth day, rousing her from her bed and into the wagon of a passing traveler, willing to take them as far as the abandoned caverns outside the city. Once there, they'd been on foot, climbing and following the silver path. Damari didn't know how she knew where to go, she simply did. The mountains seemed to be communing with her mind, whispering soft comfort in her ear. Letting her know she was on the right path. The path Navaria had set her on from the moment they met.

Damari huffed, hoisting herself up onto a flattened boulder, her shoes scraping on pebble and stone dust. Lathan pulled himself up after her, a strained groan slipping between his lips as she turned to face him.

"You're going to collapse, Lathan," she said.

Lathan fell back against the round stone behind him, head tilted back and eyes closed.

"Take off your shirt."

Lathan opened one eye to look at her. "I'm fine, Damari."

"Why do you torture yourself?" Damari smirked, resting her hands on her hips. "Do you fear for your modesty?"

Lathan chuckled. "No."

Damari sighed, reaching for their water skin. She moved toward him, popping the cork from the top. Before he could protest, she grabbed a handful of his hair and pulled him down, pouring a steady stream through his hair and down his back. Lathan shuddered.

"Thank you," he murmured, his forehead resting on her shoulder.

"Please, Lathan," she choked slightly, tears threatening. "Make this easier on yourself. I don't know what you're trying to hide but—"

"All right. I'll take my shirt off for a moment. But turn away."

Damari stepped back, frowning. "Why?"

Lathan cupped her cheek in his palm. "Trust me, Damari. Turn away."

She popped the cork back on the water skin and turned her back. Gently, Lathan took the water from her. His soft exhale let her know he was removing his shirt and the next moment, she heard the sprinkling of water on the stones.

Damari bit her lip. *Don't ... you promised ...*

Slowly, she looked over her shoulder. A gasp slipped out before she could stop it. He'd turned away from her, facing the stones now as he drenched himself in water, but at the sound of her sharp breath, he turned his head, eyes widening. She paid no attention, instead staring at his marred skin.

His broad back was striped with scars, some curving across the side of his stomach. Scars from the battles he'd fought for her brother to obtain the Mother City, Sunkai. She hadn't realized how much of Lathan's blood had been shed in the name of Roderick Kael. She was sickened at the thought.

When he faced her completely, she resisted another gasp, her eyes fused to the thick, jagged scar that crossed from his right shoulder to the opposite rib. How he had survived them, she didn't know and she didn't want to know. Without thought she stepped forward, pressing her palm flat on the largest scar across his ribs.

"Oh, no, Lathan," she whispered, sniffling. "I-I'm so sorry."

"They're just scars, Damari," he answered just as softly, covering her hand with his.

"But once they caused you pain!" Damari sobbed, squeezing her eyes closed. "I cannot bear to think of you in pain. I cannot bear to think my brother caused all of this!"

"In the past, yes, he did. But not anymore, Damari." He pinched her chin between his thumb and finger, tilting her head up. She forced her eyes open, staring back into his. "Let's leave these hurts in the past where they belong. Now, we look to a new dawn."

Damari nodded. Lathan reached to put his shirt back on, but she grabbed his wrist, stopping him. A frown creased his brow when she took his shirt from him and tossed it behind her.

"A new dawn," she repeated. "No more hiding from me."

The corner of his mouth twitched in want of a smile, then he dipped his head in acquiescence. Damari started to turn, Lathan's gentle hand on her shoulder urging her as she reached to pull herself up onto another pile of boulders.

"Damari!" Lathan hissed.

She stumbled back, bumping into his chest. Damari glared at him, but he didn't notice, pointing instead ahead of them. Her gaze followed his finger and her breath caught.

Three small children crouched on the stones up ahead, heads tilted curiously, and bright eyes stared unblinking at them. The two boys were shirtless, wearing only thin brown britches, while the girl wore a thin dress of the same color, no sleeves. Damari took a hesitant step forward to get a closer look. The boys had their heads shaved on one side, the way she remembered Krow's to be and the girl's hair nearly reached her waist and glittered with a silvery tint unexpected in one so young. Their skin was darkened from the sun, one of the boys' darker than the other two with piercing eyes the color of fire.

"*Almaër Dominje*," one of the boys whispered, pointing at her.

Damari's skin rippled with a sudden chill and Lathan's grip on her shoulder tightened.

"Come," the little girl said. "Come meet the First Mother."

Damari looked up at Lathan, who merely gave her a soft push before preceding her up the incline. She kept a hold of Lathan's arm as they climbed, both pausing for a moment when they came to a staircase, carved directly into the stone. Lathan smiled at her when she hesitated, his lips grazing her temple.

"Stay close," she breathed. His eyes softened, sobering to a warm glow which acknowledged the seriousness of their situation. He supported her with a hand to her elbow, keeping close to her side.

The children ran ahead, always out of reach yet always in sight. They climbed for what felt like hours, the stones never seeming to change as they went higher and higher, the children's giggles echoing on the wind whenever they stopped to look back at Damari and Lathan.

Finally, the steps gave way to a flat cliff. Damari took a moment to catch her breath, leaning against Lathan's side. The wind whistled all around them, warm and comforting. Lathan even seemed to relish it, tilting his head back as the breeze swept over both of them. Damari's back tingled and she frowned, her magic waking suddenly in the pit of her belly.

She opened her eyes and looked around.

"Lathan." Damari stepped away from his arm. "Lathan, where are the children?"

His head turned back and forth, searching. Damari moved across the cliff, heading for the edge. Her heart skipped a beat when she looked down, Lathan's shadow falling over her when he stopped at her side.

The cliff dropped sharply into a ravine, surrounded by walls of stone, dozens of staircases carved into them leading to the village below. Hundreds of houses, some built right into the walls of the mountains, were arranged below them, surrounding the roaring waterfall crashing to the sparkling pond below.

People milled about, women in brown robes and veils carrying baskets. Children leaping and playing in the pond. Men stalking about like bodyguards, keeping a close watch on each staircase.

"We found them," Damari whispered. "What now?"

"Now we find the First Mother." Lathan took her hand and turned for the closest staircase.

They stopped short, Damari gasping when Lathan shoved her partly behind him. The man and woman standing between them and the stairs seemed strangely familiar. Her in her brown robes, and him shirtless with his head half-shaved.

The woman tilted her head, her fiery-tinted hair glistening in equal glory with the ruby red dragon skin peppering the left side of her face. The man stood nearly a foot taller than Lathan, his sun-kissed skin glaring in the heat and dark golden hair shimmering.

"Who is this foreigner who speaks of the First Mother?" the woman asked, her deep voice gravelly.

"Lathan Jandry of Sunkai," Lathan answered cautiously. "And you?"

The woman's lips curved in amusement. "I am Malindra, Daughter of Hadroul's Mountain, and this is my husband, Evingar, brother of the First Mother."

Damari inched out a little from behind Lathan. "You're Navaria's brother?"

Evingar looked at her strangely, his dark eyes making her squirm the longer he remained silent.

"Our children told us of your coming," Malindra continued as if Damari hadn't spoken.

"Those three scamps were yours?" Lathan smirked.

Malindra laughed, a smooth pleasing sound that calmed Damari's heart. "Yes, my sweet babies. They have reached the age of belonging more to the mountain than to their mother."

Evingar leaned over, whispering something in his wife's ear. She nodded, stroking his cheek gently before her honey-colored eyes pierced Damari.

"You must come, *Almaër Dominÿe*. It is time."

Damari moved forward, but Lathan grabbed her arm.

"Time for what, exactly?"

Malindra and Evingar both tilted their heads at the same time, more curious than offended by Lathan's distrust. Damari twined her fingers with Lathan's hoping her touch offered him some reassurance when Malindra spoke again.

"Do not fear, Lathan Jandry. Navaria Lightmaker, Daughter of Hadroul's Mountain, Mistress of the Crystals and the *Almaër Dominÿe's* First Mother, has summoned you."

The houses were carved into soft squares with flat roofs, each one glittering in the sunlight either bright silver or pure onyx. Within the circle of the mountain, the ground was surprisingly soft with rich soil and pastures for the horses. There was a coolness within the houses. The strange stonework offering shelter from the unrelenting rays of the sun.

Damari clutched her necklace in her fist as one of the mountain women tied the rope tight at her waist. They'd insisted she change her dress before seeing Navaria, draping her instead in the mountain women's garb of brown robes, rope belts, and leather boots. She didn't mind really. The only part that troubled her was their haste to separate her and Lathan.

The men seemed to surround him the moment they stepped into the village, urging him away. Damari barely heard Malindra's reassuring whispers in her ear as she was pushed in the opposite direction into one of the houses.

"There," the woman helping her said as she finished with the belt.

Damari looked at her, eyes narrowing slightly. She'd been introduced as Lyssia, a young Daughter of the Mountain according to Malindra. Her brown skin was flawless, save for the dark emerald dragon scales spreading across her right cheek and down her throat. Lyssia was different from Malindra and Navaria. Her dragon skin hadn't spread as far as theirs had, dark hair only lightly tinted with a green glow and her pearl-colored eyes were as normal as any human's.

Like mine, unless I spread my wings. Damari bit her lip.

"Come." Lyssia beckoned, lifting the tapestry from the door. "Your *Chalqüin* is ready also."

At the mention of Lathan, Damari rushed forward, pushing Lyssia aside. She stopped short when she saw Lathan. He grinned at her, raking a hand through his hair as he stood in between two of the mountain men. They'd taken his clothes too, dressing him in the tall black boots all the men wore, a thick black leather belt holding up his brown britches and his chest and torso bare. Unlike them, however, they'd not shaved his head and Damari breathed a sigh of relief, closing the distance between them.

"Strange, yes?" Lathan muttered, eyeing the men to either side of them. "I don't know whether to feel like a prisoner or a guest."

"Me too." Damari giggled behind her hand, reaching across with her other to brush their fingers.

"*Almaër Dominje*," Lyssia said, poking Damari in the arm nervously. "Navaria Lightmaker is waiting for you!"

Lathan put his arm around her shoulders, drawing strange looks from the men as they followed Lyssia. Damari bit her lip.

"I don't think they approve of you," she whispered.

Lathan's eyes sparkled. "Do you approve of me?"

"Of course I do."

He arched a brow. "Then let them think what they wish."

Damari placed her hand over his where it rested on her shoulder. They followed Lyssia through the village. Children paused in their play to stare, women whispered as they passed, and the men moved about their business impassively, sparing only a momentary glance for Lathan. Lyssia paused at the waterfall, reaching beneath the collar of her dress to pull out a silver chain with a perfectly round emerald pendant hanging from the end. She kissed it softly, then signaled them forward, guiding them along a path behind the roaring stream.

Damari kept close to the mountainside as the sunlight faded behind them, glowing through the thick wall of water. The further they went, the darker the cave became until, ahead, she caught sight of the faint glow of torches in iron sconces on the wall. Lyssia moved with ease, barely sparing a glance over her shoulder at them. The hall widened and Damari trailed a hand along the darkening stone, smooth and soft beneath her fingertips. The stone was swiftly changing from the natural gray of the mountain to marble black, swirling with silver.

Her breath came faster as they left natural stone behind them, entering a chamber made entirely of onyx stone, carved with care and grace. Lathan sensed the change in atmosphere as well, his grip on her tightening and eyes rounding in awe. Damari found herself smiling. There was something almost familiar about this place something that felt like ...

Home. More like home than anywhere else.

"What is this place?" she asked, breaking the silence.

Lyssia looked over her shoulder. "This is the heart of Hadroul's Mountain. We now approach Hadroul's Chamber, where the Mistress of the Crystals and her *Chalqüin* husband live."

"They're married?" Surprise laced Lathan's voice.

"They returned to us man and wife. It was expected." Lyssia shrugged her shoulders and turned away, continuing on.

"He lived then," Lathan said, lowering his voice so only Damari would hear. "I honestly wasn't sure she could save him."

"What exactly did she do for him?" Damari asked.

"I'm not entirely certain. A spell perhaps? There was mention of her surrendering her mortal soul."

Damari's brow rose. "Can she really do such a thing? To save another?"

"I've always heard of the Mountain People possessing powerful gifts but never truly believed the rumors. Until now."

"But what does it mean for her?"

Lathan wouldn't look at her, his gaze on Lyssia's back. "I don't know, Damari."

"We have arrived," Lyssia's voice echoed off the walls.

They stopped before two doors rising high in golden splendor, the carving of two dragons etched intricately across the front. Lyssia pressed her palm to one, pushing it open as if the thick panels weighed no more than a feather.

Hadroul's Chamber opened before them, a wide empty hall with pillars framing the aisle and the floors uncovered to reveal smooth black marble. Lathan kept close to Damari's side when Lyssia gestured for them to precede her. Not even the whisper of the wind could be heard this deep within the mountain, only the sound of her own breath.

Then her eyes locked with the woman she swore in her heart she never wanted to see again. Navaria sat at the other side of the chamber, her hands resting calmly on the arms of her throne and her sapphire-tinted hair hanging over her left shoulder in thick, twisted braids. Golden eyes Damari remembered so well gleamed at her, unsurprised but pleased.

"You found us," Navaria breathed, her voice barely reaching them across the large space.

Anger surged in Damari's gut, and she pushed Lathan's arm away, storming forward.

"Who am I to you?" she demanded, her own voice rising to a frustrated shout. "What do you mean you're my First Mother? What is the *Almaër Dominje*?"

"I mean exactly what I say, Damari," Navaria purred soothingly. "I am your mother."

"No. My mother was Lila Kael!"

"She was the mother you knew. I am your blood mother."

Damari shook her head, tears welling.

"Lila Kael knew who you truly were. It's why she gave you the necklace you clutch so desperately." Navaria nodded to Damari's hand.

She hadn't even realized she'd taken hold of the pendant.

"She knew who you were always meant to be, and she protected you as best she could. Even from your own father and siblings."

Lathan reached for her, pulling her hand from the necklace and twining their fingers together.

"So I am not a Kael at all?" Damari rasped. "My whole life has been a lie?"

"No, Damari, no." Navaria's own eyes glimmered. "Who you are has not changed. Only where you came from. I left you in the arms of the Kael woman so you might live to see this day. You are the *Almaër Dominje* and since Winter has come, you must take your rightful place and be reborn to our people, so you may protect us from the storm."

"I don't understand," Damari whispered, wiping tears from her cheeks. "What am I supposed to do?"

Navaria folded her hands in her lap, knuckles whitening, and eyes piercing. Krow stood at her left shoulder and Damari took notice of him for the first time since she entered the hall. His hard gaze was steady as his eyes moved subtly between her and Lathan.

"We are the People of the Dragon. Long ago, when the first of our kind was given life by the Creator, he turned against the light and entered darkness. For centuries, we were creatures of the Abyss. We followed the Evil One's ways and served his purpose. Until the first *Almaër Dominje* was gifted to us by the Creator Himself. She was beautiful. Pure. From her line, I came to be. She guided our people back to the light and to the Creator, though every day is a struggle against the evil that once stirred within us." Navaria paused for a breath, and Krow rested his hand tenderly on her shoulder. "I was not born to be the *Almaër Dominje*. But you were. I was one of the chosen, meant to raise the future of our race."

"But you didn't raise me," Damari hissed. "You abandoned me."

Navaria winced. "For that, I am sorry. But I gave you away to the Kael family for your own protection."

"What do you mean?" Lathan asked before Damari could speak.

"The Abyss entered the heart of your true father, Damari," Navaria whispered, yet her voice echoed on the cave walls. "He tried to murder you in your crib, and with what strength was given me, I protected you. I tried to kill him."

Damari inhaled sharply. "Tried?"

Navaria looked away, her eyes closed. "He fled with the darkness still inside him. I knew he would not stop unless you were far away. I gave you to those I trusted ..." Navaria looked up at Krow, a wobbly smile tilting her lips. "I gave you to my True Heart, and he did what was best. He laid you in the arms of the Kael woman and gave her the necklace to offer you when your fire awakened in your child's heart. She knew we would come for you one day."

Damari took a step forward, tugging Lathan with her. "And then?"

Navaria met her eyes again. "Then I hunted the one with the darkness. I found him and I attempted to expel the evil from his soul. I succeeded but ..."

"He died," Damari finished for her, knowing the truth in her heart. "Ridding him of the evil killed him."

"Yes." A tear slipped from Navaria's eye, but she wiped it away quickly. "Finding him took years and even after, we feared the Abyss would try to enter another's heart to hunt you. It was the coming of winter that spurred us to Sunkai. Only the *Almaër Dominje* can protect us from winter's chill. Only *you* can keep the storm at bay so we will not become vulnerable to the Abyss again. For if Adlae Sundragon were to fall, the Abyss would guide winter to our shores to tempt us back with his protection ... or kill us all with the Frostling magic."

"You believe I can protect an entire nation of your people?" Damari rasped.

"I *know* you can. You are the *Almaër Dominje* and when you and your *Chalqüin* are reborn in the waters of Hadroul's Mountain, you will be an unstoppable force."

"But Lathan is not one of the Mountain People." Damari looked up at him, fear pounding in her heart.

"He might still be reborn," Krow spoke now and they both looked at him. "If the Creator has chosen him for you, then he might take the power of the Haven Star upon himself with the rebirth, making him immortal, as I am."

"And me?" Damari whispered.

"Your youth will be prolonged, but you will only be immortal if you relinquish your mortal soul in a pledge of everlasting love for this man." Navaria gestured to Lathan.

Damari looked up at him, smiling. "I would—"

"No." Lathan shook his head, grasping her shoulders. "You cannot make such a decision now. You are speaking of eternity. I would gladly live one, even if it meant I only had a few years with you."

"You think I wouldn't do the same for you? Why should you make the sacrifice and not I?"

"Because you bear a burden I cannot possibly understand. You would be living an eternity with this power. A weight you could never relinquish. Such magic will wear you down. If you choose immortality, there is no going back. You would be here until the day the Creator calls all creatures upon the earth to His realm."

Lathan raised his gaze to Krow. The two men stared at each other, a silent understanding passing between them Damari couldn't comprehend.

"But I would live those years with you," Damari whispered.

"Make sure that's what you truly want. An absolute eternity with this power and no end." Lathan cupped her face in his palms.

"If I wait," Damari hesitated a moment, "then you must wait also. You will not go through the rebirth until *you* are certain you want an immortal life. Promise me, Lathan."

Lathan's eyes darted slightly then he leaned in, lightly kissing her lips. "All right, Damari. I promise."

When Damari turned back, Navaria was standing before her. Her heart leaped in surprise, but Navaria smiled, raising a hesitant, trembling hand to touch Damari's hair.

"You look like Evingar," Navaria whispered. "You have my little brother's golden hair … and his nose." She laughed softly.

Damari shook her head. How could this woman, who looked no older than Damari herself, be her mother? How was any of this possible?

By My hand, I give eternal life. A soft voice murmured in her ear.

Damari froze, listening.

Live, for the kingdom is for those who trust in My love, My mercy, My faithfulness. For your people, I give this gift, so you might see the world restored to My glory.

A tear escaped down her cheek and Navaria wiped it away.

"The Creator speaks to you now." Navaria leaned forward, resting her forehead on Damari's. "The time has come for you to be reborn in the Waters of Hadroul. Will you accept this gift?"

Navaria raised her hand, palm facing Damari. Smiling, Damari joined her hand with her mother's, peace washing over her in waves.

"Yes. I'm ready now."

Lathan paced back and forth across the meadow, flexing his fingers on the hilt of the sword Krow had given him. He could feel Malindra's children watching him from where they sat beside the lake, heads tilted and eyes wide. They'd been like that for hours, never once taking their eyes off him.

Navaria and Damari had left him and Krow behind in Hadroul's Chamber after Navaria told them her story. Lathan watched Damari go with a small amount of trepidation bubbling in his chest. He didn't like her being out of his sight for too long, especially when neither of them fully understood what was about to happen. Only her smile put him at ease long enough for her to disappear deep within the mountain with her First Mother.

"Thirsty?"

Lathan turned to Lyssia. She smiled, holding out a simple wooden cup, filled with a dark liquid. He hesitated, a strange, spicy scent wafting up to him.

"You worry too much, Lathan Jandry. This is a juice made from our mountain trees. Please taste. It will quench your thirst and fill your belly." Lyssia raised the cup a little higher, attempting to put it to his lips herself.

"All right." Lathan half-smiled, taking the cup. He tilted his head back, swallowing the drink in one gulp.

The thick liquid went down smoothly, rolling sharp, bitter spice over his tongue which turned sweet at the last moment. He smiled, handing back the empty cup.

"Thank you."

"Lyssia," Evingar's deep voice interrupted and they both turned. "Malindra is in need of your assistance."

"Of course, Evingar." Lyssia spared one last warm glance for Lathan before hurrying away.

Evingar approached, hand resting leisurely on his sword hilt. Lathan tensed when the man came to a halt before him, irritated to no end that he had to look up at him. Evingar seemed to sense his agitation, smirking in return.

"You are certain this is what you want? The Haven Star shines tonight and will not do so again for another fortnight."

"I'm certain," Lathan replied. His eyes darted back and forth, searching for Damari. "She won't know?"

"Not until her own rebirth. She will sense a change in you, but she will not know what the difference means." Evingar paused, his broad chest swelling with a breath. "You were meant for the mountain, Lathan Jandry. I see in your soul your intentions. Like so many other *Chalqüins* before you, you seek your fate in secrecy to spare the one you love. If our women could stop us, they would."

Evingar smiled fondly, his eyes distant as he remembered something Lathan wasn't privy to. Lathan straightened his back, tilting his head up.

"Tell me what I must do to be at her side."

"You will be leaving everything behind, Lathan Jandry. When this is done, you will belong not only to the mountain, but to the Haven Star and our people as well."

"I understand. I am ready, Evingar."

"Then come."

Krow's voice boomed behind him and he turned, staring up at the man who should've died days ago, had it not been for Navaria. Krow approached, placing a strong hand on Lathan's shoulder.

"Follow and become our brother, Lathan Jandry. Forever and to death."

Lathan grasped the man's wrist, staring straight into his eyes when he replied,

"Forever and to death."

The Tower of the Dead

Akaria sat at the top of the stairs, humming softly as she plucked at the hem of her dress. Adlae stared at her, her hand clasped firmly in her father's as they waited for the small ghost-child to move.

"Why have you brought me here?" Adlae whispered, looking up at the wispy image of her father.

"Everything I did in life, I did for you and your sisters," Vihaan replied. "I need you to know that, my daughter. For what comes next will try you, but I must do this."

Adlae frowned. "I've always known that, Father. I never doubted for a moment you did everything you could for us. Brae, Mirae, and I ... we loved you. We loved you with all our hearts."

Vihaan smiled. "And I loved you."

Akaria raised her head, stabbing them with her ageless eyes.

"She is ready, Vihaan."

When Adlae looked to the child again, she was gone, the stairway to the roof of the tower clear.

"Ready for what?" Adlae rasped, her breath coming harder.

"Forgive me, daughter. But they have a message, and you must listen if you wish to save Nfaros."

"Father, what—?"

The door to the roof flew open, a harsh winter wind raising Adlae's hair all around her. Outside, the shadows descended. Shrieking and thick they swirled in the air before her. Reaching for her with invisible claws. She spun away, her eyes widening when she came face to face with her father.

"Let them take you, daughter. Let them show you what they must. Dance with the shadows, Adlae."

He shoved her through the door.

Adlae screamed as the shadows swallowed her in darkness.

CHAPTER NINETEEN

Molderëin

Clea ran her fingers along the back of the throne, the rough stone scraping her fingertips. She didn't mind the sting, her mind drifting to the events of the past few days. Nothing had gone the way she'd planned, and now, here she stood, draped in a velvety gown of royal blue, her hair braided in the Molderëinian fashion, waiting for Grange Molten to come fetch her for the coronation ceremony.

Molderëin hadn't been this peaceful in years, at least according to Grange. From the moment she'd stepped into the tower, the entire city shifted. Even Rheatha commented on how quiet the streets were, her fear of the city she'd been born to waning in light of the change in the air. Clea couldn't understand, no matter how many times it was explained to her.

My uncle gave me the Sword of Kings because he knew … but how? How did I not know? How could Brecken keep such a thing from me? Clea rested her hand over her heart, feeling its sudden pounding.

"We are of royal blood," she whispered, her voice echoing in the empty hall. "Brae could've been queen, and Brecken knew all the time."

She shook her head, the weight of such a betrayal stinging more than anything else. What would Adlae do when she found out? Worse, what would Raphaela do? If Brecken was, as Clea suspected, still trapped by the evil sorceress, then Clea declaring herself the Heir of Molderëin would not bode well for her oldest brother.

He said I could save us all …

She breathed deeply, tilting her head to look at the ceiling. "Blessed Creator, please let my brother be right."

"He was."

Clea turned, watching Morgren saunter into the room. He stopped halfway to the throne, his gaze moving over her from head to toe.

"You look beautiful, little one."

"I still don't understand," Clea replied. "Why me, Morgren? Why me and not Brecken?"

"In Molderëin, the youngest is the heir."

"And they will just accept me?"

"No. You will have to fight for what you've been given."

Clea's cheeks puffed with a breath. She stepped down from the throne, meeting him in the center of the room. A hint of winter's wind touched the tower, whistling against the thick stones. The cold would never completely touch Molderëin, not unless Adlae Sundragon wished it too. Yet as close as the wind was, Clea found herself in doubt.

Where is she now? Where are my brothers and my sister now? Clea's heart rocketed into her ribs, the feeling of being trapped overwhelming her. She closed her eyes, calming herself as best she could as she set her mind to something else.

"Have you found the Summer Flower yet?"

Morgren's eyes darkened. "No. I know only it is in one of the towers and Grange Molten has been avoiding me."

"Hmm." Clea massaged her temples. "Izeana and Rheatha?"

"Safe. I've advised them to remain in their rooms as often as possible."

"Ryker?"

"Keeping the men in line. They are within the city walls, but are following your orders. They won't come near the towers until they receive your permission."

"Good." Clea turned away, moving toward one of the windows overlooking the overpass leading to the center tower. "There's something wrong here, Morgren."

"This is Molderëin, Clea. There's always something wrong here." Morgren snorted, an obnoxious eye-roll following.

"No, Morgren. Within these walls …" Clea rubbed the knot in her chest, her eyes flooding. "Someone of power is in pain here."

Morgren sobered, reaching to touch her arm. "Grange?"

"No. No, he's fine." Clea tried to breathe, but it was getting harder.

She trembled, a drop of sweat rolling down her temple as her power surged through her, struggling against the weakness of her mortal soul.

Morgren anchored her, his hand firmly supporting her arm when her knees knocked together. Clea breathed in and out slowly. She closed her eyes.

"Whoever it is, she's strong. Very strong and she's not of Molderëin." Clea gasped, opening her eyes.

She released her magic, stumbling against Morgren's side as the weight of the magic lifted from her.

"We have to find that flower," Morgren mumbled.

"Soon. First, can you do something for me?" Clea faced him.

"Anything."

"Distract Rhoydaen and Grange Molten. He's not let me wander to the other towers since we've been here, and I am tired of being confined to either this throne room or the Queen's chambers. Send Izeana to me right away, I'll need her."

"Clea, I must advise against ..." his voice faded when Clea eyed him wearily.

"No more advice. Just this once, Morgren, don't be my advisor. Be my loyal soldier and follow orders without question."

Morgren's lips thinned, but he nodded before marching away. Clea turned, leaning back against the windowpane, hugging her ribs. When she first entered the tower, she could feel the Summer Flower reaching out for her, refreshing her power, but the longer she went without finding it, the faster the feeling faded from her senses. And her lightning show on the street with the *Kläerjaen* hadn't helped any. Drawing on nature's power was always draining for any creature of magic, but Clea hadn't seen another alternative.

The door to the throne room creaked. Clea opened her eyes, turning toward the sound. Izeana stepped inside cautiously, her dark eyes big with worry.

"My lady?" she squeaked like a mouse.

Clea forced a smile. Faking strength was easy enough for her, especially in front of poor Izeana who, more than any other in her company, needed reassurance while they were in Molderëin.

"Morgren said you had need of me?" Izeana stepped a little closer.

Clea hastily closed the distance between them, taking the young woman's hands.

"I need your help, Izeana. I intend to roam the towers and if I am seen, it would be best if I wasn't alone. Will you accompany me?"

"Of course, my lady. What do we seek?"

"I don't know, Izeana." Clea took Izeana's arm, turning toward the doors. "I suppose I will know her when I see her."

"Her, my lady?"

Clea's brow furrowed, creasing the bridge of her nose. "Yes, her. I know something I shouldn't, and yet, I do not know what I know."

"Riddles, my lady?"

Clea laughed softly as they left the throne room, turning down the hall to the stairs. "You don't mind, do you?"

"Not at all, my lady. But … what shall I say if we are seen?"

They reached the bottom of the stairs and Clea pushed open the door, a warm breeze catching at her skirt as they stared across the long, curved bridge leading to the center tower.

"We are just walking, Izeana," Clea replied, guiding the young woman out onto the bridge. "That's all. Just walking. These are, after all, the Towers of the King. I am going to be crowned Queen of Molderëin in a matter of hours. These towers will become my home, and I want to see them."

Izeana nodded as they paused at the center of the bridge, looking out over the city. Very few people were on the streets at this time of day. Just a few women hurrying home from the market with baskets tucked under their arms. Clea urged Izeana faster to the other end of the bridge, shoving the latch aside before thrusting the door inward.

The stone scraped loudly, echoing on the walls as the door opened to a spiral staircase, leading down. Izeana shuddered as Clea closed the door behind them. Without a word, they began their descent, taking their time round each turn until they reached the first hall. Clea took a deep breath as they silently went to work, peeking in every door, searching for someone Clea didn't even know.

As the hours passed, Clea could feel Izeana watching her. The girl's worry was thick in the air between them. She knew Izeana thought she was fading into the madness of her magic. But the more they searched, the stronger the feeling another creature of magic was in these walls became.

They came to the bottom of the tower, one last narrow hall leading deep within the structure. Izeana gripped Clea's arm when they faced the dimming light at the end of the corridor.

"My lady, I-I think we s-should return now. The coronation will begin soon." Izeana tugged on her sleeve.

"Just a moment, sweet one. There's … something …" Clea strode forward, the tingling warmth in her chest unmistakable.

She let go of Izeana, stopping in front of the door at the end of the corridor. Her heart plummeted into her stomach, the chains wrapped tightly around the latch alerting her this was not a room, but a dungeon. A prison.

With a gentle wave of her hand, the locks released, sending the chains crashing to the floor. Another twist of her wrist and the door flew open, rebounding against the wall. Clea squinted in the dim light, leaning through the doorway until her vision began to clear.

Something moved, a dark form squirming in the corner.

Clea shrieked when her eyes adjusted to the darkness, lunging forward and falling to her knees.

"No!" she gasped, her hands hovering over the form of the little woman. "No, no, no …"

The woman turned her head, her amethyst hair glistening even in the darkness of the room. Dried blood stained her clothes and her back was covered in fresh cuts, gone unattended for far too long.

But it was her face Clea fixated on. The soft, beautiful lilac dragon scales covering nearly half of her face … and the long, jagged scar marring their beauty. The woman looked up at Clea with white eyes blazing, her pupils thinned to horizontal lines.

"My lady, she is of the Mountain," Izeana whispered, coming cautiously to Clea's side.

"I know." Clea leaned in, carefully resting a hand on the woman's shoulder. "Who did this to you? Who dared do this to a creature of the Mountain?"

The woman merely stared at her, the pain in her gaze tearing Clea's heart to shreds. She didn't need her to say anything, she already knew the answer. Clea's lip curled as she helped the woman to her feet, pulling her tightly into her arms, the same name thundering in Clea's head like the beat of a drum.

Rhoydaen Molten.

Clea gently helped the Mountain woman onto her bed, carefully avoiding the fresh cuts crisscrossed on her back. The poor woman moaned, her head lolling to the side on the pillow. Clea's throat tightened and she looked away, unable to bear seeing another creature of magic in such pain.

Clea still didn't know how she and Izeana managed to get all the way back to her chambers without being seen half-carrying the Mountain woman. Thankfully, the servants were so occupied preparing the throne room for the coronation, they hadn't been near the back spiral stairs where she'd snuck Rhoydaen's prisoner to safety.

"I don't understand," Izeana whispered, drawing Clea's gaze. "Molderëinians always stayed away from the People of the Dragon. They knew better than to grasp for power this way."

"Not all of them, apparently," Clea muttered, pouring water into the bedside basin. She soaked a cloth through, wringing it between her hands before placing it gently on the woman's forehead.

The Mountain woman shuddered, a small whimper slipping between her lips. Then she opened her eyes, their diamond-like splendor gleaming under the candlelight.

"You," she whispered, her voice rough with dryness. "I did not know when you would come for me, but I knew you would."

"How?" Clea stroked the cloth down the woman's cheek, trying not to stare at the scar that cut through her otherwise flawless dragon skin.

"I am one of the last of my kind. My sister and I were born with the Sight. I saw you in my visions, come to rescue me. You bear the *Klärjaen* and will redeem all of Molderëin."

Clea's hand paused on the woman's forehead. "Rhoydaen Molten did this to you, did he not?"

She winced. "Yes, he did. He is a selfish, cruel man. His son is good but powerless until you walked through the gates of the city. If you'd not found me first, he would have come for me. All he has wanted since my arrival is to set me free."

"He knew what his father was doing to you and did nothing? Why didn't he say something to me if he wanted to free you?"

The Mountain woman smiled. "He fears you, as do many in Molderëin already. You are a powerful woman, Clea Jandry."

Clea perked up, surprise bringing a small smile to her lips. "I seem to be at a disadvantage. You know my name by your visions, but I still don't know yours."

The Mountain woman sat up a bit, reaching to take Clea's hand. She took a breath, her pupils shuddering into horizontal slits and her skin glowing.

"I am Kalea Lightmaker, Mistress of the Diamonds, Daughter of Hadroul's Mountain, and Sister of the First Mother. I am your humble servant, Clea Jandry, forever and to death."

In the Heart of the Shadows ...

Breathe, Adlae. Don't give up, breathe.

"I can't ..."

Don't fight. Just breathe and listen. Listen to their voices.

"I'm dying, Winter."

This is not meant to be your end. This is meant to be your beginning. Listen to their message.

Adlae closed her eyes, and listened.

CHAPTER TWENTY

The Tower of Righteousness

Breath steaming before her face, Mirae crouched beside the frosty oak tree. The Tower of Righteousness loomed before her, the dark stone wall encircling it barricading her people on the outside. The soft sounds of women singing within the tower reached her ears, and a knot formed in her throat. The gentle Sisters and Brothers of the Creed wouldn't approve of her violence, nor did she wish them to come to any harm. Yet they would, without doubt, be standing at the very center of the conflict when she chose to bring her men over the wall. At this time of the evening, they would be at solitary prayer in the south courtyard.

Brecken shifted at her side and she glanced his way, fingers tightening around the hilt of her sword. They'd barely spoken since leaving for the tower, a heavy weight falling over both of them. She could almost see him taking the burden of her people on his shoulders. Struggling beneath the new responsibility of leading men and women into battle. He'd left one army behind to lead another and, for whatever reason, Mirae hated it.

I should've sent him to find Noelle, not handed my army over to his command. She held her breath, glaring at the wall.

"Look there," Brecken hissed near her ear, pointing at the south side of the wall. "Only two guards. Your bowmen could take them out from this distance, yes?"

Mirae nodded. She turned to her left, where Jaeger sat crouched behind another tree. He was staring at the tower, his nose and cheeks red from the icy wind and eyes colder than winter's storm. Jaeger hated stone structures, as most Woodlanders did. She knew he thought she'd chosen the woods.

That she would choose the woods even had she taken back Sunkai. He couldn't understand her love for stone cities and marble palaces.

Taking Righteousness was a small step in the quest to put Adlae back on the throne. If they could take all of the towers across Northern Nfaros, it would give Adlae a much stronger hold on the country. A hold she desperately needed.

Mirae curled her free hand around her necklace, a tear threatening to fall from her lashes. She'd not felt Adlae's presence for hours, and she was troubled. The shadowy cloud, drifting between Kaldon and Quintaria, could be seen for miles, and she knew it was for Adlae. She didn't understand how she knew, she simply did. Now she could no longer feel her sister's ice. Could no longer feel the strength of her big sister's heartbeat, or sense her emotions. Something was wrong and she was helpless.

Please, You did not give her back to me only to take her away again. Blessed Creator please ... Mirae exhaled, releasing the breath she'd been holding.

"Jaeger, I want Lara and Ahmet on bows. Braven and Cohdel will bring in the ladders once the guards are down. I want Griyer at Brecken's right hand and you at my left."

Jaeger grunted in response, hunching slightly as he jogged among the trees to Lara and Ahmet's position. The snow crunched beneath her boots as she inched a little further from behind the tree to get a better look at her peoples' positions.

"Where's Afra?" she asked, looking over her shoulder at Brecken.

"She stayed back with the other women to look after the children," Brecken answered, smiling warmly. "She wanted to fight."

Mirae arched a brow. "And you wouldn't let her?"

"She'll need her strength for ... after."

"I still don't understand exactly what a Passer endures. I can't imagine crossing the realms in such a way over and over again. My father used to say Passers spent a piece of their own souls every time they crossed someone from this realm until, one day, they never returned from the Creator's Realm." Mirae paused, her gaze colliding with Brecken's. "I suppose it would be peaceful that way, to simply go and never return. No pain or fear."

"I've never known death to be peaceful. Not in the life I've lived." Brecken's voice was hard, cold. A shiver rushed down Mirae's spine. "Not even the Winter Queen's death was peaceful when she handed her power to your sister. The violence of her death was evident in the body she left behind."

Mirae didn't answer, returning her attention to the tower. The singing had ceased, leaving the forest eerily quiet. She leaned forward a bit so Lara and Ahmet could see her just as Jaeger and Griyer came silently up beside her. With a soft nod from Mirae, Lara and Ahmet stepped boldly out of their cover behind the trees, bows raised.

"Here we go," Griyer muttered.

Their arrows hissed softly through the air. Two grunts, a thud, and the guards were down. Braven and Cohdel ran out, the ladders bouncing in their hands.

"Now," Mirae hissed.

The four of them hurried forward, lifting their feet high above the thick layer of snow covering the ground. Last night had brought another stage of the storm, covering the Pilvaa in more snow than the forest had ever seen during any other winter. Mirae felt Adlae's grief in every gust of the wind. In every chill of a snowflake touching her skin. Her devastation was ripe in the air, just as Mirae's was still fresh in her heart.

They reached the walls just as Braven and Cohdel placed the ladders, standing beneath them to hold them steady. Mirae launched herself on the first one, Jaeger right behind her as she climbed, sword still in hand. Brecken moved just as swiftly on the other ladder, the sound of their boots on the rungs, the clattering of the rails against the top of the wall sounding strangely louder than they should in the quiet of the evening.

Mirae grabbed the top rung and swung herself onto the wall, crouching low to the ground. Brecken appeared at her side a moment later, followed by Jaeger than Griyer.

"Tell me again how many more guards you expect below?" Mirae asked, breathless.

"Twenty at most. Roderick never thought Righteousness was important enough to heavily guard it," Brecken replied.

"You'd better be right, captain."

Mirae stepped away without another word, keeping her shoulders hunched as she jogged along the ledge to the steps. A cloud passed over the moon, causing an ethereal glow from the tower torches. The light of the fires danced across the courtyard when Mirae reached the bottom, holding her sword out in front of her.

She moved on the tips of her toes, her back scraping the wall. The courtyard was quiet; empty. Her heart thundered.

This isn't right ... Mirae raised her hand, halting the men behind her.

"What's wrong?" Jaeger asked.

Mirae looked at Brecken. He was stiff, jaw tight and shoulders tense when he looked back at her.

"Silence," she whispered.

"I know." His sword hissed as he slid it back into the sheath. "Stay here. Wait for my signal."

Brecken gestured for her to stay put, his cloak billowing behind him as he strode forward boldly, stopping just short of the tower. He presented his back to the wall, following the circle of the building round toward the other side. Mirae bent her knees, resting one hand in the snow to support herself as Jaeger and Griyer did the same, keeping low to the ground while they waited.

The hiss of a sword broke the silence of the night, followed by the distinct thud of a body hitting the icy ground.

Mirae surged forward, but Jaeger grabbed her arm, pulling her back.

"Wait for his signal, Your Majesty."

Mirae's breath struggled between her lips. What if he couldn't signal? What if the sound she'd heard was Brecken falling under an enemy sword?

Please ... please ...

A shout rent the air, followed by the clash of steel on steel. Mirae fidgeted in the snow.

Blessed Creator, please ...

An unearthly howl echoed in the empty courtyard.

"Brecken!" Mirae shot to her feet, racing through the snow before Jaeger could stop her.

She skidded around the tower just as the Wraith Spawn swung his axe. Mirae gasped, ducking beneath the loud *whoosh* of the weapon before thrusting her father's sword up. The blade pierced directly through the creature's chest, disintegrating him to a cloud of black ash in the snow.

Mirae spun, her eyes wide. The small army of Wraith Spawn charged toward her. Brecken was caught in the middle, swinging and thrusting his sword frantically in the chaos.

"Griyer!" she screamed as Jaeger reached her side. She raised her sword. "Signal Braven and Cohdel! The Abyss has come to Righteousness!"

Brecken fell back in the snow, his sword lying limp in his hand. He stared at the sky, watching the dark clouds roll across the stars, blocking their light. A rumble filled the night air, warning of another approaching storm. The snow had been laced with ice earlier in the day, making their journey across the Pilvaa even harder. The Woodland horses weren't accustomed to the cold beneath their hooves, not to mention the people themselves were averse to the cold.

He groaned when something thumped into his side, bringing him back to the center of the battlefield. The next moment, her face appeared above him, tears glossing her eyes as she shook his shoulders frantically.

"Brecken!" Mirae gasped, a small stream of blood rolling down her chin. "Are you wounded?"

He shook his head, reaching up to rub the cut in her lip with his thumb. Mirae winced, taking hold of his hand to pull him to his feet. Brecken bent low at the waist, catching his breath once he was on his feet. The once pure white ground was now stained with the blood and dust of Wraith Spawn. Mirae's men wandered about, checking injuries and searching for any remaining enemy soldiers.

"Fifty Wraith Spawn," Mirae hissed, her face twisting in disgust. "I don't understand. If Roderick and Raphaela wanted to hold Righteousness, why send such a small company?"

"I don't know." Brecken raked a hand through his hair. "Perhaps they were a warning. Roderick has held Nfaros for nearly six years and he always allowed us to believe he didn't care about the towers. Perhaps he tricked us all."

"You think the Abyss holds every tower? Truce, Tears? Even the Tower of the Night Wood?"

"The Eventide Sisters wouldn't allow evil to touch the Night Wood. But it doesn't mean Roderick didn't send men there under cover of darkness. If the Abyss truly walks the halls of the Blood Keep, I suppose anything is possible."

Mirae turned to the tower.

"Do you suppose he's here? Would he dare cross over Righteousness's threshold?"

Brecken stared at the cylindrical building, his gaze following the smooth, silver bricks from the wide stairs to the pointed rooftop. He lifted his sword from the ground, weighing the hilt in his palm.

"I suppose there's only one way to find out."

Brecken strode forward, Mirae falling into step beside him. They started up the stairs toward the tall double doors. Another rumble vibrated in the distance, making Brecken tremble inside.

"Once we clear the tower, then what?" he asked, the closer they came to the door.

"We hold it. Then we take the Tower of Tears," Mirae answered.

"Tears is bigger, Mirae."

"It's also close. And the battlements? The equipment they keep there? Adlae will need everything Tears has to offer when Roderick finally comes out of hiding behind the walls of Sunkai."

Brecken's mouth thinned. There was no point in arguing with her on the wisdom of moving so quickly on to Tears. At least not now. They stopped at the top of the steps, each placing a hand on the doors. From within, they could hear the Sisters singing. Mirae smiled.

"They sound unharmed," she whispered.

Brecken gave the doors a shove. They groaned sliding open, scraping the dusty ground. The two of them came to a halt. Brecken's heart lurched into his throat.

The Brothers and Sisters of the Creed lay sprawled across the grand hall, dried blood staining the marble floor, eyes glazed in death. Mirae gasped, covering her nose and mouth as the wind swirled the stench all around them. Brecken moved forward, the sound of singing drawing him further into the darkened room.

Three figures stood near the center of the room, huddled together, their voices echoing in the chamber. They stood in the middle of the carnage, three women holding hands and swaying, moaning out a song Brecken had never heard before.

"Sisters?" Mirae said softly, cautiously moving forward. "Are you all right?"

"You bring swords into this Righteous place?" one of the women asked, her voice booming against the stone walls.

A tremor in his hand rattled Brecken's sword. The overwhelming instinct to get out of the tower danced in his belly.

"Forgive us, Sister." Mirae slowly placed her sword back in its sheath. "We meant no disrespect. Please ... tell us what happened here."

The other two women continued to moan, swaying side to side with eyes closed as if in pain. They wore traditional black robes that covered them from collar to ankle, high white necklines tightly buttoned round their throats. Their hair was shorn to their temples, and for proof of humility, they wore no jewelry. Had Mirae not escaped five years ago, Brecken knew she would most likely have ended up here, among these simple People of the Creed.

She's not like Brae. She would have chosen this rather than a forced union.

"*He* came for us," the woman replied drawing Brecken back to the moment. She kept her back to them, not even sparing a glance their way. "There was a great storm and the ground trembled. We could do nothing to stop him. Every day he grows stronger, preparing for the final battle in the sky."

Mirae and Brecken exchanged glances and he lowered his sword. "Sister, let us take you out of this place."

He reached out to her, his fingertips brushing the Sister's sleeve.

She spun at his touch, eyes wide.

Brecken and Mirae reared back, a small shriek escaping Mirae's lips. The woman looked back and forth between them, her eyes glowing bright red in the darkened room. Her mouth twisted in an ugly smile as dark clouds began to rise from beneath her feet. Brecken knew this magic well. Raphaela used it on him every day when he was her prisoner.

"Mirae ..." Brecken reached for her, backing away slowly. "Mirae, we have to go."

Mirae shook her head, stunned and frozen in place.

"Get out," the woman hissed, spittle flying between her teeth and moistening her chin. "He doesn't want you here! Get out!"

"Mirae now!" Brecken grabbed her arm.

"This cannot be," Mirae whispered, struggling in his hold. "The Creator wouldn't do this! He wouldn't allow it!"

"GET OUT!" the woman howled, raising her hands.

His breath left him as he and Mirae were lifted off their feet, flying backward through the doors. They landed hard on the stone, the doors slamming after them. Brecken's back throbbed in rhythm with the frantic beating of his heart.

"Your Majesty!" Lara's voice cried, followed by thundering footsteps up the stairs. "What happened?"

A strong hand curled around Brecken's arm. He looked up to find Cohdel there, a concerned frown creasing his brow as he helped Brecken back on his feet.

"I don't believe this," Mirae said hoarsely. Brecken turned to her, regaining his breath as Lara assisted Mirae to her feet. "How? How could the Abyss enter the souls of the most faithful people in Nfaros?"

"Mirae." Brecken stepped toward her, placing his hands on her cheeks. He turned her away from the tower, forcing her to look at him instead. His fingers tingled at the surprisingly soft touch of her skin, one hand gliding up to caress her hair. "She didn't kill us."

"But Brecken, you saw her!"

"There is goodness in her. Look how many fell because their souls wouldn't allow the Abyss to enter! Those women ..." his voice faded, unable to speak aloud what he was thinking.

Tears brimmed in her eyes, nearly overflowing with understanding. "They're going to die, aren't they? If they keep fighting, they won't make it. That's his plan isn't it? He's trying to kill the last truly pure souls in Nfaros."

"I don't know, Mirae. But if that is what he's trying to do, he won't succeed. Because Adlae is a force he cannot touch. She was made pure by the Creator's hand. She won't let any more of her people fall, you know this."

Mirae's hand lifted, covering her necklace.

"Yes," she murmured, though her voice was laced with doubt. "Yes, I know."

Mirae took hold of his wrists, pushing his hands away from her face before turning. A lump clogged his throat for a moment, and he didn't know why as he flexed his fingers at his sides, skin still tingling from touching her.

"I should find Jaeger." Mirae wrapped her arms around herself as a frozen breeze swept over them, prelude to the inevitable snowfall. "We need to post guards around the tower and find a way to reach those women. If there's a chance we can save them, then we have to try."

"Of course," Brecken agreed.

Mirae walked away without another word, Lara at her side whispering comforts. Brecken watched her until she disappeared around the side of the tower, nearly forgetting Cohdel's quiet presence at his side. He glared at the man.

"What?"

The corner of Cohdel's mouth twitched, nearly smiling. "I said nothing, Brecken Jandry. I find it curious how you watch her, that's all."

"What is there to be curious about? She's my queen's sister. I am here to help her succeed."

"Hmm." Cohdel rubbed his chin thoughtfully. "There is more than that."

"Don't be ridiculous." Brecken started down the steps.

"You watch her the way I watch your sister."

Brecken froze, staring across the courtyard blankly. Cohdel slowly joined him halfway down the steps, slapping him on the shoulder.

"Do not fret, captain. I won't say anything."

"Good. Because you're wrong." Brecken scowled at the man, stepping away. "I loved my wife. I love her still, even though she's gone. To suggest I see Mirae as anything other than my sister by law and my ruler is preposterous."

"I said nothing of love. Only that you fear losing her, the way you lost your wife. Take care, Brecken Jandry. In these troubled times, having a vulnerable heart is dangerous." Cohdel preceded him down the steps.

Brecken moved on, putting Cohdel's words from his mind as he rejoined the Woodlanders. There were more important things to think about than the guard's intrusive observations.

Like the fate of those poor women inside and Mirae's determination to take the Tower of Tears next.

The Gracian Wood

Raphaela raised her skirt above her ankles as she walked among the trees, the snow soaking into her shoes, attempting to freeze her. She hummed softly, numb to the cold even as the wind intensified, pulling at her hair and dress.

Brecken's escape from her prison had been ... unfortunate. She'd had so many plans for him. So many different ways to make him regret what he'd done in turning his back on their future.

To make him regret breaking my heart. Raphaela scowled, moving deeper into the woods. The dark clouds overhead roiled the further she went, whispering to the magic in her belly. Her scowl faded to a smile, the rustle of the creatures she'd summoned growing louder behind her.

Raphaela didn't need to turn to know the Wraith Spawn had answered her call. *He* said they would. He'd assured her they'd come the moment she called. Adlae Sundragon had reached the Tower of the Dead, which could only mean one thing.

The time has come.

Raphaela stopped suddenly, angling her head back sharply to look into the blackened sky. She lifted her hands, black coils rising from her palms. Her body trembled with the strength of the power he'd given her.

"Tell me your will. Tell me what you want me to do. Tell me where to send them next!" Raphaela groaned, her eyes rolling back.

A cloud descended on her, and she screamed. Tendrils wrapped tight around her, shaking her, infusing her.

Then they released. Raphaela fell to her knees gasping, hugging her ribs as the pain began to abate. Something growled in front of her, and she stilled. As slowly as she could, she raised her head. A laugh slipped between her lips when she saw the creature. Black and slick, the animal crouched on all four feet. Jagged claws dug into the snow beneath it, supporting a long, thin body and wiry wings. The animal's nose nearly touched hers, his long snout huffing and gray teeth protruding from its upper lip.

"A *Brakari*," Raphaela whispered. She lifted her hand, resting her palm on the creature's forehead.

Beady red eyes watched her as curiously as she watched him. In that moment, she knew what to do. Standing, she turned her back on the *Brakari*, facing the legion of Wraith Spawn behind her.

"You will go to the Aulend Forest and wait," she shouted for all of them to hear. "Wait for the one who thinks she can take these Woodlands without a price."

Raphaela grinned, her eyes brightening with excitement.

"Wait for Mirae Sundragon to come to the Tower of Tears … then kill her."

CHAPTER TWENTY-ONE

The Mountain Lands

Lathan slowly approached the dark pool of water, Krow and Evingar flanking him. The cave whistled with a soft breeze, the opening at the top allowing white light to shine down on the water, shining like ebony stones. Lathan tilted his head back, looking through the opening at the star above.

His heart lurched, a sense of familiarity about the glistening white globe in the sky. A soft, seven-pointed star, larger than any other in the sky, glowed fiery gold amongst the sea of white dots all around. He smiled, resting a hand over the center of his chest to alleviate the excitement and fear suddenly filling his gut. He could feel Krow and Evingar standing close now as he came to the edge of the pond, looking down into the dark liquid. They each rested a hand on his back, more to hold him steady than pressure him to take the next step.

"The Creator will decide if you are to be reborn a Son of the Haven Star, Lathan Jandry," Krow's voice rumbled at his ear. "Understand what is asked of you. To become immortal, you must surrender your soul. To serve the *Almaër Dominÿe,* you must release the human life you once lived to the Creator forever."

"I understand," Lathan whispered.

"This is a hard life, Lathan Jandry," Evingar added. "You are truly a man of honor, sacrificing everything you know for our *Almaër Dominÿe.* I will be proud to call you brother."

Lathan nodded, the air in his lungs beginning to ache. He looked up again, watching as the star shifted closer to the center of the sky.

"The time has come," Krow announced. "The Haven Star will not return to the waters of Hadroul for another fortnight. Step now into the blessed water, Lathan Jandry, and see what the Creator wills."

Lathan moved forward, barely taking his eyes off the star above as he put one foot than the other into the pond. He went slowly, the water rising toward his knees now. Behind him, Krow and Evingar crouched by the water's edge, a deep purr coming from Evingar. Then Krow spoke.

"*Fer baërne gorth. Por técli et soberân, Chalqüin,*" Krow paused, then he began again, "*Fer baërne gorth. Por técli …*"

He spoke the same words over and over again, some sort of incantation. His voice bounced off the walls, filling the silence. Lathan moved deeper into the pond, the water up to his waist, until he stopped in the very center.

Bending his neck back, Lathan stared at the star, his heart thundering harder until he could barely hear Krow anymore. Something whispered on the wind, making his head spin. The water suddenly rose in temperature, changing from a comfortable warmth to boiling. Lathan grunted, trembling in the center.

The ground went out from beneath him. A strangled shout tore from his throat before he went under, his mouth filling with the sharp, tangy taste of the water. Lathan struggled, legs kicking and arms pumping as invisible hands dragged him down … down … down …

Then he saw it. The Haven Star, growing larger and brighter, shutting out everything else. Even making the pain of the water filling his lungs and stinging his eyes vanish.

The Creator will decide if you are to be reborn a Son of the Haven Star …

You are truly a man of honor, sacrificing everything you know for our Almaër Dominje …

To become immortal, you must surrender your soul …

Their voices filled him, covering him in peace. His arms went limp, his heart slowing as the warmth of the star surrounded him, easing the pain.

Lathan surrendered.

Molderëin

The towers fairly trembled with the ringing of the bells. People crowded into the throne room, standing to either side of the scarlet carpet spread from the door to the stone chair waiting for her. Her heart pounded harder against her ribs, most certainly leaving a bruise from the inside out. She clasped her hands tightly in front of her, the blue velvet gown feeling heavier than it had earlier in the day as she took the first step into the throne room.

The bells chimed louder; the *Kläerjaen* suddenly heavier at her hip. Everyone watched her walk up the aisle toward Rhoydaen Molten, his head held high and a cold gleam in his eye chilling the warmth of the room from her. Beside the throne, stood his son, shoulders hunched tensely and hands fisted loosely at his sides. To the left, her people. Morgren and Rheatha, arm in arm. Izeana and Ryker holding hands.

Then her gaze fell upon the crown in Rhoydaen's hands. The simple, golden circlet glittering with six white diamonds at a soft peak in the front. In moments, the crown would grace her head and she would be declared the Savior of Molderëin. The long lost royal, finally returned to the throne.

Her head spun, all sense of why she'd come here in the first place gone. In this moment, her need for the Summer Flower waned beneath the pressure of a dying country. A country no one cared about. A country that had fallen into savagery due to the selfishness of one man. Even her own weakening soul seemed trivial compared to the work she needed to do here.

Save them all … that's what he said. I could save them all.

Clea Jandry knelt before Rhoydaen Molten, keeping her hands before her and her head bowed. The bells had ceased. No one moved. Not even a mouse could be heard in the sudden silence of the room.

"Before us kneels the bearer of the *Kläerjaen*. By this sign, she has declared herself the Heir of Molderëin, the one prophesied to save our people from darkness and restore our country to greatness. The Savior of our nation and a true creature of magic under the hand of the Creator," Rhoydaen's voice boomed throughout the room.

Clea tilted her head back, looking at him the very moment he looked down at her.

"Do you, Clea Jandry of Quintaria, take this crown? Do you swear to protect the people of Molderëin and return our country to greatness? Do you swear to remove all evil from our midst and uphold the will of the Creator in all things, restoring Molderëin from the Abyss so we may once again shine in the light?"

Clea took a breath. "I do."

Rhoydaen's mouth turned down for a moment, his hands shaking where they held the crown. Then he bent forward, resting the light circlet upon her hair.

"I crown you Queen Clea of Molderëin, Protector of the Stone Lands and Keeper of the Summer Flower. Rise and take your place."

He turned, clearing the path to the throne. Clea rose, lifting her skirts above her ankles as she climbed the steps, turned, and settled on the throne. The room erupted in applause, men and women cheering, children laughing.

Clea raised her hand and the room fell silent. Her gaze skittered to the side and Izeana smiled, her head dipping slightly.

"As your queen, I have sworn to remove all evil from Molderëin," she said, her voice loud to her own ears. But she pushed on. "I now call forth one who has sworn to be my humble servant, even before this crown sat upon my head."

Clea stared down the aisle as the doors opened. Kalea strode down the aisle, her presence followed by gasps and exclamations. She wore one of Clea's dresses, a simple brown gown with a matching belt, her shimmering hair wrapped in multiple braids atop her head and her white eyes sharp. She stopped before the throne, bowing her head low in respect to Clea before turning her cold gaze on Rhoydaen.

"Morgren Lanfira and Grange Molten," Clea called.

The two men came before her, bowing low at the waist.

"As your queen, I hereby order you to arrest Rhoydaen Molten for crimes against a creature of magic, a Chosen One of the Creator, and a woman of Hadroul's Mountain. Under these charges he will face trial and judgment according to the laws of old."

Rhoydaen's enraged howl echoed on the walls of the Towers of the King.

The Mountain Lands

"Where is he?" Damari twisted her neck, looking over her shoulder at the closed doors to Hadroul's Chamber.

Navaria touched her arm lightly and she turned back, staring into the woman's warm gaze.

"He will come. But we cannot wait any longer, Damari. The time has come."

"I-I can't! Not without Lathan."

"You must." Navaria took both her hands, backing up.

Damari followed, gripping the First Mother's hands tighter. The silk white dress was thin, cool against her skin. After she accepted her fate, Damari had been whisked away to Malindra's house where she'd been scrubbed from head to foot before they lifted the gown over her head. Somehow, the dress fit perfectly, falling lightly on her skin, the long sleeves clinging from shoulder to wrist and the low back leaving enough bare so her wings could spread free if she so wished, no fear of destroying the fragile material.

Her feet were bare, but she didn't feel the heat of the stones beneath them. If anything, the mountain felt cool to her and she realized, for the first time in all her life, the temperature of this land was comfortable for her.

If I can't bear the cold in the North, how am I supposed to protect these people from Winter? How am I supposed to help Adlae win back Nfaros? Damari trembled.

"Hush," Navaria cooed, placing her hands on Damari's cheeks. "Do not fear, Damari. The rebirth will embody you with powers you do not have now. The rebirth will awaken what you have buried deep inside you."

"How ... how did you ...?"

Navaria smiled. "You are flesh of my flesh and blood of my blood. I know you, as well as I know myself."

Damari's heart sang.

Navaria guided her from Hadroul's Chamber, deeper within the mountain. They followed a dark, narrow hall, Navaria taking every turn in the shadows like she knew them by heart. Damari kept a firm hold of her hand until the hall opened to a large circular room. At the center, a lake glistened under torchlight.

Damari stared at the great expanse of water rippling in the heart of Hadroul's Mountain, hardly believing what she was seeing. Malindra, Lyssia, and one other woman with topaz dragon skin on the right side of her face, all stood by the stone steps leading down to the water. Navaria gave her hand a small tug, urging her toward the lake.

They stopped at the steps and Damari faced Navaria, her chest tightening.

"I don't know what I'm supposed to do," she whispered.

Navaria pressed her cheek to Damari's. "You must awaken what you have held prisoner in your soul all these years. Allow the water to take you where you need to be, and when you return, you will be the *Almaër Dominÿe*."

Damari closed her eyes, leaning against Navaria for a moment longer before she turned toward the lake. She stepped down onto the first step, the water catching the hem of her dress. Once waist deep, she presented her back to the lake, reaching for Navaria and Malindra. They each took one of her hands, anchoring her as Damari lightened her body, her feet and legs floating up until she was lying flat on the surface of the water.

Her hair soaked through, swirling all around her head as Malindra and Navaria gave her a small push, sending her gliding toward the middle of the lake. She was suddenly weightless, her body rippling along the surface of the water, taking her far from the shore. Damari stared at the ceiling, watching the firelight dance in shadows on the glittering stones. The beauty stole her breath.

Damari smiled, all other sounds muted by the water in her ears. Her fingers fidgeted, clapping against the water. There were no words to describe what she felt now. Something about the water sent flutters rushing through her belly, followed by a scorching heat she'd felt once before.

In the sea after the shipwreck. Damari gasped.

An invisible energy sucked her down, pulling her beneath the water. She twisted and spun, sinking faster than possible toward the bottom of the lake, then …

Damari gasped, falling face first on green grass. She coughed, water sputtering out of her mouth, her dress clinging to her body, chilling her to the bone. When she raised her head, she froze.

She was in the middle of the woods. Beautiful, lush trees surrounded her in a circle with golden and red leaves fluttering from their branches. The grass was soft and fresh, crisp with brand new life. The sun glimmered down, not a winter sun but a spring sun. Not a breeze touched her, yet the trees swayed, as if dancing to a silent song.

"Navaria?" Damari called, rising from the ground. "Navaria, where …?"

Her voice faded when she turned, staring into sharp, crystal blue eyes.

The creature was magnificent. Her smooth, shimmering scales pure white, round eyes protruding from a gorgeously structured face and three horns rising in gentle slopes at the nape of her neck. Her long, wide snout huffed a breath at the sight of Damari. Smoke rose from her nostrils and Damari giggle, despite the ferocity of the creature.

Then she rose, her belly round beneath her, front claws raised and curled near her chest. Behind her, perfectly sculpted wings rose, expanding a thousand feet in each direction. Damari's neck strained back as she watched the creature raise herself on her hind legs, her thick tail curling round one of the nearest trees.

You must awaken what you have held prisoner in your soul all these years …

Navaria's words tumbled in her head. Damari's eyes filled with tears and she took a hesitant step forward. The animal shrieked, her neck stretching high, head tilted back as the sound pierced Damari's ears.

With a heavy bat of her wings, the dragon shot off the ground, flying straight toward the sun and out of sight.

CHAPTER TWENTY-TWO

The Caravan Road

"Hurry with the tents, boys! The sun has nearly set!"

Jabon bounced in the saddle as his horse cantered down the line of the camp. Another ear-splitting crack made him turn sharply toward the wall of ice surrounding them. The further the sun set on the horizon, the more the wall began to break down. His heart lurched in his chest, every breath shaky with the fact Adlae hadn't returned.

If I do not return by tomorrow's sunset, then you must pursue Mirae... her voice whispered in his ear.

Jabon scowled, pulling hard on the reins to guide his mount toward the forest. Glaydin still stood there, as unmoving as ever before. Jabon swung from the saddle once close enough, striding to the Mountain man's side.

"The wall is coming down," he said heavily, his breath clouding against the frozen block.

"If you must go, Jabon Malaki, then go," Glaydin growled. "I will not leave here until she returns."

"Do you think I would so easily abandon her?" Jabon hissed. "If I must send the men on, I will. But if she doesn't return at the last ray of light, I am going into that forest."

Glaydin nodded, a spark of approval gleaming in his eye. Jabon looked over his shoulder, watching the soldiers pack the wagons and ready the horses. The wall had protected them from everything, including winter's wind, offering the men a day of relief from the harsh weather. How Adlae managed it, he didn't know. He would much rather have had her here, with all her icy magic and frozen demeanor, then the relief she offered by trapping them on the open road.

Another crack rent the air and this time, even Glaydin jumped, his gaze straying from the forest to the wall over their heads.

"We have to move," Jabon said, taking a cautious step back.

The sun was nearly set now, the sky turning shades of orange on the horizon as it began to disappear behind the tree line. The ice wall roared, trembling in a fury. Jabon and Glaydin turned, racing back toward the center of the camp as the wall came crumbling down in a mass of broken ice and snow dust.

Something crashed into Jabon's back and he grunted, falling flat on his belly. He spun around, raising himself up on his elbows as he watched each section of the wall crumble, falling in piles of crystal stones all around the encampment. His shoulder throbbed where such a stone had hit him.

Glaydin grabbed his arm, lifting him to his feet with ease as the roar continued to echo in his ears, even though all the ice had settled. The wind had no barrier now, blowing into his face and freezing his skin. Jabon breathed deeply, slapping the snow dust from his sleeves.

"Do you see anything?" he asked, looking to the woods.

Glaydin didn't answer, taking careful steps toward the piles of ice pressed against the tree line. Jabon looked back at the men.

"You men start shoveling away the ice! We make for the Pilvaa as soon as the road is cleared!" he ordered, his voice resounding across the empty plains.

"Jabon Malaki."

He turned at the sound of Glaydin's voice, going still.

She climbed over the pile of ice, her staff gripped tightly in her hand, clicking softly with each step she took. Her bare feet were pearly white, but she didn't shiver from the cold as she tiptoed over each large frosty rock. Her white dress with the golden eagle etched at the center caught the light beautifully, glowing as if freshly washed and her white hair hung loosely all around her shoulders.

"Adlae," Jabon breathed, stumbling slightly in his rush toward her.

He and Glaydin reached her together, staring up at her where she'd stopped at the top of the pile of ice, staring at the army behind them.

"Adlae?" Jabon raised his arm toward her, his fingertips reaching just short of her hand. "Are you all right?"

She didn't answer; didn't even look at him.

"My lady," Glaydin murmured. "What did you see? What did the shadows tell you?"

His words made her eyes twinkle and, slowly, she looked down at them. A gentle smile spread her lips, the beauty in her blue eyes taking Jabon's breath away. Then, she whispered.

"We're going to win."

CHAPTER TWENTY-THREE

The Aulend Forest

"How much farther, Uncle Maxx?"

Maxx looked down, his arm tightening around Noelle's trembling little form. The smoke in the distance rose in a perfect silver spiral toward the sky, the touch of magic in the stream making it glitter. The frozen air stole his next breath, making his heart skip a beat. There'd been no choice, not after what he'd seen. Lathan and Damari were too far from him by that time, and trying to find Brecken would have achieved nothing. He'd been through enough already.

There's only one person who can help her. Maxx cringed at the thought.

"See the smoke, Little Bit?" Maxx whispered. "Not far now."

Noelle's head bobbed against his chin and she settled, wrapping the warmth of her own cloak around her. The storm had been consistent, a thick snow falling all around them catching in the trees so only a light sprinkle touched them as they followed the path as best they could. Maxx had lost the Woodland Path hours ago, the thick blanket of snow on the ground making it impossible for him to find the stones.

Noelle shivered again and he pulled her in, willing his body warmth to seep into her. Better he die of cold than her. Not after everything he'd done to find her.

Not after all the trouble I've gotten myself into. Creator's Night I hope she doesn't kill me. Maxx took another breath as the trees parted to a clearing.

One large tent was erected in the center of the clearing, arching into a round roof with a hole at the center to release the smoke. The four horses strapped to the nearest trees skittered and whinnied at his approach. Gently, he dismounted, cradling Noelle on one arm as he went.

The tent flap swung and, in seemingly one motion, the four women he sought stepped out, weapons at the ready and a glow surrounding them. Maxx set Noelle down and she rushed behind him, clinging to his leg as he raised his hands in surrender.

"Please," he whispered.

"Why have you come here?" *she* asked, glaring at him despite the warmth in her velvety eyes.

"I need your help, Gwylan," he replied, ignoring the way the other women moved subtly toward him, prepared to strike at the first sign he was hostile.

"I thought not to see you again," Gwylan commented, curiosity lighting in her eyes. She tilted her head slightly. "What do you want?"

Maxx lowered his hands carefully and then turned, bending on one knee in the snow so he would be eye level with Noelle.

"Sweetheart," he whispered hoarsely, eyes stinging. "Show these ladies what you showed me, hmm?"

Noelle hesitated, looking back and forth between him and the women. "But ... but Uncle Maxx ..."

"It's all right, Noelle. They can help. Please, Little Bit, show them."

Noelle's tiny chest swelled with a breath, and then she nodded. Maxx pinched the bridge of his nose when she turned away, facing Gwylan. Before him stood a child with a woman's soul and he had no idea when it happened. Yet it had.

The sharp sound of Gwylan inhaling brought him around. His gaze fixed on Noelle, watching as her face lit with a smile, her small hands moving in circular motions in front of her over and over again. White light began to gather between her palms, sparking and spitting like fire. Then, in a single fluid motion Noelle sent the sparks flying into the air.

They shattered—the way glass shatters on marble—shooting thousands of sparkling lights across the sky. The child laughed softly, then her eyes rolled, the magic draining her face of blood. Maxx caught Noelle's limp body in his arms, the sound of her strained, but steady breaths catapulting his heart into his chest.

His eyes locked with Gwylan's.

"Can you help her?"

To Be Continued ...

ABOUT THE AUTHOR

ERICA MARIE HOGAN was born in New York but now calls Texas home. She has three cats and two dogs, was homeschooled, is a member of American Christian Fiction Writers, and when she's not writing, she's reading. Erica can be found on Facebook, Twitter, and Goodreads, along with her monthly blog, "By the Book: Diary of a Bookaholic."